AN ACT OF SI
THE COURAGE O
FIGHTI

William J. Krandel: The Marine Corps Commander of the Rapid Deployment Force was as devoted as he was inexperienced. When the mission to Do'brai, Africa, went wrong, he was left with ten men on a heat-seared runway—all fighting for their lives. . . .

Robert Gould: The daring Air Force Major was the elite pilot of the TAV—TransAtmospheric Vehicle—the fastest machine in the world. Against deadly odds he flew toward the ultimate challenge—a surprise landing in a red-hot enemy zone. . . .

Delores Beckman: In a man's world she was trying to prove herself. When Air Force One fell into terrorist hands, Gould didn't want her as the second TAV pilot—but he had given her her rating, and now she was ready to fly. . . .

Hujr ibn-Adi: Half Filipino, half North African, he was a man who spread the most brutal forms of terror without remorse. Now he was on his most spectacular mission—and walking into a web of even deadlier treachery. . . .

Sandoval Montoya: The first Mexican-American President of the United States was feeling the pressure of his office—and dreamed of getting out. Suddenly, he was fighting for his life. . . .

RETURN TO HONOR

"Tightly plotted, characters you care about, fast paced. . . . I greatly enjoyed reading *RETURN TO HONOR*. I'll be watching for Beason's future work."

> —Robert Adams, author of the *Horse Clans* series

"Beason's acute eye for military detail and his portrayal of characters of courage and conviction mark him as a promising new storyteller."

> —Patrick Lucien Price, editor, *Amazing Stories*™

RETURN TO HONOR

DOUG BEASON

POCKET BOOKS

New York   London   Toronto   Sydney   Tokyo

A substantially different version of a portion of this work appeared in AMAZING STORIES℠ under the title *The Man I'll Never Be*, copyright © 1987 by Doug Beason.

The quote preceeding Chapter 10 is used with the kind permission of its author, Robert A. Heinlein. The quote is taken from TIME ENOUGH FOR LOVE, copyright © 1973 by Robert A. Heinlein.

An *Original* Publication of POCKET BOOKS

POCKET BOOKS, a division of Simon & Schuster Inc.
1230 Avenue of the Americas, New York, NY 10020

Copyright © 1989 by Doug Beason
Cover art copyright © 1989 James Mathewuse

ISBN: 0-671-64809-8

First Pocket Books printing February 1989

10 9 8 7 6 5 4 3 2 1

POCKET and colophon are trademarks of Simon & Schuster Inc.

Printed in the U.S.A.

To my wife and daughters—
Cindy, Amanda and Tamara—
who put up with me.

ACKNOWLEDGMENTS

To Dr. Tom Tascione, for giving me the idea for this novel, and Dr. Don Erbschloe, for reviewing and commenting on the draft manuscript. Boston's "A Man I'll Never Be" provided me with much inspiration during the writing. And to John F. Carr at J. E. Pournelle and Associates for first accepting the novelette on which this novel is based; to Patrick L. Price at AMAZING STORIES℠ who first published the novelette; and most importantly, to Paul McCarthy, senior editor at Pocket Books, who had patience with the slush pile and had faith in me.

DRAMATIS PERSONAE

MAJOR ROBERT GOULD, USAF—TransAtmospheric Vehicle pilot, Edwards AFB, California

MAJOR DELORES BECKMAN, USAF—TAV pilot

COLONEL MATHIN, USAF—Commander, USAF Test Pilot School, Edwards AFB

LT. COL. WILLIAM J. KRANDEL, USMC—Commander, 37th Marine Battalion: Rapid Deployment Force, Camp Pendleton, California

MAUREEN KRANDEL—his wife

BRIGADIER GENERAL ALLEN W. VANDERVOOS, USMC—First Marine, Air Wing Commander

CAPTAIN HARVEY WESTON, USMC—Headquarters Platoon Commander, RDF

GUNNERY SERGEANT DAVID BALCALSKI, USMC—Battalion First Sergeant, RDF

PRIVATE ARROSH HAVISAD, USMC—Communications expert, Alpha Squad, RDF

DRAMATIS PERSONAE

LANCE CORPORAL FRANCIS MORALES, USMC—Alpha Squad Leader, RDF

LANCE CORPORAL KENNETH HENDERSON, USMC—Bravo Squad Leader, RDF

PRESIDENT SANDOVAL MONTOYA—President of the United States

MANUEL BACA—White House Chief of Staff

G. PERCIVAL WOODSTONE—Vice President of the United States

AMADOR TRUJILLO—White House National Security Advisor

CPO YOLI AQUINBALDO, USN—Steward aboard Air Force One

CPO RAMIS SICAT, USN—another steward

HUJR IBN-ADI—terrorist

DU'ALI AL-ASWAD—another terrorist, Hujr's assistant

GHAZZALI ABU-HAMID—Head of the Arab Liberated Hegemony (ALH)

ABD AL-RAHMAN IBN-MUHAMMED IBN AL-ASH'ATH—President-for-Life and Commanding General, Do'brainese Militia Forces

GENERAL FARIQ KAMIL—Chief of Staff for President Ash'ath

COLONEL JOSEPH MCGIRNEY, USAF—Aircraft Commander, Air Force One

DRAMATIS PERSONAE

MAJOR LAYNAM, USAF—Copilot, Air Force One

LIEUTENANT COLONEL GEORGE FRIER, USAF—Commanding Officer, U.S.S.S. *Bifrost*

MAJOR STEPHEN WORDEL, USAF—*Bifrost* crew member

HONORABLE DIETRICH GRUNZIMMER—West German Chancellor

SERGEANT DONALD CLEMENTS, USMC—Marine guard assigned to Air Force One

GENERAL "BLACKIE" BACKERMAN, USA—Chairman, Joint Chiefs of Staff

COLONEL WELCH, USAF—Presidential Military Aide, assigned to the National Emergency Command Center

CAPTAIN JIMMY McCLUNEY, USAF—F-15 Wild Weasel Flight Commander

FIRST LIEUTENANT CHIU, USAF—Missile Launch Officer, Vandenberg AFB, CA

COLONEL RATHSON, USAF—Commander, 2nd Aircraft Delivery Group, Langley AFB, VA

ABBREVIATIONS

AC—Aircraft Commander
AFSATCOM—Air Force SATellite COMmunications
ASL—Above Sea Level
ATC—Air Training Command
AWACS—Airborne Warning And Control System
Base Ops—Base Operations
BIGEYE—U.S.S.S. *Bifrost*
Check—short for checkride, a graded flight examination
CINCSAC—Commander IN Chief Strategic Air Command
CP—Command Post
CRT—Cathode Ray Tube
CSOC—Consolidated Space Operations Center, Colorado
    Springs, CO
CYA—Cover Your Ass
DIA—Defense Intelligence Agency
EM—Electromagnetic
EMP—Electromagnetic Pulse
FE—Flight Examiner
FOB—Fractional Orbit Bomb
FTC—Flight Test Center
ICBM—InterContinental Ballistic Missile
IFF—Identification Friend or Foe
IP—Instructor Pilot
INS—Inertial Navigation System
IR—InfraRed

13

ABBREVIATIONS

JATO—Jet Assisted TakeOff
JP-4—high-grade jet fuel
JP-12—super-octane TAV fuel
MRBM—Medium-Range Ballistic Missile
NECC—National Emergency Command Center
NSA—National Security Agency
O-7—Brigadier general
PAX—passengers
PCS—Permanent Change of Station
PLF—Parachute Landing Fall
SAC—Strategic Air Command
SCRAM—Supersonic Combustion RAM jets
SDI—Strategic Defense Initiative
SIE—Self-Initiated Elimination
SLBM—Sea-Launched Ballistic Missile
SMART—Super Maintenance And Readiness Truck
TAC—Tactical Air Command
TAV—TransAtmospheric Vehicle
TDY—Temporary Duty
TLF—Transient Living Facilities
UPT—Undergraduate Pilot Training
U.S.S.S.—United States Space Station
VUHF—Very Ultra High Frequency
ZULU—Greenwich Mean Time, measured from Greenwich, Great Britain

The "born leader" is a fiction by "born followers." Leadership is not a gift at birth: it is an award for growing up to full moral stature. It is the only award a man must win every day. The prize is the respect of others, earned by the disciplines that generate self-respect.

Major General Louis Metzger
Commanding General
Third Marine Division

RETURN TO
HONOR

ⅢⅢ Prologue ⅢⅢ

1200 ZULU:
WEDNESDAY, 29 MAY

264,000 + Feet ASL

Mach 25—over fifteen thousand miles per hour—and no sensation of movement. The ride seemed smooth enough; the buffeting that accompanied the TAV's launch was nothing compared to the eerie silence that now permeated the craft. They were stuffed in the TransAtmospheric Vehicle tighter than sardines in a can: twenty-four marines, all clutching their rifles, all depending on their hotshot air force pilot to bring them safely back to ground.

Where they could get killed the instant they scrambled from the TAV.

Gunnery sergeant Balcalski shifted his weight, trying to get comfortable. Now that his weight had returned, the webbed seating straps dug into his back. And the heat didn't help. You'd think that once they were above the atmosphere—over fifty miles above the ground—things would cool down. But the cramped compartment held the heat in, sapping their strength.

Minutes passes. Balcalski inched forward, and he jumped when the klaxon, set in the TAV's bulkhead, gave an earsplitting blast. The air force pilot came over the intercom: "Two minutes to landing . . . prepare your stations, marines." All around Balcalski, the marines straightened in their seats. Balcalski pushed his feet firmly against the vibrating deck and prepared for landing. They were approaching the desert at an unthinkable speed, screaming through the air, ready to disembark and spill out of the TAV to take their objective.

Balcalski glanced over at Captain Weston, the new platoon commander. As young as Weston seemed, Balcalski had confidence in him. From what Balcalski knew of Weston's background, he was a capable leader. Balcalski could count on being able to run the platoon through its motions without Weston butting in. Weston was there to observe, and he would step in only as needed. He was the type of officer Balcalski respected—one he didn't have to train; one that respected the presence of a good noncom. It was essential to have that mutual respect when going into battle.

The TAV bounced down, jarring the marines as it landed. Before Balcalski could react, Captain Weston was out of his seat and standing in the TAV hatch, yelling, "This is it—get ready to jump!"

Balcalski followed the rest of the marines as they stood and shuffled to the door in their combat equipment, careful not to trip on the bouncing deck. Balcalski felt adrenaline rush into his system as the excitement of the moment swept him up. He was first at the door, then stepped back as Weston shouted in his ear, "I'll take the first jump—make sure the rest of them get out as soon as they can after me."

"Aye, aye, sir." Balcalski shouldered his rifle. Weston clutched the sides of the hatch; a red light flickered above the door as the hatch swung open, spilling in warm desert air. Scrub brush and cactus whizzed by. The TAV bounced on the desert floor as the craft continued to slow. The intercom crackled as the air force pilot came on, excitement evident in his voice.

"Twenty-five knots . . . twenty knots . . . and *fifteen*. Marines, disembark!"

Balcalski slapped the captain on the rear. "Jump, sir!" Weston leapt out the hatch; he disappeared as the next marine took his place. Balcalski swatted the marine. "Jump!"

Twenty-one more marines followed until Balcalski was alone in the TAV. Balcalski assumed the position at the hatch, spotted the rushing ground, and jumped, hitting the desert in a parachute-landing fall. He was instantly on his feet, running toward a small building to his right. The remainder of the Rapid Deployment Force was already converging on the objective. Behind him, Balcalski could make out the whine of the TAV's engines winding down as the craft slowed to a halt.

Out of breath, Balcalski was the last to reach the building. Grasping his rifle, he stormed through the door—and froze at what he saw.

A burly, dark-haired man clicked off a stopwatch as Balcalski entered the building. The man took a cigar from his mouth and eyed the clock. "Fifty seconds. Gentlemen, you are all dead."

Brigadier General Vandervoos took a long draw off his cigar and studied the marines in front of him. They stood panting from the exertion, standing at attention. Balcalski felt his face grow red, more from embarrassing Captain Weston in front of the general than anything else. Vandervoos blew smoke away and spoke quietly so the marines had to strain to hear him: "Gentlemen, let me lay it on the line for you.

"The *only* reason the RDF exists is for rapid response. American taxpayers are paying out good money for your training; they're spending thousands of dollars so the air force can keep their TAVs on alert, twenty-four hours a day, here at Edwards. Those pilots have to pull alert, just like all of you, so that if the balloon ever goes up, they can fly you to any spot in the world to knock out enemy command posts—or to do whatever the hell the President wants you to do.

"Now, unless you gentlemen get serious about these exercises, and can get every man out of that TAV in less than fifty seconds, we might as well hang it up. We can send in the damned army cheaper than what it's costing to keep this outfit going." He allowed his words to sink in for some moments before speaking again. "Captain Weston, do you have anything to add?"

"No, sir."

"Very well, I'll see you outside. Carry on, men." Vandervoos stomped out the building, leaving the marines at attention. A trail of cigar smoke rose behind him.

Weston eyed Balcalski. "Run the men through the simulator until they get that time down. Next time we go up in a TAV, I want the general's socks blown off."

"Aye, aye, sir." Weston didn't have to elaborate to let Balcalski know he meant business; it was the first time Balcalski had seen a general officer dress down a platoon.

Weston hurried out of the building to catch up with the general. As the officer left Balcalski turned to the men. He relaxed minutely before growling, "All right—let's hit the bus for Pendleton. We're swinging by the simulator on the way back—and unless that time gets down, you can forget any weekend passes."

The grumbling was less than what he expected, but then again, it wasn't every day they got their asses chewed by an O-7. It made Balcalski realize how important their job really was.

ⅠⅠⅠ 1 ⅠⅠⅠ

2300 ZULU:
FRIDAY, 1 JUNE

To be prepared for war is one of the most
effectual means of preserving peace.

George Washington

Camp Pendleton, California

Lieutenant Colonel Bill Krandel pulled into the lot across
the street from the officers' club. General Vandervoos's
parking slot near the main door was empty, so Krandel was
still early for the appointment. Getting out of the car, he
squared himself away, making sure his shirt was taut in
front. The shirt was starched, but he still smoothed away
the wrinkles. Years of habit kept him looking sharp. It was
more instinct now than anything else. Krandel himself
couldn't tell that the shirt had been in a suitcase only hours
before. As he entered the club a voice called, "Wild Bill,
ten years and you haven't changed at all."

Surprised, Krandel turned. "Harvey Weston. What the
hell are you doing here?"

"I should ask *you* that. I'm the platoon commander for
the RDF they've geared up. And how about those silver
leaves? You must have gotten every below-the-zone pro-

motion that came your way and then some. You haven't had your 'command lobotomy' yet, have you, uh, sir?"

Krandel laughed. "Easy, Harv—the last time my old roomie called me sir was when you reported at my table, late for dinner. Besides, I've only had these leaves a few weeks."

Weston leaned forward and fingered Krandel's rank, grinning. "Still, what about this promotion?"

Krandel shrugged. "Well, I just got lucky, that's all. Got hooked up with a sugar-daddy general at the Pentagon who liked what I did and didn't think my crap smelled. Guess I was in the right place at the right time. But how about you? When do you pin on major, and what have you been doing since graduation?"

"Well, I don't pin on the gold ones till next year. I was selected with our—I mean *my*—year group, so I've got a while to go yet. But anyway, I've been out gruntin' the past few years, instead of sitting on my fat fanny at the Pentagon like you. I've been everywhere from Okinawa to Reykjavik working with the troops." He paused, then said almost wistfully, "I guess I've got to pull a Pentagon tour one of these days if I want to get promoted.

"So what's a paper pusher like you doing at an operational base?"

"I'm taking over the 37th Battalion next week from Colonel Hathaway. In fact, I'm meeting General Vandervoos tonight to discuss it."

Captain Weston cracked a grin. "Well, I guess I'd *really* better get used to calling you sir, then. I knew a Colonel Krandel was supposed to take over the 37th, but I didn't know it was 'Wild Bill.' The platoon I'm in is part of your Smilin' 37th."

"No kidding. We'll just have to work together like old times then, Harv."

"Sure." Weston glanced at his watch. He looked around and, spotting the general's staff car driving to the front, spoke up. "There's Vandervoos now. Hey, I've got a dinner date and I'm late. Got to be running off. By the way, you

married that girl you dated at Annapolis—uh, Maureen—
didn't you?"

Krandel felt pleased that Weston remembered. "That's
right. Got two little rug rats, too. How about yourself? You
weren't dating anyone in school."

"I got married about a year out of Quantico. Been di-
vorced for two years now. You know how it is—being
away from home all the time is rough on the family life."

Krandel nodded. "Sorry."

"That's all right." Weston clasped Krandel's shoulder.
"Listen, I've got to go. I'll catch you on the rebound."

Krandel shook his hand. "Take care, Harv. We'll get
together."

"Yes, sir—I'm sure we will."

Weston spun on his heels and left, leaving Krandel
blinking about the "sir" his classmate had tagged on. He
started to call after him but was interrupted. "Bill Krandel.
How do you do, son? Any trouble making it out here?"

Krandel turned and smiled. Brigadier General Allen W.
Vandervoos was as big as they allowed marines to get in
the service. His bulky frame wasn't fat—the bones were
too large to allow that—but it was solid. And his presence
was overpowering. He was a typical general officer: When
you were around him, you spoke only when he wanted you
to speak; he told you what to talk about, and when he was
finished, you stopped talking.

General Vandervoos was flanked by his aide, a youngish
but serious-looking lieutenant who politely ignored Krandel's presence.

Krandel stuck out his hand. "How are you, sir?"

"Fine, Bill. And you?"

"Couldn't be better, sir. The trip from D.C. went well,
and I'm ready to go."

"Good. How are Maureen and the kids—get them settled in?"

"We just got in from L.A. this afternoon. We spent a few
days touring Disneyland and Knott's Berry Farm before
heading down here. I've got the family put up at the TLF."

"Glad to hear it." Vandervoos nodded toward the bar.

"Let's sit down and talk, Bill. I've got some things to let you in on before you take over my battalion."

"Yes, sir. By the way, is there any way I could meet my gunnery tomorrow?"

"Sure." General Vandervoos turned to his aide, then back to Krandel. "Bill, this is Stephen Moranz, my aide. He'll help you out."

"How do you do, sir?" The second lieutenant stepped forward and briskly shook hands with Krandel.

"Fine, Lieutenant. Could you arrange that meeting for me?"

"No problem, sir. I'll track down your gunnery sergeant and have him ready when you want him. Do you have a particular time in mind?"

"Any time in the morning."

"Well, sir, the battalion finishes their run by 0630. How does 0900 sound?"

"Fine. I'll be at Battalion HQ."

"Very well, sir." The lieutenant turned to Vandervoos. "Anything else, General?"

Vandervoos waved him away. "Get lost, Stephen. Colonel Krandel and I have some catching up to do."

"Yes, sir. Good afternoon, sir." He nodded at Krandel and backed away, leaving the two alone.

Vandervoos steered Krandel to the bar. "Let's have that drink, Bill. It's 1600—the drinking light is lit."

"Yes, sir."

After ordering drinks, Krandel stood behind his chair at the table and waited for the general to sit. Vandervoos waved him down. "The 37 Smilers is a good bunch, Bill."

"That's what I've heard, sir."

Vandervoos pulled out a cigar case and offered it to Krandel. Krandel shook his head. Vandervoos drew out a cigar, wet it, and bit off the tip before lighting up. He blew smoke away from Krandel and said, "I know this is your first command, Bill, so I don't want you to feel the pressure of having to show me you're some kind of superstar. I've seen what you can do."

Krandel shifted his weight in his chair. "Thank you, sir."

"Don't thank me yet." Vandervoos took a pull on his cigar and settled back in his chair. He got a faraway look in his eyes. "Having a command is probably the best job in the world. You're on your own out there; nobody is looking over your shoulder trying to second-guess you. I never realized how much fun it was until I got my first command. The only thing that ever came close was the time I coached my daughter's soccer team. I had total control then, as you will now. And that experience is necessary. Especially if you go into combat. And with the 37th, that's a possibility."

"That's what I've heard. In fact, I just met Captain Weston—one of my classmates. He has a platoon in the 37th."

Vandervoos nodded. He looked quickly around the room and, seeing no one nearby, lowered his voice. "Good man. He just took over the RDF—are you familiar with it?"

"Well, sir, I thought that the entire 37th was assigned to the Rapid Deployment Force. They could be called to action anywhere at any time."

"That's true. Part of the 37th is on alert all the time. If the balloon goes up, our men will be on the next plane out of Pendleton no matter where the action is. But what distinguishes Weston's platoon is the way they get there. They use TAVs to get to the strike area instead of a TAC cargo plane." Vandervoos sipped his drink.

Krandel nodded. He recalled that one of his classmates at the War College had been a project officer for the TAV. It stood for TransAtmospheric Vehicle, the air force "spaceplane" dropped from a 747 mother ship. It was similar to the old X-15, but bigger and better. It took less than an hour to get to any spot on earth. The original TAV, the National Aerospace Plane, had the capability to launch from the ground, but congressionally-mandated budget cuts forced the air force to go with a cheaper craft. It wasn't perfect, but it was the best thing going.

Vandervoos continued: "There's berthing for one squad aboard each TAV. Weston's platoon will take four planes to get to the strike area."

Krandel nodded. "That's right. I've heard of the TAV,

sir, but I didn't know it would be used for the RDF. I guess it really does put meat into the rapid part of RDF."

Vandervoos answered wryly, "I'll say. And by the way, that's for official use only. The government doesn't want to broadcast the fact that we use TAVs—mostly for political reasons. It might look as though we're trying to develop a terrorist-like strike force. The entire project is what we call a 'black project'; no one quibbles about the money we spend on it, and we don't tout its existence.

"Anyway, Weston's platoon works intimately with the air force out at Edwards. We try to get the platoon at least one flight per month for training."

Krandel toyed with his napkin. "How do the troops get back, sir?"

"That's the catch. The TAVs don't have the capability to launch without the mother ship, so once they reach the strike area, they're stuck there. But any time we'd need them, it would be a last-ditch effort anyway. We'd recover the troops with traditional transports like the C-19, which means that although they can get somewhere in a hurry, they'll have to wait awhile to get back, out of the strike zone." He noticed Krandel's frown. "Don't let it disturb you, Bill. Every man in the RDF is a volunteer and knows his rear is on the line. Besides, as commander, you won't be going with that particular unit—that's Weston's job. You'll be going in with Headquarters Squad on C-19s, with the rest of the battalion."

Krandel took a long pull on his drink. The liquor felt good after the drive down from L.A. today, and he had always felt comfortable around the general. Krandel's first assignment out of Quantico was as Vandervoos's aide; the then-Colonel Vandervoos had taken a liking to the sharp young officer and had groomed him for promotion. He'd kept track of Krandel's career, and when a hand was needed to steer the tides of fate, Vandervoos had interceded, taking care of Krandel. Krandel leaned forward. "It certainly sounds challenging, sir."

"It will be. But if you can handle this, I can almost

guarantee you that once you get back to the Pentagon you'll have a star waiting for you. We need men like you in the corps, Bill. Good, sharp managers who know how to think on their feet. It's a different corps from when I was in your place. That damned Mexican fiasco has changed everything around, and it will be men like you running the corps.

"So don't step on it. Get this operational command out of the way, and you'll go a long way."

Krandel held up his glass in salute. "Thank you, General. I'll do my best."

Vandervoos returned the salute and grinnèd. "I know you will, son." He shot down the drink and turned to the hostess. "Miss, another round here, and make them doubles this time."

Edwards Air Force Base, California

As Major Robert Gould hopped the three feet from the TAV to the asphalt runway the hot desert air hit him like a bag of cement. It wasn't the heat that made him fume—it was the maintenance pukes holding up his debrief. Four o'clock, he thought. The hottest part of the whole damn day, and the friggin' Flight Test Center commander won't release my craft because of a maintenance check.

Moments before, in the still, air-conditioned coolness of the TAV, Gould had watched the shimmering air rise from the ground in front of Base Operations. That was when he'd gotten notice over the command post frequency that there'd be a "short holdup" before he could turn his TAV over to his crew chief. Colonel Mathin wanted to speak to him personally.

Gould swung his gaze to Base Ops; on top of the building an oversized billboard exclaimed:

WELCOME TO
EDWARDS AIR FORCE BASE
UNITED STATES AIR FORCE SYSTEMS COMMAND
ELEVATION 2302 FEET ASL

Although brown with dust, the white-bordered sign still managed to elicit a feeling of pride. He wouldn't admit it, but having the opportunity to fly with the best . . . to walk quietly through the O-club with his orange flight suit and just *know* every fighter jock in the place would be envying him . . . to be at the cutting edge of technology . . . it was like living in heaven. It was something he wouldn't admit to anyone, but God, it was great!

He was totally absorbed in the flying, from the TAV's gut-wrenching launch to the recovery back at Edwards. He wasn't just flying here, he was flirting with . . . *greatness*. The Yeagers of old had made their mark, and here he was—walking in their footsteps.

Ten years ago he would never have dreamed it possible. With a month to finish UPT (Undergraduate Pilot Training) he'd SIE'd to fly helicopters, giving up forever his chance to fly fixed-wings.

His wing commander had a shit fit: Here was Gould, Willie's top stick, pulling a "Self-Initiated Elimination." And why? Because it turned Gould's stomach knowing he'd to have to live up to the fighter-pilot image. He was a good pilot—and he knew it. But the partying and carrying-on that went with the fighter-pilot mentality just wasn't his style.

Ever since he'd turned down fixed-wings, he'd been incessantly told: "Are you out of your ever-lovin', woman-chasin', beer-drinkin', ring-knockin', one-each-issue, sex-crazed mind? What do you mean, turning down a chance for fighters for a piss-pot *helicopter?* Are you nuts?!"

Sure it was crazy—but it was something that, at the time, he just had to do. And still he managed to get to the top, albeit through the back door. His only regret was that he never got to fly a "heavy"—a jumbo jet—so that when he retired from the air force he could ease on into a cushy civilian job flying for the airlines.

But no matter. Here he was: Local boy makes good. He made it to the top without flying fighters. He was lucky to be assigned to Edwards straight out of choppers. Sure, it had never happened before; and sure, he'd had trouble transitioning back to fixed-wings from choppers, but who cared? He knew there wasn't any truth to the story that he was the President's long-lost cousin. He'd made it here on his own.

Besides, saving CINCSAC's ass, when SAC's ubiquitous Airborne Command Post had crashed in the Great Salt Lake, hadn't hurt his chances for entrance to Test Pilot School either. The general had told him, "I'll get you anything you want," when Gould plucked CINCSAC from the water.

So here he was. Number-one honcho on the TAV circuit and being held up on the flightline by some lard-ass, non-rated colonel. Why on earth they'd put a nonpilot in charge of the Flight Test Center still puzzled him. The "new air force" had certainly gone to hell.

He squinted through the heat toward Base Ops. Still nothing. The motorcade from maintenance was nowhere in sight.

As he scowled he heard the sound of feet hitting the ground. He wiped a small bead of perspiration that began to gather at his lip and jerked his head toward Base Ops. He said, "It'll be a while yet; looks like the debrief is going to be delayed."

Major Delores Beckman rolled her eyes and leaned against the side of the TAV. Her orange flight suit contrasted with the blackened camouflage painted on the TAV. The camouflage was a compromise settled on by the various generals on the air staff. Exhaustive studies had shown it didn't matter *what* you painted on the aircraft; as it turned out, the enemy would either detect the plane by radar or from the glint off the windshield, so it really didn't matter. The camouflage was the result of a two-year piss-ing contest among the generals, a compromise struck so that no one would lose face.

Delores crossed her arms over her breasts. "Command Post still insists we stay put until maintenance does their thing. They promised it would be only a few more minutes. Do you want me to go ahead with the postflight?"

"Sure, I'll grab the front if you get the back."

"Right."

Delores sashayed away, the flight suit swaying slightly at the hips—tight around the buttocks, but sagging around the waist, not complimenting her at all.

Gould shook his head slightly, thinking to himself, I've seen worse. Delores perplexed him. Not only was she one of the few women at Edwards that he had failed to get to bed, but she was a superb pilot. It just didn't seem right: Hot pilots *have* to be hot in bed, but from all indications, she was not playing the game at all. He'd taken her out a couple of times in the month she'd been there—no steady thing—but she'd let him know in no uncertain terms that they were playing by *her* rules.

As a flight examiner, he was in a position to force her hand—flunk her on a check ride in one of the TAV's if she didn't ante up—but damn it, he was better than that. He didn't need to fall back on some hoked-up position of FE to get what he wanted. And if she was going to play the game that way—well, he thought, we'll just see, Miss Delores Beckman—you may be a shit-hot pilot, but you're not going to mess with my gonads. No siree. I'll play your game and win, damn it.

Gould yanked the checklist out of a zipped top pocket and strode around the front of the TAV. He checked off items as he came to them, ensuring the craft had not sustained damage from its semiballistic flight.

He was at the next-to-last item on the checklist when he heard an approaching vehicle. He hastily looked over a Pitot tube and the VUHF antenna before scrambling under the TAV's fuselage to greet two staff cars, a SMART maintenance truck, and a bus that served as the crew van.

A chubby colonel, his blue short-sleeved uniform shirt

untucked in the back and a paunch bulging over his belt, nodded a greeting to Gould. "How ya doing, Major?"

"Fine, sir." Gould straightened slightly and halfway forced a salute.

Colonel Mathin ignored the salute and walked around the TAV, staring up at the scorched fuselage. The craft still emanated heat from its reentry, but it had quickly cooled in the dry air. He patted the low-slung vessel and turned to Gould. "We're taking her off flight status until we can get her completely checked out. I don't want any of the other birds to go up until we find the glitch you reported. Which flight controls were you having trouble with?"

Delores appeared behind Gould and held out a notepad. The colonel grunted a greeting to Delores, ripped the top form off the pad, and studied it. He spoke to no one in particular: "Pitch thrusters." Then, looking up at Gould, he said, "I would have thought you had trouble with the new JATO units we installed. There hasn't been any trouble with the pitch thrusters since we upgraded them last year. What happened?"

"Well, it wasn't me, sir—I was the examiner on the flight. Major Beckman was AC; she noticed the sluggish response once we were entering the atmosphere." He turned to Delores. "Do you want to fill him in?"

"That's right, Colonel. We were rounding the top, about one-fifty klicks up, when I couldn't get a nose-down attitude."

Colonel Mathin looked at her from the corner of his eye. "Then why didn't you declare an emergency?"

"Didn't have time. I rotated the TAV using the roll thrusters, tweaked the yaws to get us pointing to the right —which was actually "down" by that time—then rolled us around again with the thrusters to get the right attitude."

The colonel raised his brows. Gould smiled, wiping the grin from his face as the colonel looked his way. Colonel Mathin said to Gould, "Well, are you going to override her and declare an emergency, Major, or what?"

Gould thought for a minute. "How long will the TAVs be in the shop, Colonel?"

"For an emergency, we'll have to ground the fleet. No telling how long we'd have to keep them there. But if you don't override her by declaring an emergency, we can only ground *this* bird until the problem is fixed. Then it's free to fly again, even if every TAV in the inventory has the same problem. You know the rules, Major."

Damn bureaucracy, thought Gould. Shut down the whole friggin' operation for nothing more than probably a blown fuse. He ran a hand through his hair. "Major Beckman passed her check ride, Colonel. Once she regained control of the TAV there was no need to declare an emergency. I'm afraid there's nothing more I can add to her report."

Mathin reddened. "Very well, Major, but it will be your ass if this happens again." He nodded curtly to the two and spun around, barking orders to the gaggle of maintenance personnel who had congregated around the trio during their discussion. The SMART truck pulled up to the TAV; an airman ran out and attached a wire from the truck to the craft, grounding the TAV by bringing it to the same electric potential as the truck, circumventing any chance of having a spark arc during the maintenance and subsequent refueling.

Gould pulled his flight briefcase out of the hatch and made his way to the crew van that had pulled up alongside the TAV. Delores caught up with him as he entered the van and signaled with her eyes for him to join her in the back. Gould scooted into the back seat; Delores sat in front of him, turning around to face him as the van started up.

"Thanks."

He shrugged. "Sure, no biggy."

"They would have taken me off flight status until the emergency was investigated—and with the shortage of maintenance personnel, it might have been months before the incident was cleared up."

"You passed the check ride, so you didn't have anything to worry about. The emergency, if there was one, was entirely a judgment call. Look, Delores, this isn't UPT. We're not quite as Mickey-Mouse as ATC out here, but you've still got to cover your six. If you screw the pooch up there and don't cover yourself, you're gone. Period. No questions asked.

"But on the other hand, if you jump the gun, like calling an emergency too early and the emergency *doesn't* pan out, then that's just as good as screwing up. Mathin will transfer you out of here so fast your head will spin. He can't afford to have TAV pilots who are too timid to put their asses on the line. But he also can't afford to have TAV pilots who end up killing themselves. You have to toe a fine line flying these babies. And today it looks like you passed the first test." Gould sat back in the seat and stared out the van window.

Delores was quiet for some time before saying, "Uh, thanks, then. If there's anything I can do in return . . ." Her voice trailed off.

He just nodded. "Don't worry; now that you've qualified on the TAV you'll start pulling alert with the rest of us soon enough. There'll be plenty of chances to pay me back in the alert shack—you'll be bored stiff after the first week of waiting around." Actually, he *could* think of something she could do, all right, but chances were it wasn't what she had in mind. Anyway, he was just too damned tired to convince her of that tonight.

The White House, Washington, D.C.

"Mr. President, I really think you ought to reconsider. If you go on this trip without stopping in Great Britain, it would be a slap in the face to their Labour Party. Especially when you consider the campaign support they gave you." The White House chief of staff, Manuel Baca, stood rigidly in front of President Montoya's desk.

Sandoval Montoya—forty-third President of the United States of America, youngest son of Ronaldo Montoya, and father of three daughters—sat unyielding. He held Baca by the eye. In the two years of his presidency, Baca, his chief of staff, had cracked open the door to the presidency to an unheard-of extent. Slowly but surely President Montoya was beginning to feel his power erode.

He no longer made decisions, he *reacted* to recommendations. Recommendations that were brought in by his chief of staff and sanitized into something that Montoya would think was acceptable. And it wasn't just here, in this office. It was everything in his life—even Rosanna had the girls present their plans to him like an overstudied, overstaffed GAO behemoth. He couldn't get back home to Santa Fe without his itinerary running up and down the bureaucracy.

Well, it *wasn't* acceptable! He tapped his fingertips together and spoke quietly. Honed to perfection while he was governor of New Mexico, it was the little power game he played that forced people to listen. And once he had them straining to hear what he was saying, he had them.

"Manuel"—he drew out the vowels—"we have to remember why we're going; I just don't have time to stop in Great Britain." He counted off points on his fingers. "One, the Brits don't really give a damn if we show up or not. They've got their Soviet oil, so what we do doesn't matter to them anymore. The Labour Party is such a small minority in Parliament that it wouldn't make any difference if we gave them Texas; they'd still buy Russian oil.

"Two, I've gone to Europe two years in a row. I've got to honor the NATO accord and attend that meeting. If I don't, I'll lose Germany's confidence.

"Three, Israel's going to fall, and soon, if we don't pump that money into their economy. The Arab Liberated Hegemony is poised on their borders with everything but the kitchen sink. All they're looking for is an excuse to attack. And if we treat Israel the same way we did Mexico, we're going to lose a lot of damned fine people."

"But Mr. President, you yourself know how touchy that would be—remember why you were elected. And keep Mexico out of this. If you try to equate the Israeli situation to what happened to Mexico, it's over for you." Baca stared at Montoya.

Yes, I remember, thought Montoya. If it wasn't for the widespread sympathy to "Let Mexicans Rule Mexico," I wouldn't be here now.

After Nicaragua, El Salvador, and Panama had been "liberated," the American public started to get alarmed only when the revolution in Mexico had reared its ugly head. But as before, the well-orchestrated propaganda from the revolutionary left presented the United States the slogan: "Let Mexicans Rule Mexico!"

Years of bigotry—treating Mexicans as "little brown brothers in the South"—and uncontrolled corporate greed had fueled the sentiment that the United States should leave well enough alone. The epidemic reached proportions unheard of in the past, outsoaring the anti-American sentiments reverberating from the rest of Latin America. And as a result, once the flow of émigrés started flooding the southern U.S., Americans openly defied the no-immigration policy. Quarter was given to any illegal alien, and support for this activity was openly sanctioned.

The previous administration had felt the heat from the conservative element to "do something and do it now, damn it!" And even the more moderate pro-Western nations lifted their brows in concern. Mexico was violently turning socialistic, and it seemed that nothing could stop it.

So in anticipation of an aggressive regime inheriting Mexico, the previous President ordered an assault on Mexico City. The purpose: install as titular head a native Mexican friendly to the U.S. (although her Harvard education was widely blown up in the press), and generally give the Mexican constabulary time to secure a stable government.

The assault failed. Network coverage by U.S. journalists brought the fighting closer than ever before to the American home. Vietnam was no comparison: Live footage of Americans sweeping through Mexico City's streets, felling nine-year-old snipers, tore at America's gut. Within three days the resounding cry of *"Come home!"* permeated the nation. "Let Mexicans Rule Mexico!"

So strong was the sentiment that outspoken attacks on

the President resulted in the outright capitulation of American troops. This was no "peace with honor"; the troops retreated with their tails between their legs. The American military was pared to the bone, and a new national feeling of isolationism became the norm. It had been two years since Montoya rode to power, but he still appealed to everyone who had any sympathy at all for the Mexican's dilemma.

Yes, Montoya remembered well. He couldn't afford to let the public appeal falter. Especially since—one month to the day after he took office—he was present in Mexico City when the Socialist People's Democracy of Mexico declared that the United States of America would no longer be blacklisted; they would be treated as any other country and be given the right to barter for Mexico's oil on the world market. So for the first time in fifteen years the United States would not have to buy Mexican oil on the black market. Once again, gasoline was plentiful. And cheap. President Montoya was tied too closely to Mexico to forget.

Montoya spoke firmly. "I remember, but Israel may still go the same way as Mexico." Montoya melted down his chief-of-staff's gaze and punched at his intercom. "Judy, continue to make arrangements for the trip to West Germany and Israel on Air Force One. We'll be leaving three months from today. Manuel will be out shortly with the itinerary."

He removed his finger from the button and settled back in his chair. He folded his hands and studied Baca. Things have changed the past few years, thought Montoya. Here is my most influential advisor—my friend—and this wrestling match we play at gets more serious all the time.

After some moments Montoya finally said, "Let me know what you propose I do about the trip."

"Yes, sir." Baca turned and left the room. As he left Montoya tapped his fingers together, satisfied that this round had come out in his favor.

Camp Pendleton

Gunnery Sergeant David Balcalski was drunk. So drunk, in fact, that when he left the bar to go to the bathroom he couldn't find his zipper. He looked—he searched the entire bathroom, on his knees under each stall, and on top of each toilet—but he . . . just . . . couldn't . . . find it.

And of all the times to lose his zipper, this had to be the worst. Swigging pitchers of beer since noon had left him feeling very uncomfortable indeed. He thought he was going to pop.

So Gunnery Balcalski, thirty-one-year gyrene veteran, went in his pants. And it felt so good, he went again.

Balcalski staggered out of the bathroom and looked blearily around the room. A khaki flash caught his eyes. "Hey, Sergeant . . . over here." One of Balcalski's drinking buddies was a blur at the end of the bar, waving Balcalski to join them.

Balcalski lurched out and made a headstrong effort to go nowhere in particular. He stumbled out into the hot desert, and the fresh air nearly floored him. The sunlight was almost unbearable. Squinting, he started to weave his way back to the Top Three Quarters—normally a five-minute walk from the NCO Club—but taking the path Balcalski was inventing, he would probably get there around sunset. If he was lucky.

But he didn't worry. In the three years he'd been at Pendleton, he hadn't been lost once. At least not for very long. In his thirty-one years of marchin', gruntin', spittin', and polishin', he'd been at Pendleton about ten years altogether. The place brought back memories to him, but right at this moment he couldn't exactly remember what those memories were.

Nor did he care.

On impulse he took a sudden left and within fifty feet

found himself in front of the Top Three Barracks. Originally built as the bachelor officer's quarters, the Top Three offered a little more luxury in the way of "goodies" than an ordinary barracks would have. And through his drunken haze Balcalski looked forward to one of those goodies: a bath that he could lounge in without having to worry about a roommate with which to share it.

He staggered up the wooden stairs and found himself looking in the eyes of a second lieutenant. Balcalski jerked to attention and almost fell backward off the stairs. The lieutenant reached out and steadied him. Balcalski grew red in the face. "How do you do, sir? I'm sorry—"

"So today's your birthday, Sergeant." It was a statement, not a question.

"Yes, sir. And I'm on leave, sir . . . only time I take leave this time of year, sir—"

"I know, Sergeant. That's why I'm here. General Vandervoos sent me to *request* that you stop over tomorrow morning and meet your new C.O."

Balcalski started to sober up. "Colonel Krandel? But sir, he's not supposed to be here until *after* the weekend."

"I know, Sergeant. He wanted to get a jump on things and requested that you meet with him tomorrow morning." He looked the grizzled sergeant up and down. "I suggest you try and get over whatever it is that you've been doing. And, if you don't mind"—the implication was clear—"do Colonel Krandel the honor of cutting your leave short and showing up tomorrow morning. Don't bother with the morning run; the reception's at 0900 in the staff room. Of course, General Vandervoos can't order you off leave for this, do you understand?"

"Yes, sir." Like hell I understand, he thought. I'm probably twice as old as this kid, but he understands just as well as I: When the marines say jump, you don't argue about whether jumping is legal or not, you ask how high.

The lieutenant smiled, but before he left he nodded toward the growing stain at Balcalski's crotch. "And don't forget to change your pants, Sergeant. Wouldn't want to break out in a rash down there."

"Yes, sir. Good evening, sir."

"Good after*noon,* Sergeant. It's only sixteen-thirty."

"Yes, sir. Good afternoon, sir." Balcalski turned as the lieutenant left, fumbled for his keys, and let himself in. Struggling out of his pants, he held the trousers up. *Shit,* he thought. No wonder I couldn't find the damn zipper—my pants have buttons.

Do'brai

Hujr ibn-Adi squatted in the twilight by the outside corner of the temple. He played with two small silver coins, nervously moving them around in his hands. The coins scratched together, grinding dirt into fine sand; children cried shrilly to one another over the din of merchants closing their hutches. Late night at the market; it brought back a flood of memories.

It was hot in Do'brai—the humidity never got above five percent, and the dry wind seemed to sap the life out of you. He adjusted his *kefiyeh* to sop up the sweat that stood at his brow.

Hujr waited for the late-night bazaar to close before moving past the temple. This place where he used to roam as a child now signaled greater things to him. It was not yet time to reveal himself to those who called him home. He didn't want to tip his hand and make the fact known too early that he was here. Even though he felt the majority of the Do'brainese were behind him, there were spies in the walls, and those who would turn him in for the money on his head. He spat to the side, thinking of the bounty levied by the imperialistic countries. They would leave him alone if they weren't prodded by the United States.

The years in Bulgaria, training with Libya's Arab Liberated Hegemony, had instilled the lessons well. How many others could boast of infiltrating the Philippine hierarchy? Adept coolness was his trademark in assassination. His three hits and one maiming were textbook examples of terrorism, used and quoted by the Jihad.

Hujr was caught between worlds. Loathing the Filipino features inherited from his mother, he unhesitatingly used the distinctly un-Arabic features to further the thrust of the ALH. His father, a career diplomat from Do'brai, had met and married his mother while assigned to the Do'brainese embassy in Manila twenty-six years before. Moving his family when he became Do'brai's ambassador to Egypt, Hujr's father was caught in the crossfire of the military coup and was found in a deserted prison, hours after the coup had failed. His father's eye sockets were blackened holes, burned out by torches in interrogation; his fingers, when pried open from his fist, had dug through his hand to the bone during the questioning.

Hujr still shook with rage at the thought of his father's death. Running away from home, he turned to the only organization in the region that promised to help him get the revenge he so desperately wanted on his father's killers. The Arab Liberated Hegemony transcended all geographical boundaries. Fueled by the radical Jihad sweeping the Middle Eastern countries like a firestorm, the ALH grew more militant and daring in their worldwide expansionism.

They welcomed Hujr into their ranks. The Philippine assassination had been his first assignment for the ALH. And now he was a legend.

So Hujr was a local hero, if not an infamous global one, for his role in the key assassinations that led to the downfall of the Philippine Islands. He was well-known now, and he was highly sought after.

He continued to turn the coins through his fingers, waiting and watching for the bazaar to close. When the time finally came, he swept back his *abiyeh* and made his way toward the center of the village.

He knocked at a back door, and as it opened dust swirled at his feet. A hand beckoned him inside as a grunt of recognition came from within. He was offered water and, drinking from the *ibriq*, thanked the servant with a nod before being escorted to the inner chamber.

The room was large by any standard. The mortar walls were covered by patterned rugs; the ceiling hung low, and a fan lazily freshened the air around him. The room was dark to his eyes, but he recognized the *shahib ibn-Yazid*—the guerilla leader—at once.

Ghazzali abu-Hamid had not changed in the years since Hujr had first met him. He was still water-fat; too much time living the politician's life. But when he tore himself away from the United Nations tirades, the incessant meetings with peace negotiators, and the worldwide trips, Ghazzali still commanded the admiration of his men. The force that made the ALH work was embodied in the man. Charisma oozed from him, surrounding and drowning you in its zeal. One couldn't help but get caught up in the fervor.

Hujr nodded to his leader and kept silent. The man sitting next to Ghazzali was a stranger. The man sat at Ghazzali's left—the place of the superior—so the implicit respect flowed from Hujr.

Ghazzali nodded to Hujr. "Welcome, my friend. You are well?"

"Well enough to fight, my brother," recited Hujr, completing the ALH pact.

"Good." Ghazzali twisted to a more comfortable position but did not invite Hujr to sit. Hujr stood loosely, relaxing. Ghazzali spoke to Hujr, still ignoring the stranger to his left. "We are pleased with your latest accomplishment. I take it you had no trouble getting back to Do'brai."

Hujr shrugged. "No more than usual. I had to hide out and take the long way home, but other than that, I've made it unnoticed. It has been over two years since I've been here; it is good to be back."

Ghazzali nodded. "This is my first visit here, and I, too, feel at home. I take it you've managed to get enough rest in the meantime?"

"If you mean so that I can train for another mission—yes."

Ghazzali smiled for the first time. He motioned with his hand for Hujr to come forward. "Excellent. Then may I introduce a friend of mine . . . one that both of us are going to work for. This is General Fariq Kamil."

Hujr kept the puzzlement from his face, but Ghazzali read the uncertainty in his eyes. Ghazzali said, "You've been gone from Do'brai a long time, my brother. General Kamil is better known for his position. He is the new commander of the general staff for Abd al-Rahman ibn-Muhammed ibn al-Ash'ath."

General Kamil spoke without expression. "I have heard of your talents. I welcome the chance to work with a fellow countryman. President Ash'ath has a proposition that will make you one of the most famous men in the world. Are you interested?"

Hujr answered without skipping a heartbeat. "Perhaps."

⫴ 2 ⫴

1230 ZULU:
SATURDAY, 2 JUNE

Find out where the people want to go, then hustle yourself around in front of them.

James Kilpatrick

Camp Pendleton

"Good morning, Sergeant."

"Good morning, sir." Gunnery Sergeant Balcalski snapped a salute, holding stiff until Lieutenant Colonel Krandel returned the greeting. Krandel sharply dropped his hand and faced the battalion. Moments before Krandel had watched from the side as the men formed up; they joked among themselves, cautiously ignoring Krandel's presence. Balcalski showed up on the scene and took control. The grizzled sergeant commanded instant respect from the men. Even though Balcalski was enlisted, the men treated the gunnery sergeant with a touch of awe. They seemed almost too eager to follow his commands.

It was as though the sergeant had charmed the men, but it was deeper than that. He said the right things at the right time; he was a natural. Krandel brushed the thought aside and concentrated on the men.

Krandel was dressed as the rest of Balcalski's men were:

45

red jogging shorts, white socks pulled high up the legs, black, low-topped sneakers, and a smartly ironed T-shirt emblazoned with UNITED STATES MARINE CORPS. The men of the 37th Marine Battalion stood in well-ordered platoons behind the sergeant; behind him was the battalion flag. Four men carried guidons, one for each platoon, adorned with battle streamers that marked the accomplishments and landings on battlefields of past years.

Krandel felt pleased. The men looked sharp, and except for a little redness around Balcalski's eyes, the 0530 roll call went without a hitch. Krandel moved close to Balcalski and spoke in a low voice, "Don't mind my presence, Sergeant. I've heard a lot about you and your men. I suppose the officers aren't running with us this morning?"

Balcalski looked embarrassed. "Well, sir, it's Saturday, and Smiler tradition is for the enlisted men to run to each platoon commanders house—wake them up with esprit, sir."

"With the final stop at the battalion commander's house, I take it?"

"Yes, sir."

"Well, no use breaking with tradition—except let's add a new one."

Balcalski cocked an eye at the new battalion CO. "Sir?"

"Let's hit General Vandervoos's house first. I want to let him know that Colonel Krandel is alive and well."

"Aye, aye, sir." Balcalski turned to his men. "Battalion —on my command: right, *face;* double time, *harch.*"

The group of two hundred men lurched off under the lead of Krandel and Balcalski.

Do'brai

Hujr ibn-Adi felt alive again. Just forty-eight hours earlier he was evading border guards—his own—to make his way back to the city. Do'brai didn't officially recognize the ALH and had even signed a multinational agreement to erase terrorist groups; Hujr was persona non grata in his own homeland. But what a country *says* and what a country *does* are two entirely different things. And now, with a stomach full of *kush-kush,* Hujr settled back and slowly pulled on a hookah laced with hashish. His country was so civilized—unlike most places where he usually traveled. It was good to get back where he belonged.

But his leisure was timed, for he knew that soon he would discover why he had been summoned. Whatever it was, General Kamil had dangled a hint of it. Hujr took another puff on the pipe and let the sweet-smelling smoke roll out of his mouth and into his nostrils. It was Ghazzali who spoke first.

"How was your food? Have you supped enough for your next starvation?"

Hujr laughed, coughing on smoke. He waved his hand in front of his face. "My next starvation? Surely I do not have to starve to be in the service of General Kamil."

Kamil growled, clearly not pleased with the direction in which Hujr was taking the conversation. "If our plan is to succeed, then *no* chances should be taken. If you have to die, then it would be but a small sacrifice for the whole."

"For the whole." Hujr nodded. If there was nothing else he took seriously, he realized that the success of the whole depended upon the expendability of the parts. The members of the ALH could not dwell on their own fate; the Jihad must be advanced. And even though Hujr demanded a price for his actions, he still realized his place.

Hujr leaned forward and put the pipestem on a cradle. "So what is it that you require of me?"

"Your heritage . . . and your skill. To accomplish perhaps one of the greatest coups in history."

"Is that all?" Hujr answered. The hashish made him cocky; Kamil reddened but did not voice any disapproval.

Ghazzali seemed slightly amused. He said, "The information I give you will have to be minimal. If you are discovered, it is best that the entire plan not be revealed." Ghazzali turned to his left and pulled out a paper.

"You must make plans to travel to the United States."

Hujr's eyes grew large. "Tonight you will leave Do'brai and travel to Cuba. There you will select the equipment you will need; your equipment will be smuggled to West Germany while you fly to Mexico. From Mexico City, it is a simple matter to get across the border to the United States. Once there, you must be extremely careful. Your compatriot, Du'Ali al-Aswad, is waiting for you in Washington, D.C.

"Later, you will rendezvous with your equipment in Germany. Neither you nor those transporting the equipment will have any knowledge of the exact whereabouts of the other. Until, of course, you arrive in Germany."

"Why is the equipment in Germany if I must go to the United States?"

"That will come later." He handed over a packet through which Hujr flipped. "We have identified three prospective marks in the United States, one of whose identities you must assume. You will have three weeks once you are in Washington, D.C., to determine which mark will enable you best to accomplish your mission.

"If you are picked up, you must deny everything. *Nothing* must cause this plan to fail. Too many people are depending on you. The Jihad will surely suffer if you fail."

Hujr absently put his hand into the *abiyeh* and turned the coins between his fingers. "And my payment?"

"Ah, yes." Ghazzali turned and snapped his fingers. A servant appeared from out of the veiled wall. "Zaynab— bring her." The servant nodded and disappeared. Ghazzali turned back to Hujr. "The usual money, plus an extra to encourage you to make it back to Do'brai."

A young woman was shoved into the room. She picked herself up from the ground and stared defiantly at the three. A smile tugged at the corners of Hujr's lips. "The extra?"

"Of course. She's quite wild and will make a fine concubine."

"Where did you get her?"

"Does it matter? But if you must know, she was picked up in a raid across the border. Spoils of war, and all that."

"I must try out the merchandise to see if it's worth it—"

"Only if you succeed."

Hujr nodded. He placed the coins back in his pouch and relaxed in his chair. "When do I leave?"

General Kamil shifted his weight and spoke up. "Tonight. We'll have you out of the country by daybreak."

"Good . . . there's no time to waste."

At the words, Ghazzali clapped his hands. "Remove the wench."

As they dragged the young woman away she managed to spit; Hujr lurched back and wiped at the spittle that reached him. The general laughed—happy, it seemed for the first time all night. Hujr reached for his pipe and drew on the coarse-smelling hemp. "She will do fine . . . if she keeps her temperament."

ⅢⅢ **3** ⅢⅢ

1430 ZULU:
MONDAY, 13 AUGUST

No pain, no palm; no thorns, no throne: no gall, no glory:
no cross, no crown.

William Penn

Mexico City

Hujr pulled down his sunglasses and ignored the man coming toward him. Behind him passengers were still exiting the gate; to his front, the long customs line split into two: one for returning nationals and the other for foreigners entering the country. As the man approached, Hujr set down his suitcase and pushed his sunglasses back on his forehead. The man picked up the piece of luggage and did not shake Hujr's hand.

"We have you on the next flight to El Paso. From there, you will connect to Washington, D.C., through National Airport. Du'Ali will pick you up."

Hujr pulled down his sunglasses and glared. He spoke in a low tone, barely audible to the man. "Do *not* mention that name."

Silence, then the man lowered his eyes. "I understand."

Hujr pushed the glasses back on. "You have the passport?"

The man withdrew an envelope from his pocket with his free hand. Passersby ignored the two and scurried to the growing line in front of customs. "I have included an identification card and Citibank checks you can cash once you're in the United States; the signature is matched to your handwriting, and the plane tickets are with the checks. You will not be contacted again until you reach Germany."

"When does the plane get to Washington?"

"Three-thirty in the afternoon."

Hujr nodded. "That leaves me plenty of time to start working tonight. Very well . . . get us through customs."

The man did not answer but instead led the way to the side of the customs counter. Reaching the bored police officer at the front of the line, he flashed a wallet and spoke in Spanish. "I am escorting Mr. Resavoo on to the embassy—I have his diplomatic pouch."

The customs officer glanced at the wallet ID. The Do'brainese chargé d'affaires's picture was intimidating. The official wondered little about political maneuvering but knew very well about the bribes that accompanied expedition of certain individuals through customs. Especially those associated with Do'brainese diplomatic passports. The customs official looked the other way and waved them through.

Once Hujr and his escort were away from the customs area they changed direction and looped back toward a sign that pointed toward outgoing flights. They arrived at the Pan American desk; the Do'brai chargé d'affaires obtained Hujr's boarding pass and delivered it to Hujr, who was standing away from the main crowd. Although the air conditioning was cranked up to high, the room was almost unbearably muggy and hot. Short sleeves and casual clothing marked most of the travelers.

Hujr wordlessly accepted the boarding pass and didn't say goodbye when the Do'brainese official left. When the flight was called, Hujr inconspicuously boarded without looking around.

Camp Pendleton

"Pick up your feet, you lardasses! Do you want to get your pecker shot off? If you keep moving the way you're going, I'll have to wrap it up and send it home to your sweetie— then what is she gonna do?" Gunnery Balcalski bawled at the men in front of him. The 37th Marines jumped out of the mock-up TAV and rolled to the sliding runway, keeping their rifles close to their bodies. As they hit they popped up and sprinted to the side, off the slidewalk, sprawling on the ground before advancing. The slidewalk rumbled past the opening, causing some of the marines to stumble as they jumped from the hatch. Most of the men made the six-foot jump without any difficulty, but there were a few who'd forgotten their PLFs—or who'd grown sloppy, thinking that the parachute landing fall was only for "Legs." The PLF was designed specially so the men would land on the fleshy part of their bodies—the calf, thigh, buttocks, and back—so they would absorb the force of the fall and not hurt themselves.

Balcalski moved closer to the mock plane's hatch and waved his right arm. "Speed out, men! You've got fifteen more seconds to get out of there or you're dead. Go, go, go!"

The last few men exited the craft nearly on top of one another. The last marine leapt from the hatch and with a smack dropped his rifle as he hit the man below him. The chattering and yells from the background—words of encouragement shouted by the men—grew deathly silent. The marine rolled off the slidewalk and snatched up his rifle, only to be stopped by Balcalski.

"Havisad!"

The marine snapped into a brace. "Yes, Sergeant."

Balcalski glared for a full ten heartbeats. When Balcalski finally spoke, Havisad had to strain to hear him over the roar of the slidewalk. "Havisad, you've been out of

Basic for two years. *I've* been out of Basic for thirty-one. The last time I saw a rifle dropped, the man who dropped it bought a Mexican bullet through his right lung. And the last thing I remember him doing was cursing himself, thinking that he could have gotten the sonofabitch who shot him—*even when he was dying*. But he couldn't. And do you know why?"

"No, Sergeant."

"Because he dropped his damned rifle, that's why, Havisad. He couldn't shoot back because he didn't have his damned rifle." One of the marines coughed; Balcalski looked around. In the distance, a jeep was driving up to the mock-up. It looked like the battalion C.O. Balcalski waved for the next squad. "Get your fannies up there. On the count of three, take the exit again. This time, I want every other man to roll to the right and cover the man behind him. Now move."

As the jeep crawled closer Balcalski saw that his guess was right on mark—Lt. Col. Krandel and Captain Weston, the platoon C.O., were both decked out in camouflaged battle gear. An enlisted driver shared the front with Krandel; Weston rode alone in the rear of the jeep.

Krandel was turning out to be all right. A little gung ho, maybe . . . but Balcalski had heard rumors that this was the colonel's first operational assignment. He'd do fine if he wouldn't try so hard not to screw up.

Balcalski turned back to Havisad; he'd given the marine plenty of time to think over his mortal sin. "Private, the 37th doesn't allow mistakes. It's not only your ass that will get shot if you screw things up—it's the platoon's." Balcalski pointed with his eyes to Havisad's rifle. "Drop that rifle once more and you're out of here. If I don't shoot you with it first. Understand?"

Havisad stood rigid. "Yes, Sergeant."

"Then get the hell back with your squad; you're wasting my time." Balcalski turned and barked, "Morales!" As Balcalski turned away Havisad sprinted off to join his squad.

A corporal left the group and trotted up. "Yes, Gunnery?"

Balcalski jerked his head at the jeep, which had pulled off the road. "I'll be taking the colonel and Captain Weston through the mock-up. Run the men through—and make damn sure there aren't any mistakes this time."

"Gotcha, Gunnery." Morales stacked his rifle with Balcalski's as the squat gunnery sergeant went off to join the officers.

"Afternoon, sir." Balcalski held the salute until both Krandel and Weston returned it.

"Good afternoon, Gunnery," returned Krandel. "How are the men doing?"

"Fine, sir. Would you care to watch them run through the exercise?"

Krandel nodded. "Lead the way." Balcalski positioned himself to the right of and slightly behind the men as they moved toward the mock-up.

As they walked the officers were silent. Balcalski noted that Krandel's boots, although flawlessly shined, still had the look of new leather. His uniform was immaculate, but there was an unbroken-in look about it: neatly pressed, the creases looked as though they could cut paper. Krandel seemed to move naturally, but it still appeared to require some effort.

Balcalski took note of all the details he spotted but didn't allow Krandel's greenhorn tendencies to worry him. He had helped plenty of inexperienced officers through the years; it was part of a good sergeant's job. But Krandel was different. Not only was Krandel inexperienced in the field, but he was the *youngest* senior officer that Balcalski had helped. He'd just have to be more careful that he didn't step on Krandel's toes.

Krandel allowed Weston to lead the way. When they reached the mock-up Weston nodded toward the exit hatch. The hatch was tightly closed, simulating the craft in flight. Weston said to Krandel, "The men are strapped in the TAV in harnesses, not unlike what they would use in a C-19 if they were parachuting in from drop planes. The difference is that the TAVs can swoop into the staging area and land before the bad guys know what's going on."

Krandel grunted. "What do you mean, swoop in?"

"Well, sir,"—the "sir" from Weston sounded natural; Krandel pretended not to notice—"the TAV is coming from a semiballistic orbit, so it is slowing from about Mach 25 to its landing speed: 130 knots. The TAV rolls to a stop, and the men disembark while the craft is still moving. That way, the men are spread along the target area in whatever pattern we want them. The main reason for using the TAV is for fast response, and I guarantee that my marines will come through on that for you."

Krandel walked around the mock-up and peered into the darkened body. It took a few moments for his eyes to adjust from the glaring sun. Twenty-four marines, twelve to a side, were strapped in the webbing attached to the sides of the TAV. They remained motionless, staring straight ahead. Krandel pulled his head out and said, "Well, let's see them do it."

"Yes, sir." Balcalski leaned inside the craft. "All right, Morales, take the men through the paces."

Morales bawled at the men, "Prepare for landing." In one motion the marines grabbed the siding, bracing themselves for the landing. In the background a diesel engine coughed once, then caught as the moving slidewalk started rumbling in front of the hatch. After a few moments, allowing for the slidewalk to get up to speed, Morales shouted above the din of the machinery, "Prepare to disembark: Stand in the door!"

The men unfastened their strappings. Krandel and Weston moved around to the side of the craft. In front of the TAV mock-up the slidewalk raced past the opening. Morales stood in the hatch. The corporal grabbed the sides of the opening and crouched.

Balcalski put his mouth to Krandel's ear. "The slidewalk is moving at fifteen miles per hour in front of the opening.

When the men jump, they hit the mat and roll. It's the closest thing to having a moving TAV that we can get. This way the men can train for any exit speed by rolling to the ground and getting in their positions."

Balcalski was interrupted by Morales's yell. "Exit, Smilers!"

Morales leapt out, hit the slidewalk, and rolled to the ground in a modified parachute-landing fall.

One after another the marines exited, all hitting the slidewalk and rolling away, until the last man successfully left the craft. Balcalski allowed himself a hidden smile and said, "Finished, sir." He glanced to his stopwatch. "Fifty-six seconds—slightly under two seconds per man."

Krandel raised his brows. "Impressive."

Weston nodded. "Good work, Sergeant. But work on it. I want them all out in forty seconds. Every second saved will mean that much more time to accomplish the mission."

"Aye, aye, sir." He turned to Krandel. "Anything else, Colonel?"

"No, thank you, Sergeant. Carry on."

Balcalski saluted, then spun and left to join the men. Krandel turned back for the jeep.

Krandel spoke half to himself. "Your men looked impressive, Harv."

"Thanks. Alpha squad is the best I've got. Bravo and Charlie will probably be out here all tomorrow afternoon until they get it right."

"Do you go through the mock-up with them?"

"I go with Delta squad; they've usually got the fourth TAV. We're coming out tomorrow morning, if you'd like to watch."

"I think I might do that. What would I need to do if I wanted to join you on the mock-up?"

"Join us?" Weston stopped and looked surprised.

"Sure, why not? The battalion C.O. should be qualified in TAV landings if he's going to lead his men, shouldn't he?" They stood by the jeep and turned back toward the

TAV mock-up. Krandel's driver stood at parade rest at the other side of the jeep, quietly ignoring the conversation.

Weston put a foot up on the jeep and answered slowly. "Well, sir . . . I suppose so. But won't you be going in with the rest of the battalion? They won't be using TAVs to get to the combat area. My platoon is the only one that uses the TAV."

"There's always a chance I could come with you."

Weston chewed on his lip. "You're going to have to run through PLF training to get checked out first."

"Well, set it up. I want to be able to go with your squad tomorrow morning."

"Are you sure, sir?"

"Look, Harv. If I'm going to have any credibility telling your men to risk their lives in a TAV landing, I've got to be able to do the same things they do."

Weston answered skeptically. "Yes, sir. I'll call HQ and have them ready the course. One hour?" Krandel nodded. Weston moved to the other side of the jeep to where the driver stood. He reached in and pulled out a mike and made his request. Finished, he clicked off the mike and said, "Let's go on over, sir. They'll be ready when we get there."

Krandel grunted his reply and climbed into the front of the jeep. Weston climbed into the back after them, and they sped off.

Edwards Air Force Base

The TAV crew chief leaned over the nose of the craft. Supported by an elevated roller, the master sergeant pulled back from the potpourri of electronic gear and wiped a hand across his brow. Even in the shade of the sprawling hanger the temperature climbed above one hundred degrees; the only respite was the relative absence of humidity.

Major Robert Gould climbed up the shaky steel ladder to

the top of the portable roller and squinted at the guts of the TAV. The heart and soul of the TransAtmospheric Vehicle lay in front of him. Megamyriad light fibers, some not more than fractions of an inch long, connected the brain of the TAV to the rest of the craft.

Gould pulled his head out of the nose section and quizzed the crew chief. "Any idea on how much longer it's going to take?"

The master sergeant wiped his hands on his fatigues; the heat had forced him to strip down to a V-necked T-shirt. "No, sir. Depends if we can get the avionics hooked up." He reached past Gould and grabbed a pack of cigarettes. He shook the pack and offered one to Gould. Gould shook his head. The sergeant took one out and stepped back from the equipment before lighting up, careful not to get any debris into the control system.

Gould said, "What's taking so long?"

The crew chief drew on his smoke before answering. He pointed with his cigarette. "See them fibers, sir?"

Gould glanced at the spaghetti mess of color-coded wires. "Yeah."

"Well, when we finally tracked down that glitch you found, Systems Command let a contract with MacDac to upgrade the avionics to fiber optics. They tore out all the electrical wiring and replaced it with those fiber bundles—after, of course, they sold the air force a couple of million-dollar conversion units to transmit and receive the light impulses. Seems that the light fibers are EMP-proof; that way you won't have to worry about your baby going down in a nuke war. Anyway, Systems Command knew that TAC would never have grounded their TAVs to install the upgrade—so when we brought the birds in to find the glitch, the engineer types jumped all over us, wanting all their new bells and whistles installed."

"Great." Gould pulled back and moved to the side of the roller. The gashes where the JATO units could be attached barely disrupted the sleek aerodynamic lines of the craft. Even though the crew chief seemed optimistic, it seemed that more and more problems kept popping up. Gould was getting frustrated. Flying was his job—not waiting around for some newfangled engineering gizmo to adorn his craft.

Gould had lobbied Colonel Mathin and had managed to convince the higher-ups to let some of the TAV pilots take up one of the F-22s. He argued that keeping pilots grounded was just asking for trouble. And the F-22s weren't being used, so why not let the TAV pilots take them up for a spin? Blowing off steam was always good for the soul.

Gould didn't know exactly why Mathin went along with his request, but thank goodness he did, because half his squadron would have been climbing the walls right now without some sort of diversion.

Even so, it was getting old. He wanted to get back to some real flying.

The White House

Montoya shook the last hand and waved goodbye. He ducked into the Red Room and nodded to the Secret Service agent guarding the doorway. The agent voiced a polite "Good afternoon, Mr. President" but was really much too busy watching the door to continue the pleasantries. Montoya continued up the stairs, thinking that unlike New Mexico, the D.C. area was certainly not the land of *mañana*. He felt a fleeting longing for the old days in Santa Fe when he was governor and *nothing* was so important it couldn't wait until the morrow. Blue-corn enchiladas at the Shed for lunch, margaritas and nachos at the Pink Adobe before dinner, opera parties at Chimayo . . .

But those days were gone, and all the wishing in the world couldn't bring them back. But sometimes he wondered. He kept thinking that since Nixon had resigned and still got a pension, then maybe . . . just maybe he could do the same. But of course, he wasn't willing to put up with a Watergate debacle just to take an early retirement.

Grantland Percival Woodstone, the vice president of the United States, was waiting for him in the Oval Office. The vice president stood—not entirely because he wanted to, but because the others in the room did—when Montoya entered. Montoya nodded a greeting. This was probably the best benefit of the job: forced respect.

And with someone like Woodstone it felt good to take advantage of the system. Not that he didn't like the man; Montoya just didn't trust him. After all, Woodstone was the only outsider in the White House clan, the only gringo, the only one not from the southwest.

Montoya felt uneasy around the Harvard-educated vice president, but the voting support Montoya got from the Northeast more than made up for the feeling. If he could just get used to that damned nasal drawl . . . sometimes Montoya felt as though Percy was amused by him. It made him uneasy.

Montoya rounded his desk and sat; the others took their seats as soon as he was settled. Chief-of-staff Baca cleared his throat. "How did it go, Mr. President?"

"The ladies' luncheon? Fine, I suppose. That is, if you care for speaking to a nest of clucking hens for forty-five minutes. What's on the agenda?"

Baca glanced at his notes. "Cabinet meeting at two, then the House Whip has a special favor to ask at four-thirty—"

"That damned military budget again. Can't you keep him off my back until the Senate tears it apart? Once they get a hold of it, he'll be begging on his knees to have me pass *my* budget."

"I think that's what he had in mind, Mr. President. He wants to, uh, head you off at the pass, if you will. If he wasn't from the biggest military-industrial state in the union, I think he'd be backing off."

"Fine, then. Go ahead and let him in, but don't schedule him for more than fifteen minutes. Anything else?"

Baca shot a wary glance at the vice president, then said, "The annual German-Israeli trip is all set up, sir."

"Good. Any flak from the Brits?"

"No, sir. At least, not as much as we expected. I still have to brief Mr. Woodstone, and I have arranged for the NSA to set up the advance team."

The vice president looked up and spoke with a slight but noticeable nasal drawl. "Trip? What trip is this?"

Baca drew in a breath. "The German-Israeli trip the President is going on in three weeks."

Woodstone looked pleased. "Oh, yes. That one—your annual trek of appeasement." He turned to Montoya. "Now, Sandy, I'm sure everything will be all right while you're away. I'll just have to rearrange my plans so I won't be in Connecticut that week. Is there anything else you might want me to do? I'm heading off to Florida for the National Committee meeting tomorrow. They're drawing up the new platform and wanted me to open the thing for them. With the rest of my schedule, I probably won't see you until right before you take off. Any problem with that?"

No problem at all, except I won't trust you while I'm out of the country, thought Montoya. "No, just keep in touch. We'll have to take the usual precautions before I leave. By the way, Manuel will be staying here to help you out; Amador will accompany me on this trip."

"Anything else, gentlemen?" No one spoke. Montoya nodded toward the door. "Well, it's Cabinet time." He stood. "Lead on, Percy—I'll follow you in this time."

As they left Montoya felt much better. He *knew* that Grantland Percival Woodstone hated to be called Percy.

The bar was full, but not crowded. The singles scene at the Tombs was dying; school was out, and the coeds from Georgetown that usually frequented the hangout were conspicuously absent. In addition, smoke wafted through the air, getting into Yoli Aquinbaldo's eyes. The steward rubbed his face and turned to his roommate. "Ramis—we try next door?"

"*Aiah.*" The other steward nodded. "Leave tip?"

"I'll get it." Yoli dug through his trousers and pulled out

a five. It was easy to forget that only a few years ago he was shining shoes at the American Officers Club in Bagio; at the time, five dollars would have been an unexpected windfall: a nice dinner, and a jeepney home, to boot.

Signing on at Subic Bay with the U.S. Navy was the best thing he'd ever done. He'd signed up just before the government toppled and the United States got kicked out. Clark, Subic Bay, and Mactan were all closed, and for the first time in over sixty years the American presence was not wanted in the P.I. Still, the navy was good to him. They'd taken care of him, fed him, clothed him . . . he even had enough money left over to send some home every month.

And it was true about hard work in the U.S. He'd worked his tail off as a steward and was selected just six months ago for duty with Air Force One. Yoli Aquinbaldo —twenty-four years old—had reached the pinnacle of his naval career. When he retired and returned to the P.I., the tales he'd have would keep the barrio talking for years. It was not every day that one could claim to have served the President of the United States as a steward.

Yoli left the five-note on the table and pushed his chair back. As he got up a stranger moved to the table and smiled at the two. "Good evening." The words came in Tagalog.

Yoli looked up with a start. "Hello—it's not often one hears the tongue of home." The stranger was definitely a fellow countryman, but the features were strangely different. Yoli couldn't quite place it, but the man was not a full-blooded Filipino. . . .

"I was just about to have a drink when I overheard you speaking: I thought you were one of my countrymen. It is an unexpected discovery. May I buy you a drink?"

"*Aiah*. And my friend?" The stranger nodded; Yoli motioned for Ramis to sit back down. He held up a finger to the waitress. "Please, again."

The stranger smiled. "If you don't mind, I, too, have a friend that would like to join us." He turned and motioned with his head toward the door. A dark-complected man came from the corner and smiled at the group as he pulled out a chair and sat. "This is my good friend, Du'Ali."

Yoli offered a greeting, but the newcomer just nodded and smiled; this one was *not* Filipino, but he was his fellow countryman's friend. Yoli shrugged it off. He was too polite to pry. And after all, a free drink is a free drink.

⫿⫿⫿⫿ 4 ⫿⫿⫿⫿

2200 ZULU:
MONDAY, 3 SEPTEMBER

If you make people think they're thinking, they'll love you: but if you really make them think, they'll hate you.
                                                                    Anon

Edwards Air Force Base

"Any other questions, Major Gould?"

"Just tell me once more, this time in plain English, how much clearance I'll have with the JATO units."

The aeronautical engineer looked puzzled; his eyes grew vacant, as if they were focused to infinity, and his face grew slack. Only after a moment of thought did the youngish captain speak. "Well, if your TAV was loaded to the gills, you wouldn't have a snowball's chance in hell of taking off. On the other hand, if she was completely stripped down, she'd shoot up so fast you'd probably be able to kick in the scramjets as soon as you rotated."

Gould shifted his weight to his right foot and said with a slight bite, "I know that, but what if I were taking off with a higher-than-normal load? What could I expect out of her?" He slapped a ream of paper on the briefing table. Charts and tables filled the pages. "I've spent the last day and a half on alert trying to figure out what the hell this stuff means; I can't make heads or tails out of it. I don't want to understand it—just tell me what I need to know."

The aeronautical engineer looked surprised. "Oh, sure. Just a second." The vacant look came back over the captain's face, but this time he was reading the papers that Gould had slapped down.

Damned aeroengineers, thought Gould. The air force is full of non-rated pukes—non-pilots—who think they're God's gift to mankind. You ask them what time it is and they tell you how to make a friggin' watch.

Gould bristled at putting up with the aeronautical engineers that populated Edwards. He'd heard that back in the good old days—the Yeager days, that is—the pilots wouldn't put up with this shit. The entire preflight checklist consisted of the test pilot running out to the bird, "kicking the tires, lighting the fires," and he was airborne. None of this nonsense of having some non-rated nipplehead, whose only operational experience was going to graduate school, telling *him* what to do.

After all, it *is* the air force, isn't it? Not the damned United States Engineering Corps.

The TAVs were retrofitted with JATO units and now had the capability of taking off on their own in emergencies—instead of being dropped from a 747 mothership. But up to now, all of Gould's takeoffs with JATOs had been made with the TAV empty of any cargo. All he wanted to know was how much weight he could safely take off with. He never could get a straight answer from an engineer. If they told him just once what he needed to know, he'd be happy.

The captain pushed his glasses back to his forehead with a finger. He pointed at a sail-like diagram on the paper. "Well, if you were carrying a full complement—"

"Full complement of what?"

"Of anything—people, equipment, fuel, cows—whatever." The captain sounded impatient. He pointed at the diagram again. "Look. If your TAV was packed with, say, just people—and *only* people—then you'd barely be able to get the TAV up to three thousand feet, plus or minus fifty feet. From there, you'd have enough fuel so that if you dove at the ground, you'd gain just enough airspeed at about one hundred feet to kick in the scramjets. After the scramjets kick in, you wouldn't need the JATO units anymore, and you could go semiballistic."

Gould lifted an eyebrow. "One hundred feet."

"You wanted to know the limits of the envelope, didn't you?" He put down the paper, removed his glasses, and rubbed his eyes. "You know, Major, I'd never try it myself. You'd be pushing the TAV to the max, and with the ground effect at that altitude, I'm really not sure if the scramjets could handle it." He put his glasses back on and smiled.

Gould swept up the papers on the briefing table. He smiled back, just sweetly enough to look sarcastic. "Well, I'll tell you what, Captain. I'll remember you said that when I'm saving your ass. You engineers are going to be an endangered species if you let a little problem like scramjet capability worry you."

The captain dropped his smile and turned slightly red. "Good *day,* Major."

As he turned to leave, Gould made a quiet kissing sound after him. "Good day, Captain." Couldn't these non-rated guys take themselves a little less seriously? He gathered up the material and made his way back to the alert facility.

Andrews Air Force Base, Washington, D.C.

Colonel Joseph McGirney tapped the checklist on the back of the seat and whistled to himself. The flightline at Andrews was just visible through the cockpit. The taxiway and concrete apron were in front of him, as were the guards and barricades that separated the base from the governmental fleet of planes. Most people mistook this plane for *the* Air Force One when, in fact, any of the 767s on the concrete bearing the United States seal could serve as the President's offical transport.

But it was for this plane that the President had a special affection. The "Enchilada Air Force's flagship," serial number 0014, was the President's favorite. Montoya had even had a special ceramic vat installed on board oughtought-one-four to cook everything from Indian bread to fried ice cream. Chimayo blankets, turquoise stones embedded in the ashtrays, and paintings of yuccas and impossibly blue canyon skies decorated the interior. Inside, it was a piece of the President's home.

Even the specially scrambled phone ironically reminded the President of Los Alamos, the weapons hamlet not thirty miles away from Santa Fe that had birthed the first atomic bomb: In the remote chance of a nuclear attack, the phone would connect him directly to the National Emergency Command Center and the SAC generals charged with deploying and launching nuclear weapons.

McGirney whistled to himself and turned from the cockpit. The plane checked out fine. Once it was certified airworthy, the Secret Service would make a final sweep of the plane and seal it up until time for the Germany trip, two days from now. International flights required a little more planning than the intracountry jaunts he'd been handling lately. He looked forward to the flight; there was a woman he wanted to look up once he hit Ramstein. Her husband and he were best friends, and when the husband happened to be gone on TDY, he and his best friend's wife didn't do too badly either.

As McGirney stepped from the cockpit into the cabin he nodded at the stewards just arriving. "Gentlemen."

"Good afternoon, Colonel. How are you today?"

McGirney glanced at the name tag. Yoli Aquinbaldo—one of the Filipino stewards. And Ramis Sicat, the other, was also Filipino. Damn, these beaks were good . . . bend over backward for you, and as friendly as can be. He had a sudden memory of R and R at the Manila Intercontinental . . . a young, brown-skinned dancer . . . she could smoke a cigarette in the damnedest way. . . .

"Afternoon, Mr. Aquinbaldo, Mr. Sicat. I'm fine. Are you gentlemen going on the flight?"

"Oh, no, sir. We're only the backup crew; we've got to double-check what the primary stewards have done. We'll just freshen up a bit before they bolt the plane up."

"Fine." McGirney slapped Aquinbaldo on the shoulder. "Too bad you couldn't make this trip; it's going to be a dandy. See you men later."

"Yes, sir." As he left he heard faint sounds of Tagalog drift from the hatch. McGirney started to get up for the trip. He made plans to take his wife out tonight, buy her a nice dinner, and the day after tomorrow the fifty-mile rule would go into effect: fifty miles from home and *nobody* is married. He was humming as he saluted the guard standing by the barricades.

Camp Pendleton, California

"I wish you'd spend more time with the children."

"Uh?"

Maureen Krandel paused before repeating herself. "I said, I wish you'd spend more time with the children."

Bill Krandel put down the pamphlet he was reading and looked at his wife. She was dressed in her nightclothes—in the short baby-doll nightie he liked—but he hadn't noticed her joining him in bed. He rolled onto his side and pulled off his reading glasses. "I spend time with them, hon. What are you talking about?"

"I'm talking about coming to see Julie's ballet recital, or visiting Justin's school with me. You can't just keep bouncing them on your knee and sending them off; you've got to get more involved in their lives."

"What do you mean, sending them off? I try to pay attention to them whenever I can. I'm just so damned busy with this job, I can't afford to go traipsing off with them every time they have a recital or something. I'm getting paid for this job, you know—not for watching the kids. Besides, what does it matter if I'm not at every little thing they do? They don't notice."

Maureen was silent for a very long time. Krandel reached over and held her chin with his hand. Her face was soft. Tiny crow's feet had just started to frame her eyes; how long was it since he'd really looked at her? "Look, I'm sorry—but I told you I took a second wife with the corps when I graduated from Annapolis. Tell you what. I promise to spend some time with the kids this weekend. We'll go to the beach and make a picnic out of it, okay?"

She didn't say anything, only nodded. Krandel patted her bottom and went back to his reading.

Edwards Air Force Base, California

"This is worse than SAC. At least those mofros have friggin' conjugal visits. And now that they've gutted the bomber force, I hear that SAC crews don't spend more than one week out of six on alert. None of this one-in-three bullshit. My pecker will fall off from inactivity if this keeps up."

"Stow it, Gould. Do you want Delores to hear you?"

"That wouldn't be such a damned bad idea." Gould peeked around the corner and grinned, lowering his voice. "I could go for a little nooky right about now. In fact, that sounds pretty damned nice. I'd even use the pool table if you guys would promise to leave us alone. You know what they say: It's what made the preacher dance and the choir sing—"

Gould was interrupted as Delores walked briskly into the

ready room. Her orange flight suit seemed to glow as she entered. The room grew quiet; a cough punctuated the silence, causing Delores to swing her eyes away from the Notams she was reading to the three TAV pilots sprawled on the alert shack furniture. An unwatched late-night movie played quietly in the background.

"Don't stop on my account."

"Wouldn't dream of it, Delores. You might say there was just a, uh, pregnant pause in the conversation. Yes, sir . . . pregnant pause. Wouldn't you say, Jim?"

"Right, Gould. Anything you say." The pilot stood and strode toward the exit. He directed his remarks to the third pilot. "How about a set of one-on-one crud?" He shot a grin at Gould before continuing. "We could play it on the pool table, if it's free."

"Gotcha." The two pilots left for the back room, leaving Gould and Delores alone. They sat in awkward silence for a moment before Delores spoke.

"Okay, hotshot. What gives? What was that all about?"

Gould spread his hands. "Nothin'—honest. Just slingin' the shit, that's all." He grinned at her and put his hands behind his head.

"I'll bet." She stared at him for a moment. "Jeez, Bob. Can't you grow up? We've been here two days, and we have another week to go cooped up in this pen; try to keep your glands from popping all over the place, would you?"

"I can't help it if I'm a likable guy."

"Oh, yeah." She moved to the cold drink machine in the corner and punched the button on the dispenser, and a fruit juice popped out. Peeling off the top, she sipped through a tiny straw that came with the box. "So this is what it's like to pull alert."

"I warned you it would be so exciting you wouldn't be able to wait for the next time."

"And I'll probably be lucky enough to draw it with you again, no doubt."

"Hey, I'm not the flight scheduler. If you've got a gripe, see Colonel Zazbrewski. He's the one who rotates the pilots. There are sixteen other TAV drivers you can get hooked up with if you've got a complaint."

"All right, settle down." Delores removed the straw from her mouth and walked over to the couch where Gould was sprawled. She hesitated, then sat on the armrest. Gould remained with his hands behind his head, keeping silent. Delores waited a moment, then said, "Look . . . I'm sorry. I'm just trying to fit in, and I guess I'm trying too hard."

"'S all right."

Silence persisted for seconds longer, then: "Look . . . Bob."

"Uh."

Delores played with the straw, ducking it in and out of the juice and keeping her eyes off Gould. "Bob, I know I've been standoffish—"

"I said it's all right."

"I know, I know." After a moment she stood and pushed back her hair; her voice sounded shaky. "You wouldn't believe all that I've had to put up with. It may sound trivial to you, but it's just so *hard* to ignore."

"Like . . ."

"Mostly nothing too overt. Sexual innuendos . . . pointed suggestions . . . you know."

"No, I don't." Gould surprised himself with his concern.

Delores's ears grew red. "Well, my IP at Willie threatened to fail me on a check if I didn't put out for him—"

"He actually *tried* . . ."

She shook her head. "No, not explicitly. It wasn't a threat . . . but the invitation was there, and the consequences were as plain as day." She crossed her arms over her breasts and looked away. "It's hard sometimes, being a woman and working with men." There was silence for several moments. "I'm sorry I snapped at you."

Gould struggled upright on the couch. This was *weird*. It wasn't half as bad as the guilt trip that nympho he'd met at Nellis had tried to lay on him, but still . . .

He managed to say, "I understand."

"Do you?"

"Sure."

She smiled at him. Gould felt as though he could reach out and touch her face, or just say something nice to comfort her, but the moment seemed too unreal.

The spell was broken when the other two pilots strode into the room laughing. They stopped abruptly when they noticed the silence in the room. "Everything all right? We didn't mean to interrupt. . . ." One of them raised a brow at Gould.

Gould didn't even bother to wave him away. "Forget it; we're just watching the tube." He straightened and turned up the TV set, forgetting about their looks and losing himself in the mindless chatter of the television.

Washington, D.C.

The apartment was well-lit, but the furniture was sparse. The decor made the apartment look nicer inside than outside. To Aquinbaldo and Sicat, it was much better than the barracks. They laughed shrilly as they snorted the last line of cocaine Hujr had carefully laid out with a razor blade.

Aquinbaldo leaned back on the couch and chattered, answering a question thrown at him by Hujr. They spoke in Tagalog, which was incomprehensible to anyone who might have been listening.

"Sure, but when the President calls, he doesn't mind if you barge on in. Or at least, that's what they say. We've never been on a *real* crew—our background clearances haven't come in."

Hujr seemed to pale at this. He shot a glance at his companion. "When will the clearances come through—so you can accompany the President?"

"Any day now, I suspect. Foreign nationals are looked at very closely, you know."

Hujr leaned forward and nodded at the traces of white

72

powder remaining on the hand mirror. "And you're not worried about this? What if they found out you were using drugs?"

Aquinbaldo covered his mouth and giggled. The whole question seemed, well . . . so *absurd!* "Of course I'm not worried. In my barrio you can buy anything if you're old enough to hold the money up to the sari-sari counter. And nobody talks about it. It's the same way here. There's no way they'll find out. Wasn't it like that in your barrio?"

Hujr spread his mouth and showed white teeth. "Not on Mindanao. But what's the difference? I'm enjoying so much the stories of your job." He paused. "So you think you'll have a chance to ride with the President soon?"

They broke out in another giggling fit. Dimly, through all the euphoria, a fleeting thought crossed Aquinbaldo's mind—why weren't Hujr and his companion laughing with them?—but the thought flew away in another spasm of silliness.

Hujr waited with a smile painted on his face.

Aquinbaldo shook his head. "Uh?"

Hujr repeated himself. "When will you fly with the President?"

"Oh, not until after he gets back from this German-Israeli trip; they only use experienced crews for the international flights." Aquinbaldo looked sly. "I tell you what, my friend . . . my buddy Ramis and I are the alternate stewards for this next trip. We were given the honor because of our hard work." He shook his head sadly, suddenly changing his mood. "But the chances of the primary stewards not going are small. There are just no good excuses for missing such a trip."

"I see." Hujr nodded toward his companion. "It is getting late, my friends, but before you go I would like to get rid of another line of this candy. Will you help me?"

"I think another line would help us through the night," giggled Aquinbaldo. It felt so *good* to let loose. He watched as Hujr carefully cut out a long, thin line of cocaine, then eagerly sniffed the powder after Sicat.

As the euphoria rolled over them they didn't wonder why Hujr let them snort the last two lines alone, or why Hujr was talking on the telephone in a low voice in the other room.

▌▌▌ 5 ▌▌▌

0945 ZULU:
WEDNESDAY, 5 SEPTEMBER

Ordinary men—and, above all, peculiarly little men—experience a charm, a certain pleasure, in attacking great men. There is much of the spirit of revenge mixed up with this.

Ernest Hello

Andrews Air Force Base

Major Gutteriz loved his job. As officer-in-charge of scheduling details on every presidential flight, he was responsible for everything from the crypto gear down to the meals. It appealed to him. Before he came to Washington he had served as commissary and MWR officer at Offut AFB and had so impressed the generals with his sierra hotel service that they had told the air force chief-of-staff that *this was his job*.

And he could get things hopping. As a mustang who had served nine years of prior enlisted service before coming up through OTS, Gutteriz knew the ins and outs of how to get almost anything done. He couldn't care less about the money he was making. LTU, the mammoth aerospace firm, had a standing offer to triple his salary if he ever decided to get out of the air force and work for them. He could get anything working, anytime and anywhere.

So Major Gutteriz didn't panic when, the morning before the president's flight to Germany was supposed to go, the police called from Washington General with the news that two of his stewards had been severely injured in a hit-and-run car accident. Gutteriz thanked the officers, made a memo for flowers to be sent, and looked up on the roster who the backups were for the sortie, all within a minute of the call.

Major Gutteriz made the call to Petty Officer Yoli Aquinbaldo himself. Since he had placed the two on standby, he wasn't surprised in the least when the phone was answered on the first ring. He informed Aquinbaldo to report, with haircut and a week's change of clothes, to the MAC terminal in the morning for the flight with Air Force One.

The only thing that did disturb him was that Aquinbaldo sounded as if he had a slight cold . . . and if he had a cold, then why was there giggling in the background?

But the one thing Major Gutteriz had learned as an enlisted man, and what had made him so successful in getting the job done as an officer, was that if he treated his people as mature individuals, they'd come through for him.

So he forgot the entire matter, but still made a note for his secretary to call the two in the morning, an hour before show time, to make sure they made it on time.

U.S.S.S. *Bifrost*

Lieutenant Colonel George Frier pushed through the tunnel connecting the living quarters and the operations center. He floated through the middle of the complex, stopping only when he grabbed a handhold. His feet spun forward when he stopped, so he applied a little more torque with his hands to keep himself still. Below him floated southern

India. The view rapidly changed to the soft blue stretches of ocean as BIGEYE sped toward Antarctica.

The view from BIGEYE's main portal never stopped astounding Frier. Even after the year and a half of being BIGEYE's commander, *any* view from the portal three hundred miles above the Earth's surface still took his breath away. He loved it up there. His rotund features, remnants of the hard and athletic body he had before coming to BIGEYE, were dangerously flabby from the extended period in zero-g. His heart was pumping much too hard, and calcification had started melding his joints, but it was all worth it to him. Especially because, for the first time since the crash, he was useful again.

The disintegration of his body was nothing compared to the satisfaction he felt working as commanding officer in the United States' Space-Based Observation Platform—nicknamed "BIGEYE" by the press, for its primary purpose was spying.

The cameras and sensors aboard BIGEYE were capable of reading a license plate from three hundred miles up. And if Washington wanted him to collect the data when it was dark on earth, the IR sensors on BIGEYE were almost as good as the visual ones. BIGEYE circled the Earth in a polar orbit, passing over every point on the earth—or at least passing near enough to get information—every twelve hours. It was the United States' ultimate in verification technology, and Lieutenant Colonel George Frier was the lucky son of a bitch who headed it up.

So when the buzzer sounded for Frier to check the alignment on the laser relay, he didn't think anything of it. The message came in code, preceded by a puzzling juxtaposition of three lettered words, all different. Normal procedure was to store the message with the other clandestine codes beamed up by operatives and squirt the entire sequence to NSA headquarters in Maryland. The squirt compressed the messages into the on/off bit patterns recognizable to computers and could be transmitted to the ground in a tenth of a second.

A UV laser beam was locked onto the huge dish antennas at NSA; any attempt at a tap automatically broke the loop and introduced random messages into the stream, confusing the intended interceptor and alerting NSA that the transmission was being tapped.

The computer screen lit up, acknowledging the message had been successfully sent. Frier hummed to himself and went about his duties, oblivious to the passage of time.

Andrews Air Force Base

"How's the plane?"

The crew chief spun on his heel and saluted. "Super, Colonel. The avionics and maintenance people have all given her the green light."

Colonel McGirney grunted and ran a hand along the nose section. "How about the INS?"

"Major Laynam cranked it up half an hour ago, sir. The plane knows exactly where she is down to a foot and should get you to Germany with about a ten-yard error."

"Great. Good job, Mac. Can I bring you anything from Ramstein?"

"Just some more of that Liebfraumilch, sir. And Colonel, if you'd get a catalog of German cameras at the BX for me, I'd appreciate it. I'd like to get something for the little lady next time another one of our birds goes over."

"No problem. Just keep the generals happy, Mac."

"Yes, sir!" The sergeant pulled up to a salute; McGirney returned it and climbed the aluminum stairs to the flight deck.

His copilot turned in his seat as McGirney strode into the cockpit. Major George Laynam twisted a dial above his head and said, "Howdy, Joe. All set?"

"That's a rog. The crew ready?"

"Everybody's up for it. The only problem is that the stewards were in an accident late last night; we got two replacements from the pool."

"Who are they?"

Laynam turned to a list and squinted. "Secret Service just okayed these guys: Aquinbaldo and Sicat." He put down the list and turned back to McGirney. "It's their first trip with us, so things might be a little hectic."

"Yeah, I think I met them the other day. Serves the President right. Wish I could be there the first time one of them spills coffee on him."

"Right. You'd better keep it down, though, those Secret Service guys can hear through walls."

"Good idea." McGirney stowed his flight bag and moved to the pilot's seat. They ran down the checklist, finishing up just as the President's chopper landed a hundred yards to their right. As the motorcade approached the plane McGirney jerked his head toward the back. "Let's start the war—the brass has arrived." He punched at the mike button.

"Tower, this is Air Force One requesting permission to taxi once the Frito Bandito is on board." McGirney used the code word for President Montoya—Mexican cartoon characters, chosen by Montoya and his staff to put a little humor into the otherwise dry military procedures.

The radio cackled almost instantly. "Permission granted, Air Force One. The runway is cleared for your use. Airways are cleared to thirty-five thousand feet, and choose your own heading going out. We've got a five-mile radius cleared for you."

"Thank you, sir."

"Have a good one, Frito."

"Roger that." Colonel McGirney clicked off the mike and grinned at his copilot. "Ready, George?"

"Yeah. Do you want to take it?"

"Sure. Make the announcement to the PAX and have the stewards strap in. We're cleared once everyone's on board."

"Rog."

They moved the plane down the taxiway and up to the end of the runway. McGirney waited until Laynam finished with the announcement. Once done, McGirney pushed forward on the throttles and edged the huge jet down the runway. Satisfied that the pressure was holding in the engines, he eased all four throttles forward. Still, the craft seemed to jump out of the starting blocks and bite at the onrushing air. The plane started vibrating, but once they passed eighty knots the ground effect eased the jolting.

"One hundred . . . ten . . . twenty, and rotate." He pulled back on the wheel, and the plane slipped gently into the air. The behemoth seemed to float upward. Laynam kicked on the smoking lamp and pulled up the gears in one fluid motion.

They continued with the checklist. Reaching twenty thousand feet, they took a short break. "Take her on up to thirty-eight. . . . I'll call for some coffee."

"Sounds good." Laynam rang for the stewards.

After some moments, Hujr entered the flight deck, dressed in Yoli Aquinbaldo's high-collared white steward's uniform. Hujr didn't speak. McGirney twisted in his seat and grabbed the coffee with both hands. He glanced at the steward, then at the name tag. All these Filipinos look alike, he thought. The only ones he recognized were the regulars on his flight; he couldn't tell if he had met this man the other day or not. "Thanks . . . and keep this filled for me." He turned back to the front, ignoring the steward.

Do'brai

General Fariq Kamil smiled. Today was a good day. A *grand* day, indeed. He hadn't felt this good since President Ash'ath had appointed him general and entrusted him with the day-to-day running of the Do'brainese militia.

Kamil nodded to his colleague Ghazzali, sitting and enjoying the thought of the coming coup as much as he was. Kamil leaned over and belched noisily, wiping his mouth with a sleeve, and spoke to the *shahib*.

"I have just been notified that the first planeload of your lieutenants has landed."

"Lieutenants?" Ghazzali bit into a fruit and swallowed

before continuing. He leaned back against soft pillows, looking content. *"Aides* would be a better word than *lieutenants—lieutenant* connotes a military operation."

"Which, of course, you have nothing to do with. The point is well taken. For if the military can divorce itself from this affair, then this could only be seen as a popular mandate of the people, something that occurred spontaneously. It must never get out that the Do'brai militia is backing the ALH in this venture; we have too many ties with the West that cannot be broken.

"In fact, your, ah, *aides* must not know that President Ash'ath is involved in this affair, or that I am." Kamil reached for a fruit and inspected it. He put the fruit down. "Still, the recognition the ALH will gain will be astronomical. And once the rest of your lieutenants—"

Ghazzali held up a finger. "Aides."

"Ah, yes . . . your *aides* arrive, then we will provide you adequate transportation to Kapuir."

"And the news media?"

"They were reluctant at first. They did not believe that this event would actually warrant a live telecast." Kamil brushed a crumb from his uniform and took a bite of his fruit. "But I was able to guarantee the networks that it would be worth their while."

"You did not let them know why we wanted the live telecast, did you?".

"No, no—of course not. Why should I do that when the western media cannot even keep their own state secrets quiet? I simply made them understand that His Excellency would pay for the cost of setting up their equipment and their plane fares if this did not prove to be the—uh—*scoop,* they call it—that we promised."

Ghazzali chuckled. He settled back and refused the water pipe that was offered him. He said, "Hujr ibn-Adi will bring us glory within two days. With this as a catalyst, the *'Ad* will rise to their prophesy."

Kamil took another bite of his fruit and narrowed his eyes. "You are that positive he will succeed?"

"Oh, I am certain of it. He is not yet ready to die a martyr."

"But can he be trusted?"

Ghazzali raised an eyebrow. "He will never put his own gains above the ALH. Although Hujr works for your money, his loyalty is pledged to me. Rest assured, General —even if Hujr fails miserably in his task, Do'brai will never be linked with his actions."

General Kamil tapped his fingers together. "Then it is done." He pushed himself up; the entire chamber seemed to step back at his presence. "I will rest, Yazid. I suggest you do the same. The next few days will be hectic." The bare hint of a suggestion hung in the air.

"I am with my own kind now, Fariq. Thank you, but I will remain with them until we leave."

"As you wish." Kamil strode from the room, turning as he left to catch the eye of one of the attendants. That's a new one, he thought. A young, unmarred body . . .

He nodded to the Hajib guarding the door and said, "Have your new help—that one over there—join me in my quarters. I will expect him soon."

As the general left the room an almost audible sigh of relief came from those attendants whom he had not noticed.

Mid-Atlantic

President Montoya sat in the cushioned seat at the back of the plane. The oval bed that had accompanied the previous president on board Air Force One had been removed during the last administration. The moral high ground was broken when a reporter mistakenly opened the door to the presidential bedroom and found the Vice President in bed with her Secret Service escort. After that fiasco, no matter how much the press corps was sworn to secrecy, it was soon realized that the bed was an open invitation for debauchery. Not that the presidential rest rooms were free of fooling around, but the tone had been set three years ago, and Sandoval Montoya was paying for it now.

The sweep-winged Boeing 767 was comfortable enough in flight, but it would have been better if he could stretch out and lie down. The floor proved to be too hard, so his thickly cushioned chair would just have to do.

A tap at the door brought Montoya back from his meandering. He stretched and tucked in his shirt before answering, "What is it?"

"A snack, Mr. President."

"Bring it in." He swung his feet down from the footrest and straightened in the chair. A Filipino steward backed into the chamber, pulling a cart laden with food and drink. The steward stopped just short of the President and moved the place settings around so that the President could eat.

After the steward positioned the tray, Montoya grunted his thanks and dove into the food; he hadn't realized how hungry he was. The last few hours of poring over reports and upcoming scenarios of the talks had left him famished as well as exhausted. The one nice thing about such a long trip was the opportunity to catch up on a little rest and relaxation.

The steward waited for a moment before asking, "Is there anything else I can get you, sir?"

"Eh? No, there's not." Montoya dabbed at his mouth. He studied the steward, keeping a fork in his food. "By the way, I don't think I've met you. You're new to this, aren't you?"

The steward looked startled. "Uh, yes, Mr. President, this is my first time on Air Force One. I am honored to meet you."

"Likewise. What's your name, young man?"

"Petty Officer Yoli Aquinbaldo, sir."

Montoya thought for a second. "A relative of yours was a very famous man, except I'm sure the name wasn't Aquinbaldo. The name must have changed over the years. Do you happen to know who it is I'm thinking about?"

Hujr shook his head. "No, Mr. President. Aquinbaldo is a pretty common name in the P.I."

"I see. Well, it's been nice meeting you. Good day." Montoya turned back to his meal. When the steward didn't leave, Montoya raised his eyes to the young man's face and repeated, "I said, good day."

"Yes, sir. I'm sorry sir." Hujr backed out of the chamber, almost tripping over his feet. When the door shut, Montoya shook his head. Being President wasn't that big of a deal to him any longer, but sometimes he forgot how people acted when they weren't in constant contact with him.

Edwards Air Force Base

"I forgot to tell you thanks."

"Uh?"

"I said thanks. For the other night." Delores propped her face up with an elbow on the kitchenette table.

"Oh." The TV blared in the other room, drowning out any conversation taking place in the cramped eating area; high-pitched screams from cartoon characters warbled into the room. The kitchenette was decorated with murals of experimental planes that had lived and died at the California testing ground. Gould leaned against a painting of an antique BELL X-1 and sipped his coffee, pondering Delores's statement.

Delores slipped her hand from her face and glanced at the door from where the television came. "I mean it. You didn't have to stand up for me in front of those guys."

"I didn't, did I?"

"Yes, you did. And you were very gentlemanly, too." She paused. "I didn't expect it from you, if you want to know the truth."

Gould put down his cup. "I don't know how I should take that."

"As a compliment." She studied him for a moment, then averted her eyes. "I've been trying to figure you out."

"That makes two of us." He waited for a moment, and when she didn't answer, he said, "So what's the problem?"

"I'm not sure. But I think I know."

"Oh?" He put his cup down and grinned, then put his hands behind his head and leaned back in his chair. "So, what's the hot poop on me?"

Delores sighed, shaking her head. "You know, you're really not a fighter jock, are you, Robert? No matter how much you try."

"Me?" Gould tried to look incredulous.

"Yeah, you, hotshot. Look, those guys knew you were sticking up for me all the time. If you were a *real* fighter pilot, you would have saved your ego first; real fighter pilots couldn't handle an attack on their ego."

"Now wait just a damn minute—" Gould's ears reddened as he rocked forward in his chair, his emotions unfeigned this time.

Delores held up a hand. "Hear me out. You could have kissed off any chance you might have had with me to save your ego, but you didn't. So I'm impressed. You let me see a little of the real you through that macho image you flyboys have to keep up. Now tell the truth. Are you really a fighter pilot, or are all those rumors I've heard about you true?"

"What rumors?"

Delores looked coy. "Oh, I'm sure you've heard: how you're really only a chopper pilot who couldn't make the grade—you know, not a good enough stick to handle fighters. And why the only reason you got TAVs is because you're the President's long-lost cousin . . ."

"Does it matter?"

"I don't know. Does it?"

"You tell me."

They stared at each other.

Hard.

When she spoke, her voice was barely audible. "I guess it doesn't."

Things were definitely looking up for him. Now if he just wouldn't blow it. Gould shifted his weight and said,

"And you're not keeping up that fighter-pilot image either."

"I'm surprised it took you six months to notice." She shot a glance at the door and said softly, "Maybe there's hope for you after all. We need to talk."

"Okay. I'm open for it."

"Later. When we're alone, not now."

Gould's muscles sagged a bit; he forced a smile. "Promises, promises." He picked up his coffee and took a sip. "Tell you what. After this alert, I'll show you the damnedest restaurant this side of Tokyo. They serve their meals in a miniature fishing boat that actually fits on a table. You can eat everything on it but the wood." He flashed another smile. "And you can even use the wood for toothpicks, if you want."

She grinned back at him, obviously pleased. "Sounds great. *After* the alert." She stood to leave.

Gould held up his hands. "Hey, I'm a Boy Scout."

"Yeah. And I sleep with my door locked, too, jet jock."

⠀6⠀

1500 ZULU:
FRIDAY, 7 SEPTEMBER

When you strike at a King, you must kill him.
Ralph Waldo Emerson

Ramstein Air Force Base, West Germany

"CPO Yoli Aquinbaldo, 483-68-7729." Hujr presented the doctored ID card to the marine.

The marine inspected the green ID and grinned. "You can always tell the greenhorns."

Hujr tensed slightly. "So sorry . . . ?"

"Look, you remember me from Andrews?"

"*Aih*, yes." And Hujr wasn't lying. The marine had almost frightened Hujr half to death back in the States when he had certified that, yes, Hujr's face matched that on the military ID, and yes, Hujr could board Air Force One for the flight to Germany.

The red-haired marine handed the card back to Hujr. "And I remember you. There's no way you would have gotten past all the checks at Andrews if you weren't who you were supposed to be. That's why I'm here. I'm the last say on who gets in."

"Oh."

The marine punched Hujr lightly on the shoulder. "So loosen up, swabbie. I won't bite your head off. By the way, the name's Clements. Don Clements."

"Yoli Aquinbaldo." Hujr quickly shook hands and forced a grin. He almost felt himself liking the husky man but quickly pushed the feeling from his mind . . . he couldn't take the chance of having any emotions interfering with what he had to do.

Hujr kept the grin plastered on his face and held up the bundle he carried, deciding to take a gamble. "How about this—do you need to inspect it, too?"

"I'm supposed to." The marine shouldered his weapon and peered inside the package Hujr carried. "What the hell is it?" He squeezed, and the package gave a little.

"What you say, uncultured cheese. For the President's nachos."

The marine withdrew his hand. "Well, shit on a shingle —you know, I haven't had that since the last time we went overseas, about four months ago. Do you think you'll be able to scare some up for me?"

"I will try. Maybe I'll let you try it right before the President . . . so you can tell me what you think about it."

"You don't say. Well, hot diggity shit; you've got yourself a deal." He slapped Hujr on the back. "Get to work then, Yoli-san."

Hujr's grin stiffened as he entered Air Force One. "I will." Naive Yankee, he thought. When the marine attached the Japanese honorific to Hujr's assumed Filipino name, it was a dead giveaway that the marine lumped all foreigners in the same pot. It only stirred the tumult raging in Hujr's stomach, intensifying his desire to accomplish his mission.

"We're ready, Mr. President."

"Eh?"

"The plane, Mr. President. Air Force One has received clearance to take off." The aide stepped back from the table.

"Oh, of course." President Montoya leaned forward in his seat and clasped his hands. He directed his remarks to the gray-haired gentleman sitting across from him. "Chancellor, I'm sorry to cut this short, but I'm afraid I've got to go. Schedule and all that to keep up with."

The chancellor showed strong, evenly spaced teeth. "Mustn't keep the Israelis waiting, either. I don't want to be out of their favor any more than I am. But at least these talks are helping. Maybe next year we can wrap this up."

The President of the United States nodded knowingly. Tensions between Germany and Israel had never totally relaxed, and anything that might be construed as a diplomatic faux pas had to be avoided. Montoya pushed himself up, and the rest of the room followed as if on cue. They brushed past the reporters and lesser dignitaries who clamored around the two leaders as they were ushered into a chauffeured car.

Arriving at the airport, they clasped hands, and Montoya strode up the ladder, turning and waving to the crowd—mostly U.S. military men and their families—who gathered to bid him farewell in the late-afternoon drizzle. Montoya waved one last time at the top of the stairs before entering the plane.

The President nodded to the stewards on his way back to his chamber. "Two Tecate, and wait about an hour before you bring me dinner."

"Yes, sir." Hujr jerked his head at Du'Ali; the two melted from Montoya's path.

Montoya struggled with his overcoat as he walked down the aisle. Amador Trujillo helped remove the garment from the President's back and followed him to the rear of the plane. Trujillo asked, "Well, what do you think. How did it go?"

Montoya shrugged, his back still to Trujillo. "Who knows? Grunzimmer seemed open enough. He could see my point, but he wouldn't have anything to do with signing that white paper."

"Hmmm."

They reached Montoya's chamber; almost immediately, Hujr appeared at the door carrying a tray. Trujillo motioned to the steward to place the tray on the table. Two iced mugs of beer with salt around the rims sat on the tray. As Hujr backed out of the room and shut the door Trujillo squeezed a lime into one of the beers and handed it to Montoya. "You were saying . . . ?"

Montoya nodded and took a sip. "Thanks." He flopped down on the chair and buckled in; Trujillo glanced around and found a seat facing the President. Montoya took a bigger sip and said, "Like I said, I just don't know. It could really go either way. If Grunzimmer decides to go ahead with the Eastern Bloc proposal, we are out of luck. We won't be able to tell East Germany from West, except for that damned wall still in Berlin. But that's more to keep us out than them in anymore. Anyway, it will upset Israel to no end. It will ruin the progress we've made."

"But if he does decide to go with our proposal, that'll put the reunification plan on the back burner for a while. So it's all up to him—the ball's in his court."

"Did he let you know any sort of timetable?"

Montoya said flatly, "None. And I wouldn't wait for him to decide on one, either. I think he's made up his mind and is just not telling anyone."

Trujillo emitted a low whistle. They stopped talking as the plane's engines roared in the background. The President's chamber was insulated for sound, but the noise from the jet's takeoff still bore into the room. The noise abated after a few moments, leaving Trujillo alone in his thoughts. Everything seemed to be going sour this trip, and even the President's downhome friendliness, which usually worked with international officials, had failed to help him.

Trujillo killed his beer and looked at Montoya. "Ready for another?"

"No, thanks, but don't let me stop you. Go ahead and ring for one."

"I think I will." Trujillo moved to the intercom as Montoya sank back in his chair and studied notes from the meeting with Grunzimmer.

As he rang for the beverage Trujillo hoped the flight would go smoothly. One more beer ought to do it for him. Actually, a six-pack would do the job, but that was another thing about being the National Security Advisor. The fishbowl he lived in was so damned transparent, he couldn't take a piss without someone shaking it for him. Last time he had a good drunk was when Montoya was governor and he was working as the Attorney General; it was almost expected of him to party, and party hard, back in Santa Fe. Or at least go out and get stoned with Montoya's Cabinet. Sometimes he wondered why he had ever left New Mexico.

220 Nautical Miles Due East of Paris

The sun was just setting, and the horizon glowed on the right side of the aircraft. The long day had taken its toll, and one by one the White House staff and members of the presidential press corps drifted off to sleep or quietly argued the day's doings over an after-dinner drink.

With the evening meal served and the silver and dishes stowed, Hujr slipped to the rear of the aircraft, carrying a cloth-covered vat. Under the towel he carried a newly sharpened kitchen knife. As he approached the President's chamber he nodded to a Secret Service agent, still wearing his ubiquitous sunglasses; the agent stared through mirrored frames.

Marine Sergeant Clements sat behind the agent, his weapon stowed and locked into place in a rifle setting to the left of the President's door. A small steward's station was to the right; facilities for a wet bar were there, along with cabinets and drawers that could be used for food storage. Hujr moved into the cubbyhole and placed the vat he carried to the rear, out of sight of the cabin. With his back turned, he wrapped his hand and the knife with a towel, then stepped back out into the cabin. He motioned with his free hand and brought the marine to his feet.

Clements blinked the sleep away. "What's up?"

"You wanted a taste of the nachos before I took them in."

Clements looked around and motioned with his eyes to the agent. Hujr's eyes widened at the sergeant's motion; Hujr hadn't planned on dealing with two of them. The Secret Service agent stood and approached them; Clements nodded to the vat and spoke quietly. "Aquinbaldo has some nachos he picked up at the commissary. Want to give them a try?"

Hujr thought fast and fought down his emotions. He directed a question to the agent. "If you are both going to try this, I will need some more chips. Could you bring some back from the other steward?" He had to get rid of the marine first—the sergeant was the taller of the two by a foot and would prove the most difficult to get past; he'd take care of the agent afterward.

"I'll get them." Clements twisted past the two; Hujr smiled nervously at the agent. *'Ifrit!* He'd have to do the best he could.

The agent spoke up. "I've always liked the President's nachos. What do you put on them?"

Hujr wet his lips as he tried to think fast. "Oh, I use my own special mixture: uh, tomatoes, lettuce, sour cream . . ."

The agent took off his glasses. "That sounds good; let me try it."

He brushed forward; Hujr stepped out of his way as the agent forced his way into the cubbyhole. Once the agent was inside, Hujr moved quickly behind him. The agent turned and scanned the counter. "Where did you say it was?"

"There, up above." As Hujr pointed the agent grunted, then turned his back. Hujr whipped the knife from his towel, brought the blade over the agent's head, and pulled back as hard as he could.

The man struggled briefly, but Hujr kept pulling back on the knife, keeping the agent from crying out. Hujr twisted the kitchen knife with his right hand as it dug into the agent's throat. Finally, the agent's head gave a crack as Hujr jerked the skull at an impossible angle. The agent fought back only sporadically as his life drained away. Hujr forced the knife up and down in vigorous strokes until the body sagged in his arms.

Hujr kicked open a food cabinet and stuffed the agent inside. A small pool of blood spotted the floor; Hujr wiped the blood up with a towel and straightened the tiny cubbyhole.

He poked his head out into the aisle. Clements ambled down toward the back with a bag of chips. Hujr saw Du'Ali slip from the stewards' station and knock lightly on the cockpit door. Everything was going as planned. And if he could get the marine into the cubbyhole, he shouldn't have any trouble getting to the President. The remaining Secret Service agents wouldn't make any difference; it was the first fifteen seconds that counted—if he could get to Montoya before anyone cried out. . . .

Clements stuck his head into the chamber. "Here're the chips. Now where's the hot stuff?" He looked around. "Where'd Sam go?"

Hujr tried to keep his voice from showing emotion. "He went to the toilet."

"Well, I guess that leaves more for us. Where's the dip?" He moved toward the back as he spotted the vat. "Hey, now, how are you supposed to do this?" He turned around just as Hujr withdrew his knife.

Clements spotted the knife and lashed out with his foot at the knife. "You fuckin' flip—"

Hujr sidestepped the kick and coolly dove at the marine, ducking a roundhouse from Clement's right. The knife found its way to the windpipe. Hujr twisted the knife deeper as the marine held him at arm's length; gurgling sounds came from the man's throat. Slowly, the marine's grip loosened, and Clements slid to the floor.

The whole incident had taken less than ten seconds, but Hujr breathed as if he were finishing a marathon. Gasping for breath, he peeked out to the aisle. Despite the marine's cry, the episode had gone unnoticed.

Now the adrenaline started to flow; he felt the first rush of the hormone as he turned back for the vat. Killing the Secret Service agent and the marine had pumped him up. The prospect of actually pulling off this coup put his body into high gear. It was the one thing that he had slept, dreamed, and struggled with for the past three months.

Hujr grasped the vat of plastique, pushed two electrodes into the soft explosive, and checked the warning light on the battery. A green light from the unit smirked up at him —the vat was almost ready to explode. With his right hand he closed the switch arming the bomb and swung the apparatus into the aisle.

The door was not locked; it opened at his touch. President Montoya scowled up at him as he entered; two empty beer mugs framed his features. The President put down a paper and said, "I know you're new to this, Mr. Aquinbaldo, but you've got to learn how to knock. You're interrupting me. Now what is it?"

Hujr moved into the room, keeping silent. Montoya stared up at him. The dark hair and brown eyes—the Mexican-American features that Hujr had grown to loathe —they stood for everything he had pledged to tear down. Hujr almost got cold feet, but the reality—his training and the drive to finish—brought him around.

Hujr quickly closed the door behind him, locking it. "Quiet, *'ifrit!* Listen to me."

Montoya calmly reached under his desk. Hujr leapt forward and kicked the wooden desk with his foot, slamming Montoya backward. Instantly, the confidence the President had carried was replaced by a look of terror.

Hujr held up his hand with the switch and hissed. "Do not try it again, if you want to live. Do you understand?" Montoya remained motionless. "Yes or no? Quickly—tell me." Hujr lashed out with his foot and sent the desk flying backward, again ramming Montoya against the wall.

"All right, dammit!" Tiny beads of sweat appeared on Montoya's face. He licked dry lips. "What do you want?"

Hujr moved to the desk and ripped two tiny wires from underneath the drawer, disarming the alarm. He motioned with his head to the vat he held. "Listen and understand me. I will only tell you once. If you do not understand, interrupt me. Otherwise, just nod your head. Understand?" Montoya's head bobbed up and down. "Good. I have five kilograms of plastic explosive, ready to detonate and destroy this plane. See this switch?" Hujr held up his right hand. Montoya nodded vigorously. "All I have to do is release this switch and the plane explodes. If that happens, everyone on it is killed, you and me included.

"This trigger is armed; if I'm killed, the bomb will explode. The trigger is called a deadman switch, for even if you somehow manage to kill me, the device will still explode. And you will die if I die. Do you understand?"

Once more Montoya nodded, but this time it took an effort. Hujr relaxed slightly. Montoya knew now that he was serious—and that had been the most critical part. Now that he'd won the President over, all he had to do was give the orders from here on out.

Hujr backed up, set the vat on the floor, and, with one hand still on the deadman switch, moved a chair in front of the door. Keeping his eyes glued to the President, he managed to push the couch with his right foot to reinforce the chair.

Hujr moved away from the front of the desk and sat to Montoya's right. "Mr. President, I am prepared to die if you do not follow my orders. My life is worthless to me; I can only achieve a higher glory if I die bringing you to your death. So do not try to talk me out of it, and only do as I say.

"First, you will contact the cockpit and forbid anyone to enter this chamber. If they try to enter, you will die. You will order them not to use the radio, or any other emergency device, to broadcast outside of this plane what I have done. Tell them now. Remember, if you say one wrong word, you will die."

Montoya reached for the intercom. His hand moved slowly across the desk to where he flicked on the instrument. "Colonel McGirney, this is the President."

The pilot sounded tired. "Mr. President, we already

know the situation—we've been waiting for you call. One of the stewards killed the flight engineer and has taken command of the cockpit. What are your orders, sir?"

Montoya looked up at Hujr, wide-eyed. "You didn't say there would be anyone killed. . . ."

Hujr stared him down and barely moved the deadman switch. "Remember your directions, Mr. President. I'm not playing a game."

Montoya drew in several breaths. He turned his attention back to the intercom. "Inform the rest of the plane not to try to contact me, Colonel. The steward that is holding me has a bomb—a very big one—and will blow up the plane without hesitation if anyone tries to get into my chamber. I am well, so do not—do *not*—try anything out of the ordinary. And maintain radio silence; no exceptions."

"Very well, sir."

Within seconds, Colonel McGirney's muffled voice could be heard through the chamber walls, transmitting the President's orders via the onboard intercom.

The intercom on Montoya's desk crackled back to life. "Done, sir."

"Stand by, Colonel." Montoya flicked off the intercom. A slight bit of color began to creep back into his cheeks, almost as though the initial shock of the hijacking had abated. Montoya's voice was level as he spoke. "All right, your announcement has been made. Now what do you want me to do?"

Hujr grew suddenly alert, catching the subtle change in Montoya's voice. He had to act now. He had to put down any thoughts the President might be having of trying to circumvent Hujr's plan. Hujr jumped up with the bomb and backhanded Montoya across the desk. "I said no speaking. Move away from the desk."

Montoya stood, complying; a red mark appeared on his face where Hujr's hand, weighted by the deadman switch, had hit. Montoya stood rigidly in front of the desk. Hujr approached, then swiftly planted a foot to Montoya's testicles. Montoya winced, grabbed at his groin, and doubled over. When he grasped for breath, Hujr kicked Montoya's kneecap, sending the President sprawling. Montoya curled up on the floor.

Hujr toed the President. "Once more—you will speak only if you do not understand me. Is that clear?"

"Yes."

Hujr kicked the President on the cheek—not hard enough to cause permanent damage, but well-placed, so that Montoya's cheek oozed blood.

"I said, is that clear?"

This time Montoya only nodded. Saliva and snot mixed with Montoya's blood on the carpet; the blue Presidential seal soaked up the fluids.

Hujr allowed Montoya a few moments to think about the threat, then prodded him once more with his toe. "Get back to your desk."

Montoya pushed himself up and staggered, holding a hand to his cheek. When he sat, Hujr stared at him stonily. "Inform the captain once more of the warning I gave not to attempt to break into the chamber. Anything else they try —such as a rapid decompression, a sudden dive, or firing bullets through the bulkhead—will only gain them death. Furthermore, they are to turn off all running lights, identification signals, and electronic gear."

Montoya did as he was told. He remained silent after speaking to McGirney.

Hujr allowed a smile to grow over his face. "Very *good*, Mr. President. I think we can have a working relationship. Now, instruct the captain to fly in the following heading." He reeled off a series of numbers. "He must fly directly in that heading, disregarding any airspace violations he may encounter." Hujr consulted the wall clock. "He won't have any, at least not any unexpected ones. Have him change course immediately. The steward in the cockpit will acknowledge that your pilot is following my directions. If he does not obey your orders, you will die. Now tell him."

Hujr relaxed back on the couch as Montoya groped for the intercom. The coup was going as planned, and things couldn't be better.

U.S.S.S. *Bifrost*

Space was the perfect place for the CRAY-5 supercomputer. Like its younger brother—the CRAY-4 on Earth—the CRAY-5 was fast. *Very* fast. So fast, in fact, that if the CRAY-5 were on Earth, the light impulses that coursed through its three-dimensional, solid-state brain would be affected by the local gravitational anomalies created by trucks roaring on roads two hundred meters away. Vibrations from those same trucks would cause the synchronization of the CRAY-5 to fall apart, and the computer would yammer like a moron. Not to mention what would happen when the 1.2 million parallel "brains" the CRAY-5 possessed couldn't coordinate with one another.

So the only place the CRAY-5 could operate with the isolation it needed was in space. It was housed in a module five hundred meters away from BIGEYE's main body, connected by a slender, graphite-composite tube.

Originally developed for the scuttled SDI program, the CRAY-5 had been built by Seymour Cray's disciples to process megamyriad bits of information at a speed approaching that of light. Billions upon billions of pieces of information had to be processed—and decisions had to be made to optimally obliterate incoming Soviet ICBMs, SLBMs, MRBMs, cruise missiles, bombers, FOBs, killer satellites . . . and the choices had to be correct.

So without SDI, the supercomputer—a cryogenically cooled single unit using molecular spin for memory . . . a device no larger than an old-fashioned calculator . . . a computer that could *only* work in the isolation of space—did not have anything to do.

So the U.S. Air Force put the CRAY-5 to work on board BIGEYE, processing the information that it gathered from earthbound, stratospheric, and low-flying satellite sensors. In addition, any unusual EM transmissions were screened by the CRAY; bits and pieces of radio calls from dope smugglers were analyzed right along with eavesdropping on unfriendly, and sometimes even friendly, governments. A machine that can process vast amounts of information might as well be put to use.

Lieutenant Colonel Frier was using only a minuscule fraction of the CRAY-5's total computing power playing a combat simulation game when the terminal burped at him. Frier frowned and moved closer to the screen. The status board indicated that no sensors were activated, but something had triggered the warning. Frier fingered the touch-sensitive screen.

As he ran through the options he hummed an old song —the words wouldn't come back to him, but the melody was still as clear as it had been twenty-three years before when he was an IP at Laughlin. Sometimes he could still feel the breeze off the lake and smell the dry desert. Those were good times; he was young, so he did not have anything to worry about except his students. It wasn't until years later, right before the crash, that things had started to wear on his nerves.

Damn. Why did he always have to let his thoughts drift back? The image stayed with him: an already-dead student, soaked with JP-4, bursting into flames as Frier dragged him out of the cockpit; then Frier swatting at patches of fire that tried to catch his nomex flight suit; falling down and not being able to get up—and finally *watching* his legs burn away. The worst part was the charred flesh.

No, it was the smell he couldn't shake. And when they told him he'd never use his legs again . . .

. . . of *course* the opportunity to command the *Bifrost* was something he couldn't turn down. What else did he have to live for? And pass up a chance to be productive again? There just wasn't any question about it.

He shook his head and concentrated on the screen. The spook satellites were listed in order of altitude from earth. Frier checked HERK-3's position. The satellite was a polar bird, as was BIGEYE, but was nearly two hundred miles closer to the Earth than BIGEYE. Its lifetime in orbit was exponentially shorter than BIGEYE's, but at that altitude,

HERK-3 could practically tell you the color of someone's eyes.

HERK-3 was south of the Med at the time; usually things were pretty quiet there, but something must be going on. The satellite was picking up data and dumping it, via the AFSATCOM, into the CRAY's memory. The CRAY-5 had put something together—a combination of two seemingly unrelated facts—and had thought enough of it to burp at him. Frier did not like what he saw, so he decided to correlate the information with a different sensor.

Frier reconfigured the screen and ran the CRAY through the "tell-me-three-times" routine to make sure the machine hadn't slipped a bit. When the answer came up the same, he let out a single word:

"Shit."

Frier didn't say anything more until he set up a scrambled transmission direct to NSA, bypassing the CSOC downlink. The first few mnemonics of the coded sequence read: "XVW XVW XVW . . ."

National Security Agency Headquarters, Fort George Meade, Maryland

The computer screen flashed on-off-on-off in a red and blue contrasting sequence designed to alert the operator. A beeper emitted a high-pitched warbling for the same purpose. There were four computer consoles in the room. Three of the consoles were manned, and the fourth, a training console, used exclusively by the on-duty supervisor, was idle. As the middle of the three active consoles warbled its warning a young, good-looking woman in a wheelchair jabbed at the interactive screen, silencing the alert.

The bespectacled woman glanced up at the clock. "Twenty minutes and I've won the pot. Ready to pay up?"

The two operators flanking her grumbled good-naturedly

but handed over the pot of money kept at the supervisor's console. The first alert normally didn't come until at least halfway through each shift. To win this early was certainly an omen.

The woman swung her wheelchair around after glancing at the screen. She hit a large button on the side of the console, and a hard copy of the coded message popped out of the top of the terminal. She tore off the copy and handed it to her supervisor, who stood behind her. "What do you think?"

"I think those damned field operatives are using the XVW too often. You'd think they'd save the hot labels until they've got something substantial."

"BIGEYE isn't your run-of-the-mill field operative."

Her supervisor raised a brow. "You've got a point." He pushed the paper back toward her. "Ship it off to the NECC and let them decode it—you do the honors, sweetheart."

"You wish you could, don't you." She snatched the paper and tapped at her terminal. As the message was transferred the woman counted the pot of money she'd won. It was just enough for drinks after work. Maybe she *would* show him a good time tonight.

The White House

"Mr. Woodstone . . ."

The Vice President waved him quiet.

Baca knelt in the dark viewing room at the Vice President's side. "Mr. *Woodstone*, this is urgent. . . ."

"What is it?"

"We lost contact with the President's plane fifteen minutes ago."

"Could his radio have gone out?"

"Impossible. There are too many backups on board. Besides, we lost his IFF along with radar contact. Air Force One has disappeared from sight."

G. Percival Woodstone made his first major decision acting as President of the United States of America: "Turn off the film." He stood abruptly and started for the exit as the house lights brightened. "Now, what's going on? I want to be fully briefed on this matter." He turned for the Oval Office.

Baca stood in the hallway. "Mr. Woodstone, I recommend we use the vault."

"Eh?"

"The National Emergency Command Center, sir. You'll be able to keep in touch with many more, ah, *sources* there." To Woodstone's blank stare he added, "We have a direct link with our satellite sensors in the NECC."

"You're right, as usual. I'm not used to taking over in times like these." Woodstone whirled and followed the chief-of-staff to the elevator that would take them to the basement. "What else do you know about this?"

"I'll be able to brief you in depth once we're in the vault, sir. I've only got a smattering of the original message myself. I thought it was more important for me to inform you now than to have you surprised later if the entire message took too long in getting here."

"Right." Woodstone kept in step with Baca's strides. Though a shorter man, Baca kept the Vice President hopping right along.

Woodstone felt an involuntary rush of adrenaline pound through his veins. The excitement of something *big* happening grabbed him. Kissing babies, dedicating libraries, opening manufacturing plants, and speaking to groups of little old ladies bored him to tears. As Vice President, he thought he would have a little more say in running the country—but he was really only a figurehead. He knew he'd have to be a P.R. man for Sandy Montoya when he decided to take the job, but holy cow! Enough was enough. Sandy didn't even trust him to run things on his own.

The President had even left his chief-of-staff to help run the show when he went to Europe. So he couldn't flub this one. Here was his chance to have a real part in making a Real Big Decision.

They passed the ubiquitous Secret Service man guarding the entrance and entered the command center. An air force colonel met them inside.

"Mr. Vice President, we have a briefing ready for you, sir."

Colonel Welch led him to an overstuffed chair in front of a long table. A large screen took up the front part of the room; myriad terminals manned by men and women with headsets were crammed into the back. The room was air-conditioned; Woodstone swore he could detect a hint of piñon wafting through the room.

Woodstone settled into the chair. "What's the story?"

"Fifteen minutes ago, 1949 local time, air controllers at Torrejon, Spain, lost contact with Air Force One. The President's plane is equipped with an Identification Friend or Foe transponder as well as the usual radar transponder. They are both routinely monitored through satellite relay. All contact with the plane ceased at the same time. The only conclusion we can reach at this time is that Air Force One met with an unforeseen ground obstacle."

"You mean it crashed."

"As far as we can tell, that is correct, sir." Colonel Welch pushed a button; the screen lit up with a view of Europe. "The President's route is marked in red." The screen flashed to a closeup of the Italian border. "We lost contact with him close to where the red line terminates." The colonel flashed a bright red arrow up on the screen using a laser pointer. "As you can see, the French Alps start here and extend down to here—which is south of where we lost contact with the plane. We didn't know Air Force One's exact position, so it's possible that the plane was ahead of its schedule and crashed."

"We've scrambled an air force unit stationed at Torrejon to scout the area and look for the wreckage. Plus we have some reconnaissance planes equipped with IR cameras flying down from Ramstein. With any luck we should be able to find the plane within the hour."

Woodstone shifted his weight in the chair. "So what now? What do we do?"

Awkward silence filled the room.

Baca spoke up. "Colonel, are you absolutely certain the plane went down?"

"Well, sir, of course we can't be one-hundred-percent sure until we locate the wreckage, but we've got a backup search plan. We've got an AWACS forward based at Ramstein that can get a radar fix on anything moving within five hundred miles. Plus, one of the recon squadrons from Torrejon is fanning out from where we've projected the crash site should be to where we calculate the plane could have traveled given its original flight plan."

"So you think there's a possibility the plane might not have crashed."

"It's possible, but not probable, sir." Colonel Welch put down the pointer. "Mr. Vice President, every electromagnetic signal emanating from Air Force One stopped at the same instant in time. If that occurs, then either the plane has lost all of its electrical power and the aircraft has crashed, or the units on the plane were deliberately shut off. Now, I can't imagine that anyone would shut off *everything* on the plane, even in an emergency. Even in combat our planes have their IFF transponders working."

Woodstone settled back in his chair. People spoke of the immense weight they shouldered while President, but he could only feel elation. . . . It was hard to keep it to himself. He had an overwhelming desire to inquire about how Johnson took over after Kennedy's assassination. Only how could he approach the subject without appearing callous—or eager, as he was?

His thoughts were broken by Baca's voice. "Mr. Woodstone, may I offer a few words of advice, with my background as an attorney?"

The words did not come as a request, but as a statement. Woodstone nodded. "Go ahead."

"Mr. Vice President, since we are out of contact with the President, you legally hold the power of the presidency. However, I think it would be wise to keep this information from public dissemination until the whereabouts of Air Force One may be ascertained. There are two reasons for this: first, you must be sworn in as President if the plane has indeed crashed. This must occur without any warning to the public, for although *we* are aware of the hierarchy of authority, the public's faith in our system must not be shaken. We must take care of the logical transfer of legal power in an expedient manner."

"Second, if the President's plane is not found, we must assume that the plane has been hijacked. You would still be legally in charge, assuming authority as if the President was found to be incompetent. But whatever happens, I cannot reiterate strongly enough that the public's faith must not be shaken."

Colonel Welch spoke before Woodstone could answer. "What do you mean, Air Force One could have been hijacked?"

"You said yourself, Colonel, that you couldn't imagine why anyone would turn off all the plane's communication systems. Well, I just threw out a possible scenario for you. If the plan was indeed hijacked, that could happen."

"But that's impossible! Everyone on that plane had at least a Top Secret clearance and was personally investigated by the FBI."

Baca answered dryly, "And we still have spies in our government, too, Colonel. I don't think we can rule anything out until the President's plane is located." He turned to Woodstone. "Mr. Vice President"—the word *vice* was faintly stressed—"again I recommend that this matter be kept quiet until the situation is cleared up. Until then, I suggest that you keep to the White House and run business as usual."

Woodstone's spirits soared, but he hid it well, keeping it to himself. "You're right. Colonel, excellent job—and keep me posted on any news. I want to hear as soon as you find out anything."

"Yes, sir."

The Colonel stood as Woodstone and Baca left the room. Woodstone allowed Baca to hold the vault door for him but vowed that Baca would be the first to go when the President's dead body was found. Hijacked indeed!

Air Force One—Over the Mediterranean

Hujr sat watching the President. The door to the rest of the plane was still barred by the couch, and the only light in the chamber was from a small lamp by Hujr's side.

Hujr had it easy. All he had to do was to watch Montoya and make sure he followed directions. At the other end of the plane Du'Ali was doing the real work. He'd be watching two directions at once: inside the cockpit at the crew, and out, toward the back of the plane.

The last time Hujr had spoken to Du'Ali—not two minutes before—everything was going as planned. Du'Ali reported over the intercom and let Hujr know every two minutes that everything was well. Their communication code was simple: Du'Ali spoke in Do'brainese and each time said a new number to Hujr. The last time Du'Ali had spoken, the number had been eighteen. If the number nineteen was not repeated next, Hujr would know that something had happened. Du'Ali might have been forced to make his two-minute report, but no one would know their little code. Not in Do'brainese, anyway.

All communications gear had been destroyed, beaten by Du'Ali with a heavy iron pan. The plane's running lights were turned off as well. Armed with only a kitchen knife, Du'Ali had been able to take over the cockpit. And once the crew had gained knowledge of Montoya's capture, they offered no resistance. Now Du'Ali watched both the cockpit and the rest of the plane armed with a Secret Service man's Uzi. He was in absolute control. For even if there was someone on the plane who still had a weapon, all would die from Hujr's bomb if they attempted to thwart the plan.

The knowledge put Hujr at ease. He allowed himself a slight smile with the anticipation of greeting his ALH brothers with the ultimate hostage.

French Alps

"Blue one, this is blue three—I've got a negatory visual on that IR spot."

"What was it, three?"

"Looks like some goats . . . or some other type of wildlife. It's not a plane, though."

"Roger that, three. Stand by." Captain Jimmy McCluney pulled his F-15 out of the banking turn and allowed the fighter to cruise level for a while. Playing mother hen to the rest of his flight at twenty thousand feet did not appeal to him. He was a wild weasel, a member of the new generation of fighter pilots who'd never seen combat, even in the Mexican Intervention, but who still loved to fly low and fast.

Knocking out enemy SAM and radar sites was his specialty; he was given grief by the air-to-air pilots who thought that the only thing that mattered was being an ace in combat. But Jimmy didn't care for that. It was zooming along the deck at one hundred feet with his official altitude reported as three hundred, and "Bitchin' Betsy"—the voice-actuated warning system—shitting in her pants for him to *pull up!* The excitement of rising over a ridge and just dodging a tower put his life squarely in the fast lane. There was nothing else like it. Let the air-to-air weenies play up in the clouds. It was down on the ground that he loved.

But here he was sending his flight out for this damned rescue mission. Now that he was a senior captain, he had to direct the whole operation instead of running around on the ground with the rest of the boys. That's what he didn't like about the air force. As soon as he became the best in his field, they booted him upstairs as a manager to oversee the rookies.

He flipped the toggle so he could speak to his squadron back at Torrejon. "This is Blue flight leader . . . we've pulled another negative check on area forty-two Delta. What are your orders?"

The reply crackled back almost instantly. "Move to forty-three, Blue flight. And are you recording the sweeps?"

"Roger that. We've got all our film rolling."

"Keep it up, Blue flight."

The mike clicked off. Roger-dodger, over and out. Shit, they didn't even trust them with their own visuals. They wanted some non-rated intel officer with Coke-bottle glasses to go over the recon photos to try to catch anything his flight might have missed. As if his flight wasn't the best in NATO.

Jimmy pulled his '15 into another bank to get over area forty-three. "Blue flight, this is Blue one. Copy my vector to area forty-three, Delta region, and use the same pattern for IR and visual checkout. Confirm by the numbers."

"Roger that, one—two here."

"Three copies."

"Say no more, I'm four."

"Five's got it. And by the way, one, who the hell's plane are we looking for?"

"You've got me, five. 'Ours is not to reason why...'"

"'Ours is just to do and fly.' Gotcha."

"All right, you clowns, cut the chatter and get to it."

"Roger, one. And have fun up there."

Up your ass; I just hope you're a flight commander when I come back to take over the wing, thought Jimmy. Then you'll see how much I like it up here, instead of being down there with you. He approached area forty-three and eased himself out of the bank.

U.S.S.S. *Bifrost*

Frier's eyes were glued to the monitors. One screen showed a view of the Canary Islands, just off Spain. At the edge of the screen lay the Med; a separate window on the computer screen showed the same view in infrared. A ghostly wavering filled the void where land and water stood out, demarcated by their differing temperatures. On the other screen a direct link to the CRAY-5 flashed bits of seemingly unrelated information.

Major Stephen Wordel floated into the observation chamber, scratching an itch and yawning. The second, and temporary, member of the BIGEYE crew swapped shifts with Frier every twelve hours. It kept Wordel sane and allowed Frier to run things the way he wanted.

Wordel squinted at the monitors Frier observed and looked puzzled. "What's up?"

"There's a search going on for a plane missing in the French Alps."

"So?"

"So the plane is Air Force One." As Wordel's eyes widened Frier explained. "And just in case the plane didn't crash, I've had the CRAY project a possible flight route." He pointed to the visual screen. "I pointed all our satellite sensors in the crash area and couldn't locate anything. So on a lark, I pointed them along the projected route. I've just detected an object about the size of Air Force One crossing the south side of the Mediterranean:"

"Holy . . . the President's plane crashed? Or . . . or . . . what the hell is going on?"

"I wish I knew. All I know is that we got a request to try to locate a downed plane with our satellite relays—and instead I've got something that hasn't filed a flight plan just crossing the south side of the Med."

"Could it be a civvy—a smuggler, maybe?"

"The size of a 767? Unlikely. Especially when a 767 is missing a couple hundred miles north. Anyway, there are no electromagnetic emissions coming from the plane. The satellites were barely able to pick out its outlines on IR, but we've got a lock on it now; the thing just keeps heading due south."

Wordel blinked at the screens. "So what does CSOC say?"

"We're bypassing CSOC and are scrambled directly into

the White House—National Emergency Command Center." Wordel let out a long, low whistle as the fact set in. Frier nodded. "You've got it. And we've got everybody's favorite Vice President calling the shots down there to top it off."

"You don't really think they'd actually let *him* . . ."

Frier shrugged. "Look. We've survived this long with Montoya, and he hasn't screwed things up too much. And we *are* sworn to uphold the commander-in-chief, no matter how much of a fruitcake the guy is. We do what they say."

"Yeah, I hear ya, but I still think it stinks, no matter what oath I took." He followed the trace on the screen. "Suppose that really is Air Force One. Where do you think it's headed? It's sure as hell not making a beeline for Israel."

"I'm not sure, but read this. It will blow your socks off." Frier sailed a sheet toward him. "HERK-3 just picked up a message from the ALH. It's a call for all the ALH bigwigs to congregate at Do'brai for some kind of powwow. Their last plane is in the air, heading for Do'brai, and should arrive within six hours." He pointed at the sheet. "The bottom list is all the possible airfields that Air Force One could reach without refueling . . . and look which one is at the very limits of its range."

Wordel scanned the sheet. "Do'brai?" He put down the page and frowned. "What the hell is going on?"

Frier shrugged. "I'm not sure, but maybe the White House knows. Anyway, I've got that ALH plane pegged and will wring any transmissions from it that I can." He turned back to the screen and keyed the mike. Although they were out of direct contact with the White House, the signal bounced off two geosynchronous satellites to connect them with the NECC half a world away. Once the classified voice link was established, Frier spoke.

"Colonel Frier here. We've got a negative report on that plane crash in the Alps, but we've picked up a bogey that could be Air Force One a few hundred miles southeast of where you're looking."

Silence. Then, "This is Colonel Welch. Air Force One's

flight plan did not entail going that far south, BIGEYE; if that's our plane, it would be heading for Israel. Continue your sweep for the crash."

"We realize that, Washington—but I think you ought to take a look at the data we've got. And a projection we've made with our computers on possible landing sites. We've come up with something interesting."

"Can you send it down?"

"We're transmitting now, Washington." Frier barely touched the screen. The data on the bogey and Do'Brai transferred at a blinding rate.

Wordel spoke half to himself. "I hope the sons of bitches down there are ready for it."

"They will be. They *have* to be."

White House

"Mr. Vice President, if we can rely on BIGEYE's intelligence, Air Force One is heading for Do'brai. We have to assume the President has been taken hostage, and if our analysis is right, something big is going to happen very soon."

Woodstone tapped a pencil nervously on the desk. "So what do we do?"

Baca lifted an eyebrow. "That's your decision, Mr. Woodstone. All we can do is give you advice."

"Right." Woodstone tapped furiously. *Crap*—this wasn't any fun at all. Where did the excitement go that he had first felt . . . hours? . . . no, only *minutes* ago, when this thing first popped open. Here he was, sweating like a convict in a lineup.

Woodstone loosened his collar and eyed the people gathered around him. He'd decided against having the full contingent of the NECC present, instead surrounding himself with about half the personnel; he hoped they'd come to a decision more quickly that way. But it still didn't help. What the hell should I do? he wondered.

Woodstone looked wildly around the room. "How about negotiations? There must be someone we can call. Someone who has influence . . . the Soviets? Someone get a hold of Premier Zel'dovich; he'll have an idea. . . ."

A cough came from his left; General Backerman's four stars gleamed on each shoulder as he spoke. "Mr. Vice President?"

Woodstone looked wild-eyed. "General?"

"Sir, if I may make a suggestion—"

"What about the Soviets?"

"Mr. Vice President, the Soviets have just about as much influence in Do'brai as we do. Remember when they tried to move into Do'brai with their advisors and economic aid, and how they were told to go to hell by President Ash'ath only two years ago? Also, Premier Zel'dovich is the *last* person we want to know that the President is missing."

Woodstone seemed to catch breath. He hesitated and sank back in his chair. "Please continue, General."

"Thank you." Backerman looked around the room and placed his hands on the table. "If indeed the President's plane is going to Do'brai, BIGEYE projects it as only two hours from landing. They've had a five-hour head start on us, meaning it would take seven hours for our closest jets to reach him."

Baca lounged in his chair and spoke over the murmuring. "Where would our jets come from, General?"

"The *Kennedy* is off of Cyprus right now. Its F-14 Tomcats could make it to Do'brai in about five to seven hours. But they'd have to get back with refueling; to get tankers into the area would take another six hours. They'd be coming out of Torrejon."

The silence prompted Backerman to continue. "If we launched a rescue"—he waved a hand, silencing the protests that began to sprout—"if we launched a rescue, the C-19, our fastest transport plane, would take over nine hours to get there from Ramstein. So we're stuck. If we want to get to the President within the next twelve hours, we have to launch right now. We have to make a decision and move, gentlemen."

Baca rapped on the table for attention. "General, this administration has prided itself on taking the moral high ground on human issues. I sincerely believe if we were to commit our military to a rescue attempt that is hastily thrown together, the consequences would greatly outweigh any perceived gains."

"I realize that, Mr. Baca, but we can always call these planes back. All we have to do is load our troops on board and at least get into the air—"

"No, you don't understand, General. We haven't had any contact with Air Force One for over three hours now. All we have is the intelligence gathered from our space station, and they're not even sure that the plane they've spotted is Air Force One. Can you begin to imagine the repercussions if we were to launch a planeload of Green Berets to storm Do'brai and discovered that what we thought was Air Force One was actually President Ash'ath's private jet? Maybe he's flying in a planeload of cheese from France."

Backerman snorted. "With his transponders off?"

"And I say how do we know for sure, General? President Kennedy sneaked secretaries into the White House to skinny-dip in his pool right under Jackie's nose. How the hell are we supposed to read President Ash'ath's mind?"

"Gentlemen!" Woodstone sounded tired, but he had finally calmed down. He looked beat and wasn't in the mood for arguments. "Gentlemen, I have to agree with Mr. Baca —we're not even sure it is the President's plane that BIGEYE spotted. I think we should relax and calmly discuss all the possibilities. After all, we may be worrying about nothing."

Backerman raised his voice. "Mr. Vice President, I *must* advise you that the prudent step would be to launch some aircraft—tankers, fighters, and maybe a couple of transports—just in case."

"Your advice has been noted, General." Woodstone's face seemed to regain some of the color it had lost. "Gentlemen, I suggest we break for something to eat and assemble here on the hour. Any other ideas?" Woodstone pushed himself up. "Very well, I'll see you in twenty minutes."

"Mr. Vice President?" Colonel Welch slammed the door behind him as he entered the room.

"Colonel, we're just taking—"

"Mr. Vice President, we've intercepted an urgent message—"

"In a *moment,* Colonel."

"Now, sir. It's from BIGEYE. They've intercepted another message sent from Do'brai to Kapuir. Because of the increased coded radio traffic, the NSA thought that Do'brai was running the show—setting something up in Kapuir—and this seems to confirm it. It concerns the President."

"Let me see that." Woodstone grabbed the sheet. As he read he sank into his chair. The room was silent as he scanned the paper. He read it twice before letting it drop to the table. "My God. Oh, my God . . ."

Baca frowned. "Mr. Vice President?"

Woodstone's voice broke. "It's from the ALH at Do'brai. It says the President has arrived at Do'brai on board Air Force One, and as soon as the ALH plane arrives and is refueled the President will be escorted by the ALH to Kapuir, where he will be publicly executed for his 'crimes against humanity.'" Woodstone closed his eyes. "They're going to kill him and broadcast the execution."

"When? Does it say when the execution is?"

"As soon as they reach Kapuir."

Colonel Welch spoke up. "The message says they'll take off in eight hours, General. If the ALH plane arrives in Do'brai on time, in eight hours the President will be back in the air . . . and allowing seven hours for the flight to Kapuir, in fifteen hours the President will die."

Woodstone closed his eyes. Baca leaned over the table and spoke in a low, firm voice. "How long would a fighter squadron from the *Kennedy* take to reach Do'brai?"

"Five hours."

Baca blew up. "We've spent five hundred billion dollars

in the last six years modernizing the armed forces, and you're saying it takes our front-line fighters five fuckin' hours to fly a route an airliner takes *six* hours to fly?"

General Backerman kept his cool. *"Mr.* Baca, five hours allows for our tankers to rendezvous with the fighters. We have to allow time for the planes to scramble, fuel, and calculate their flight plans. These planes are not on alert. At top speed, the '14s have a range of far less than two thousand miles, and if we want to get them back, we need the tankers. What good would a fighter squadron do at Do'brai if they couldn't get back? Never mind what they'd do if they ran out of fuel before they got there."

"But surely the *Kennedy* has tankers that can accompany the fighters—"

"Your administration turned that responsibility over to the air force last year . . . to save money," Backerman finished softly. "But there is another way—"

Woodstone spoke, his face flushed. "We'll shoot the bastards down. That's what we'll do. We'll intercept the sons of bitches before they get to Kapuir and fry their asses. They can't get away with this—"

"Mr. Woodstone." Baca stood and walked around the table. He was pale. "Mr. Woodstone, as Vice President you have the ultimate authority to make a decision. Right now, *please* listen to what the general has to say. I don't like it any more than you do. It was on my suggestion, in fact, that the in-flight refueling capabilities of the *Kennedy* be cut back, but pointing fingers won't solve anything now. This is no time for ideological arguments. If Colonel Welch is correct in his estimates, for all practical purposes we can consider the President dead in eight hours. Once the President boards that plane to Kapuir, there is nothing we can do to save him.

"So if there is anything General Backerman can come up with, no matter how scatterbrained it sounds, we've got to go with it. Now. No bickering, no arguing." He shut his mouth and looked around. Perspiration rolled down his forehead; he wiped it away with a swipe from his sleeve, then sat down abruptly.

Backerman waited a moment, then nodded slightly at Baca before turning to Woodstone. "Mr. Vice President, there is a marine unit training at Camp Pendleton, the Rapid Deployment Force, which uses the air force's Trans-Atmospheric Vehicles to lift them into the combat zone. The unit has been training to capture enemy command posts and other high-level enemy targets during a full-scale war. Now, they aren't rescue troops, but—"

Baca interruped. "How fast can they get there?"

"If I give the order now, the troops could load up the TAVs in one and a half hours. The TAVs take forty-five minutes to get anywhere in the world, so we could get to the President in about three hours—"

"Which leaves us five hours to play with." Baca turned to Woodstone. "Mr. Vice President, I respectfully request that you allow General Backerman to give the order to send that marine unit out. We don't have much time; we must act now."

Backerman waved at Colonel Welch to bring him a secure phone. As the colonel carried the phone the line trailed behind him.

Woodstone hesitated. He shook his head. "But sending in troops . . . my God, I'm not sure that Congress would allow it."

"*Now*, Mr. Woodstone. We're running short of time. If you let Congress in on this, they'll debate it for days."

Backerman interjected, "The least you could do is have the troops load up. The TAVs can orbit on the mother ship and not actually launch until you've given it a little more thought. The important thing is to get the men airborne. It will only take forty-five minutes to get to Do'brai once you give the final go-ahead."

"Forty-five minutes?" Woodstone closed his eyes. "How many TAVs would this take?"

"There are seven TAVs; four are on alert to go at any one time."

"Send two of them." Woodstone opened his eyes. "Only have two of them go, and wait for my order to commit. I want some time to think this over."

Backerman was speaking on the phone as the Vice President finished. Baca protested. "Mr. Woodstone, sending only two TAVs cuts the rescue chances in half—"

"Two, Mr. Baca. I've made my decision. I want to keep this to a minimum in case we have a debacle like those for which the military is famous."

ⅢⅢ 7 ⅢⅢ

0030 ZULU:
SATURDAY, 8 SEPTEMBER

The act of war is simple enough. Find out where your enemy is. Get at him as soon as you can. Strike him as hard as you can, and keep moving.

Ulysses S. Grant

When you appeal to force, there's one thing you can never do—lose.

Dwight D. Eisenhower

Do'brai

As Air Force One rolled to a stop the engines wound down from their high-pitched whining to a deep, dull roar. The windows in the President's chamber were still sealed, so Montoya couldn't tell if it was light or dark outside. His captor smiled widely; moments before the plane landed, the steward had conversed in rapid-fire language with whoever was on the other side of the intercom. The language was not the clipped dialect of Tagalog that the Filipino stewards used, but it still was vaguely familiar to Montoya's ear.

The steward seemed to relax once the plane touched down. Montoya didn't try to pry any information from his kidnapper. His cheek still ached from where he had been kicked. The pain in his groin was gone; all that remained was a dull pounding. He felt that he had somehow suppressed the pain, blocking out any feeling from his lower torso because of the agony.

The steward stood and motioned Montoya to do likewise. Montoya pushed himself up with effort. He stretched sore muscles and momentarily tried to work out a cramp that grew in his leg, but a sharp retort from the steward straightened him.

"When the door opens, do not try to escape." The steward motioned with his eyes to the switch he held, still connected to the vat of explosives. "If anything goes wrong, we will both die."

Montoya started to speak but, remembering the beating he'd taken, decided against it. Long minutes passed; sporadic yelling and bumps against the wall jolted Montoya out of the lull he started to experience. Finally, a light tapping came at the door. The steward moved close and put his ear against the panel; a muffled shout came from the other side.

"*Hai!*" The steward unlocked the door with his free hand and swung the door open; a man pushed through. He held the steward's shoulders, and they looked each other up and down. "Hujr . . ."

The steward bent his head. "*Labbayka Allahummah*, General Kamil."

The two broke into grins and hugged each other. The steward squatted next to the vat and gingerly removed the electrodes buried in the explosive. The newcomer carefully picked up the vat and arming device, left through the door, and returned without the device moments later. Again Hujr hugged the man, keeping the embrace for several seconds before speaking. Montoya couldn't make out what was said, but several of the words caught his attention. References to a Boeing 747 and television were the only words Montoya understood. The two conversed quietly for some time until Hujr abruptly nodded and left the compartment, neither looking back nor acknowledging Montoya when he left. His exit was unhampered by any resistance.

Only then did the newcomer turn to the President. He slowly looked Montoya up and down. "So this is the famous wetback President of the United States of America. The most powerful man on earth—supplier of arms and weaponry to the highest bidder, so full of moral righteousness that it drips on the ground. You don't look so powerful now. What do you have to say about that?"

Montoya remained stone-faced. The newcomer grinned at Montoya's silence, showing smoke-stained teeth that vividly enhanced his dark, deep-set eyes. A uniform, tight-fitting and ornately decorated, covered every inch of his body except for the head. "So, for once the great American President is speechless. You had better think up a good speech soon, Mr. President. You'll soon have the whole world listening to you."

"Who are you, and what are you going to do with my plane?" It was the first time Montoya had spoken in several hours; he was surprised at the harshness in his voice.

"Eh? So you can speak. Hujr told me he had broken your spirit."

Montoya braced himself for a beating, but when the newcomer left him alone he spoke again.

"What have you done with the passengers?"

"All in good time, Mr. President. Just remember what I said—start thinking of a good speech to make. One of those you do so well appealing to the generosity and good-will of all nations. It will make a good show for us."

He turned back to the door and spat a command. The noise outside Montoya's chamber grew quiet; people were leaving the plane. Satisfied that the plane was emptied, the man grabbed Montoya by the arm and forced him to exit.

The plane was in shambles; the aircraft was torn apart. Montoya couldn't tell if the ransacking was for souvenirs or for the cryptographic equipment carried on board Air Force One. At this point, Montoya couldn't care less.

The man shoved Montoya into the back seat of a staff car and locked him in. Metal mesh separated Montoya from the man in front. The man drove away, and as they were leaving, people stepped out from the darkness and started filling the plane again. It was almost as if the man didn't want anyone to know Montoya was there.

Camp Pendleton

"Don't answer the phone, dear. The kids are waiting in the car." Maureen Krandel's shoulders sagged. She stood outside the door, holding the picnic basket in one hand and a blanket in the other. It was mid-afternoon, and they were running late. Creases furrowed her forehead. The lines looked deeper than they actually were because of the sun's reflection off the concrete. She pleaded with her husband once more as the phone's shrill ring cut through the air. "Honey, you *promised*—"

Bill Krandel barely hesitated. "I'll be right back. The battalion knows I'm signed out on leave; they wouldn't bother me if it wasn't important. Promise."

He left the door ajar as he sprinted out of sight.

Maureen's fingers tightened around the picnic basket's handle as the ringing stopped. *Damn*—ever since moving out to California, she hadn't had an uninterrupted day with her husband. The Pentagon was bad, but this was worse. She'd lost count of the nights he'd been pulled awake, be it an unannounced exercise or one of his men locked up, drunk, in the downtown jail. It never seemed to stop.

And the children . . . the kids couldn't even say they had a father now. He'd be gone before light and home after they'd gone to bed. It really hadn't struck her until Julie had asked one night over dinner how come her daddy couldn't make her soccer games like the rest of her friends' fathers.

And Justin needed a father more than ever now. The few times Bill had been home to throw a baseball to him, Bill would wisecrack about Justin growing up as a marine brat:

living all over the world before he was eighteen, but staying in no place longer than two years.

How long would it go on? It just wasn't meant to be this way. She could see it if the pay was good, or even if he raked in the bennies like her friends' husbands who weren't in the military. She had once kept track of the hours Bill worked in a month, then divided that into his salary, but she'd been too depressed to tell him they were living below the poverty level.

He could be making more money working for McDonald's.

He wasn't in it for the pay. She'd known that since he was a butter bar, but things were different back then. They could have a good time on only a movie and a malt. But with the kids . . . she didn't want them to grow up as some fatherless pair of renegades . . . and all because of his goals.

What goals? The last time they'd talked, he dreamed of going back to the Pentagon as a full colonel . . . then making general. It could only get worse.

So this command was his ticket to glory. But what kind of satisfaction could he find ignoring the kids? And her?

Her thoughts were broken as Bill stuck his head out the door; he wasn't smiling. He wore that intense, worried look that disturbed her so much.

"I'm afraid you'll have to go without me, hon. Something's come up."

"Can you meet us at the beach?"

He shook his head and seemed tense. "No, I've got to run."

"How long?"

"I don't know—I've got to be at battalion headquarters in ten minutes." He set his mouth. "Go ahead. I'll try to get back as soon as possible. And don't mention this to anyone, hon. I wasn't even supposed to let you know I'd be gone."

She closed her eyes. "We'll wait until you leave."

He nodded, then left as abruptly as he had come.

She stood in the door for several moments before the

basket slipped from her fingers, dropping to the ground. She didn't hear the bottle inside break. She turned to the car to bring the children inside. Liquid seeped out of the basket and into the sunlight, covering the concrete with dull, blood-red wine.

Edwards Air Force Base

The atomic bomb detonated just above his bed, flashing white, brilliant light with a sound that overloaded his senses. Gould shot up from the cot screaming.

When he woke the klaxon was shrieking above his head, and his heart still yammered from the scare. He realized he hadn't been atom-bombed, and it took another second to realize the klaxon was actually *warning* him that the alert was on.

"Holy shit!" He'd slept in his flight suit; his boots were on and halfway laced by the time he hit the door running. Delores burst from a door down the hall. She was running upright and passed him as he bent over to tie his boots.

"What the hell—"

"How should I know?" Delores's voice came from outside the alert shack door, as she was already outdoors.

This can't be happening, he thought. SAC crews do this shit all the time . . . missiles, bombers, you name it. And the call always comes through: "THIS IS SKYBIRD, I SAY AGAIN, THIS IS SKYBIRD . . . THIS IS ONLY AN ALERT." And once they know it's an alert, the SAC weenies can relax.

Oh, they still do their jobs—you'd better believe it! 'Cause if they're found dicking around, that's it, bucko. Out the door with a boot in the fanny. So they practice like it's the real thing all the time.

But what the hell is this?

The thoughts pounded through Gould's mind as he finished lacing his boots. He was out the door at a run. The desert sunlight hit him like a sledgehammer. Going from the cool air-conditioned alert shack to the dry outdoor heat slowed him minutely, but he put down his head and sprinted for the second TAV.

The 747 crew was ahead of him. They must have been out the door as the klaxon first sounded, for they had already reached the 747 and were scrambling up the ladder to the cockpit.

He'd been assigned the second TAV because he could outrun Delores in the one-hundred-yard sprint, about the distance from the alert shack to the TAV—theory was they'd reach their TAVs at the same time. But Delores was already climbing onto the lifting unit, which hoisted her above the 747 mother craft and right up to the TAV's hatch.

Gould increased his pace; he reached his lift seconds later.

Once inside the TAV Gould strapped in and secured his helmet. He slapped on the touch-sensitive terminal and punched up the checklist option. The terminal screen raced through preflight check, changing with each configuration, and displaying each subsystem it queried. The TAV flight units flashed across the screen in multicolored animation.

Gould scanned the results as he settled in. "INS, commup, slave terminals . . . looks good." He reached overhead and threw what few "hard" switches he had—nearly everything was routed through his touch-sensitive terminals, doing away with unnecessary items. Gould still viewed it with a jaundiced eye. *Anything* could go wrong with computers, he believed, and personally he'd rather have a switch he could click than fool with a computer that went sick.

The craft started a slow vibration as the 747's engines ran up. Gould established a link with the 747 mother ship below him. He said, "You guys know what's going on?"

"Later, hitchhiker. We're busy down here; talk to CP if you've got any questions. Now, don't bother us unless you're going to blow us up."

Gould got the idea and switched over to GUARD. The terminal flashed an "ALL SYSTEMS GO" in huge green letters. "Command Post, this is tail number—"

"Unidentified plane, all airways are closed. Acceptance on S for Sam only."

Shit. They're only taking messages over the secure—the Sam—link. Whatever it is, they've got to be serious about it. The secure link was bounced off the two geo-synchronous satellites—DOD's AFSATCOMs—that were overhead at all times. Three thousand frequency bands were used, and in addition to voice scrambling, the chan-nels randomly jumped from one frequency to another within the band every tenth of a second. Even if the bad guys stumbled onto the frequency Gould started communi-cating on, the frequency switched too fast for them to fol-low his conversation.

And if the communication link popped out of synch, the whole procedure had to be restarted, initializing on a set of cards that were changed every day to prevent compromise.

Gould touched an icon on the terminal to switch him over to the secure link. As he reached out the TAV jerked as the 747 lurched under him. They were moving some-where. . . .

A red square flashed on the terminal. An icon of a tiny figure, the hat pulled low over its eyes, filled one corner of the square with the words "SECURE LINK ESTABLISHED" plastered underneath. "TAV niner one, this is Command Post. Do you copy?"

Gould clicked his radio. "I copy, Command Post; this is niner one."

"Stand by for message, niner one." In the background he heard a voice say, "I've got him, sir."

A moment passed, then: "Niner one, this is Colonel Mathin. Your mother ship is cleared for takeoff, and I'll brief you over the secure link while they're getting you to Pendleton. We'll hack on my time: in seven seconds I'll have 1002 hours . . . ready, ready, hack." Gould punched at his terminal; the numbers agreed with the hack. Mathin continued: "We've got an ETA into Pendleton at 1055 local. I want you in the air and ready to rocket no later than 1130."

"Sir, can I—"

"Niner one, we don't have much time, and this is important. If it were up to me, I'd have Beckman on niner two flying this mission—she'd follow orders better than you without giving me any crap—but you're the best we've got, so are you going to shut up and listen, or do I turn the mission over to niner two?"

"Copy that, sir, please continue." Gould held his breath; he'd taken things one step too far, but he had a feeling that if he was *really* lucky, he was in for one hell of a time.

"Very well, niner one." Mathin sounded relieved. "Once your 747 lands at Pendleton, you'll load up with a full contingent of RDF personnel. Your destination is being downloaded directly into your onboard computer; when you rocket, your new call sign will be *OJO-ONE*."

"That's a rog, tower: Ojo-1. Care to let me know what this mission's about?"

A long silence preceded Colonel Mathin's coming back. "That's a negative, Major. We'll have to wait until you rocket."

Damned need-to-know, fumed Gould. But at least he finally had a live one, and the whole mission probably depended on his steady hand to get them there. He also thought how damned typical it was that he didn't have the proper clearance to know where the hell they were going until he was on his way.

He wondered where the flare-up might be. No telling, but as long as they had the C-19 transports to pull them out of there, he didn't really care. In fact, he might even be able to hit the club for dinner tonight if he was lucky. . . .

The TAV jumped a bit as the 747 lumbered off the runway, throwing Gould back against his seat. The jolt was more unexpected than harmful, but Gould switched on the comm to the mother ship below. As he did the secure link automatically disconnected.

"When are you guys sending up the cocktail service? First class hasn't been served yet."

"Just sit back and enjoy the ride, hotshot. You'll get yours."

Another voice broke in over the commline. "Hey, while

you've got our hitchhiker on the line, tell Gould I'm going back to take a crap and lie down on a cot for a while. Ask him if he can do that in that excuse for an airplane he flies."

"You guys are jealous, ya bunch of lardasses. Just don't run into any commercial liners while you're goofing off down there."

The intercom shut off, leaving him in silence. He tried to relax by reviewing the TAV procedures for a fully loaded craft. If they were going to Pendleton, he'd probably be flying with the marines' whole dog-and-pony show.

It still didn't make much sense to house the marines down at Pendleton if they were supposed to be part of the RDF, but politics dictated it would save money. The RDF wouldn't lose more than forty-five minutes flight time if the TAVs were kept at Edwards and the marines at Pendleton. Otherwise, the additional cost of buildings, supplies, and even schools for the marines' kids would have to be taken care of at Edwards. Gould had to admit, as much as he despised the President's politics, it had saved money.

His terminal silently flashed down the minutes and seconds that were left before landing at Pendleton. The emergency procedures bored him to tears. He had plenty of time to rack it back and catch some sleep. It was an old habit he had picked up as a cadet at the Air Force Academy during classes.

Within seconds he was conked out.

Camp Pendleton

"Are the men ready?"

"Not yet, sir. They're still rounding up Delta squad out at the mockup. They should be arriving within five minutes."

"Good." General Vandervoos lit his cigar for the fifth time and paced across the room. He didn't puff on the stogie, so his perpetual routine of lighting and relighting the cigar kept his hands busy. Reaching the window, he turned and looked Krandel up and down. "Bill, I can't let you go. Weston's got the experience, the men know him . . . and most importantly, he's been tested under fire."

Krandel's face grew red. "General, they're my men. They'll follow me for no other reason than that they're marines—"

"And you're still a stranger to them, Bill. You're some hotshot desk jockey who thinks he'll change the whole damned Marine Corps in three months—"

"And if you didn't think I could hack it, then why did you get me here, sir?"

Vandervoos glared, then reached for a match. "You *can* hack it. I would not assign you command of my RDF if I didn't believe you could handle it." He puffed on the cigar for a moment, then promptly forgot the smoldering stogie as he started pacing again.

Krandel followed the general around the room. "Then why won't you let me lead my own men?"

"You haven't even been out on maneuvers with them, much less jumped from a real TAV—"

"But I've done everything else, sir." Krandel drew in a deep breath, fighting down the shaking that had started in his hands. "I've been through everything the men have tackled the last three months, General. Everything they did, I led the way. Period. I did it because I didn't want this situation to come up. And if it did, I wanted to be in a position to show I could hack it."

Vandervoos retorted, "But at least Weston has experience under fire—"

Krandel exploded. "That's *bullshit*. Sir," he added as Vandervoos stopped lighting his cigar in midair. "General, the only difference in our experience is that Harvey has had a real TAV flight. And that's no big deal; you've told me that before. I'm as qualified as any other marine in the mockup. Besides, if you won't let me command my own men, you'll have one of those TAV pilots as the on-site commander. Think of it: The TAV pilots all outrank Weston. Can you imagine one of those air force hot dogs commanding *marines?*"

The question hung in the air. Krandel had finally stumped Vandervoos long enough so that the general couldn't answer; he could feel Vandervoos giving in, and he had to keep at it. He strode to where Vandervoos stared out the window. "You said I'd be the best C.O. this battalion ever had. I've been through the training, I've paid my dues; now *give me the chance!*"

Vandervoos was quiet for several heartbeats before answering, his voice a whisper. "Bill, this isn't only the President's life we're talking about. If you fail, that poor excuse for a Vice President could ruin this country—"

"General, I didn't make it to lieutenant colonel because of you. If I didn't have something going for me, I wouldn't have made it this far. This isn't a test of how well you've groomed me for command; it's my ass that's on the line. Damn it, General, I wouldn't be here if I was not the best man for the job."

Vandervoos pursed his lips; as he started to speak a knock came at the door. Vandervoos called irritably. "What?"

"The RDF is assembled, sir. Captains Weston and Daniels are in the foyer, waiting to escort you and Colonel Krandel."

Krandel pressed the issue. "General . . . I've *never* let you down."

"Damn it, Bill. I know that." Vandervoos opened his mouth, then promptly shut it. He put a hand on the windowsill. The parade ground sprawled next to the headquarters building, lined by a row of palm trees. It seemed so calm out there, but it was miles away from the maelstrom that churned inside his mind.

Krandel spoke quietly. "Shall I have Weston and Daniels come in so you can tell them who's commanding this mission?"

A long moment passed. Vandervoos smashed his cigar in an ashtray and picked up a fresh one from the box on his desk. "You're their C.O.; you tell them." As Krandel's face lit up Vandervoos bit off the end of his cigar and spit. "Bill."

Krandel stopped halfway to the door. "Yes, sir?"

"I'm stepping out for a moment. Bring them in here to tell them while I'm gone. If you're going to command this rescue, you'll need to see how Weston and Daniels will react when you tell them they aren't going. Like the saying goes: If you're going to dance to the music, you've got to pay the band. And watch out. Daniels won't be bad; his platoon was the second string in all our contingencies. But Weston's going to have a shit."

U.S.S.S. *Bifrost*

Colonel Frier switched off the communications part of the screen and set the apparatus up to beep at any reception from the NECC. He'd done all he could for the time being; additional orders would be coming up at any moment, he hoped, from dirtside. Now, if they could only make a decision on what to do down there. He had all the sensing gear ready, but without the final okay from the NECC he was helpless to use it.

Wordel swam into view to his right. "How did Washington take it, Colonel?"

"The usual—they'll get back to us."

"What are they going to do? Do they realize we're running out of time?"

"They *know* it, damn it. I couldn't have been clearer. My guess is they'll want us to deploy the sonic and motion sensors around the Do'brai airport. We're not due to be overhead for another half hour—we can't get a visual until then—so I'm trying to outguess the bastards at NECC. What the hell else do you want me to do?" Frier noticed the look on Wordel's face. "Look, I'm sorry—I shouldn't have snapped at you. I guess I'm preaching to the choir."

Besides, it was the first time Frier had been able to let

out steam in a while. If something was going to happen down there, he sure the hell wanted to be on top of it.

On top of it. The irony almost made him laugh. Here he was, three hundred miles above the earth, and he wanted to be on *top* of something?

"S'all right. I shouldn't—"

Wordel was interrupted as the communications screen started angrily beeping, demanding the message be received. Frier slapped at the screen. A faceless voice yammered, "BIGEYE, BIGEYE, confirm this broadcast from NECC with echo-check, I repeat, confirm this broadcast with echo-check. I tell you three times: Sensor package deployment ordered soonest incident Do'brai; sensor package deployment ordered soonest incident Do'brai; sensor . . ."

Frier was deploying the sensor package from BIGEYE's bay as he heard the first words. A railgun accelerated the sonic and motion sensor package at velocities that would have turned any human cargo to strawberry jam. The package shot along the precomputed trajectory. Hitting the earth's atmosphere, it would be slowed by atmospheric drag. Tiny gas rockets on the package would steer it in fine-tuning its path and comparing its location to where its internal computer said it should be.

Within minutes the package would separate and impact the ground near Do'brai, saturating the area with tiny sensors that could detect any sound above a whisper from fifty yards away. The information would be relayed to any of the several intelligence satellites circling the earth, then amplified and transferred to BIGEYE, where it would be processed and shot back to the NECC in Washington.

Frier relaxed, finally satisfied that he had been able to do something constructive. "Let's get ready for that visual and IR scan of Do'brai when we overfly it."

"We've still got twenty minutes, Colonel."

"I'd rather be ready and waiting than have something go wrong at the last minute, Major."

"Yes, sir." Wordel shot out of the compartment. He

knew Frier meant business when he reverted to using military rank.

Camp Pendleton

"Room, Aa-ten-*hut!*" The room stood as one.

General Vandervoos strode into the room, teeth clenching an unlit cigar, the quintessential wing commander. Lieutenant Colonel Krandel kept pace one step behind him; General Vandervoos reached the podium and stared hard at the men in front of him. Finally he broke the silence, saying, "Take seats, gentlemen. This won't take long."

He shifted the cigar from side to side and nodded for the first slide. Krandel pushed a button; the lights dimmed, and a desert scene, pictured from high overhead, flashed on the screen. Bordering the slide were the words COMPARTMENTAL TS/RD-SCI NO FORN—DOWNGRADE IAW DOD 5200.2. Vandervoos spoke around the cigar. "This, gentlemen, is Do'brai—it's an IR scan taken from BIGEYE and transmitted to the National Emergency Command Center not fifteen minutes ago. If you'll notice, in the lower right corner of the picture there's a runway." The screen flashed again, showing a closeup. The runway was spotted with vehicles, dots that had to be people, and a single plane. "The plane is Air Force One. Gentlemen, the President of the United States is being held at Do'brai against his will."

Vandervoos paused, waited for the stir to die down, and continued. "This morning, our time, Air Force One left Ramstein, Germany, for Israel. En route, communication with Air Force One was terminated, and the aircraft was diverted to this field. We managed to track the flight but were unable to regain contact with the pilot. As soon as the aircraft landed BIGEYE saturated the area with sonic and motion sensors using over-the-horizon semiballistics; we've been able to keep in touch with what's going on to a large extent through the sensors, but we didn't have visual confirmation until BIGEYE's polar orbit brought it overhead fifteen minutes ago.

"From intercepted communiqués we determined the plane will remain at Do'brai only for a short time. Both DIA and CIA sources confirm that high-ranking ALH guerilla leaders are assembling at Do'brai . . . and that any not there are en route and will arrive within the next eight hours. This is the largest gathering of ALH guerillas since the Mexican Intervention."

He paused. "I'll lay it out for you: The President's been taken hostage and has twelve hours to live. As soon as the ALH junta is assembled they will announce his impending execution for American crimes against humanity. It will be televised by the Arab Liberated Hegemony and will be picked up by the world media"—he shook his head bitterly—"and don't think our media won't accept the feed. The ALH is going to make this execution into a three-ring circus."

He nodded to Krandel; Krandel changed the slide, throwing up an exaggerated view of Central Africa with air routes marked in red. General Vandervoos rapped on the podium to quiet the stir. "We'll only have one chance. Air Force One is refueling at Do'brai, and as soon as the last guerilla leader is aboard—in about eight hours—Air Force One will take off for Kapuir for the execution. The reason you're here is that the National Emergency Command Center wants us to rescue the President. And do it now.

"We don't have any air power close enough to help; even if we did, they couldn't do anything. After all, we can't shoot down Air Force One—not with the President on board. And once he reaches Kapuir, it's over. The place will be swarming with so many guerillas, it would be suicide to attempt a rescue there. Another option we have is to retaliate against the ALH, but with this administration's leanings, I wouldn't count on even that. So this is our only chance. We have to move now." The rumbling grew; General Vandervoos nodded to Krandel, who switched off the slide and brought the lights back up.

The room smelled of the heavy musk that came with

fifty men decked out in battle gear. General Vandervoos shot a glance at Lieutenant Colonel Krandel. Krandel stood erect and studied the men; in the back, behind the marines, slouched a row of air force types. As much as he loathed them, they were a necessary evil, their help was required to pull off the rescue.

The general cleared his throat and eyed the back row. "The air force is preparing two of its seven TransAtmospheric Vehicles at Edwards for the flight to Do'Brai. The TAVs will be cramped, but we can get two squads on board one of them. The other TAV is loaded down with enough fuel to get both TAVs back with the rescue team and the hostages.

"I know your training with the Rapid Deployment Force had you using four TAVs, but the National Emergency Command Center is willing to risk only two of them. We can cram everyone from Air Force One aboard the TAV carrying the fuel bladder—after it's expended, of course—so we shouldn't have any trouble getting everyone back." He lowered his voice. "Personally, I think those village idiots at the NECC are still worried about what the public will think. They've got that damned Mexican Intervention albatross hanging around their necks, so I want the rest of you to man the other TAVs as a backup, just in case they change their minds."

The general took the cigar from his mouth. "We figure they'll head for Kapuir at dawn, local time. That gives us six hours at the most to get you there, rescue the President, and get you back up in the air." He stuck the cigar in his mouth and glanced at his watch. "The TAVs are arriving from Edwards within the half hour; you leave here in forty-five minutes and will orbit at a predesignated jump-off point until final approval for the rescue comes from the White House. If the NECC can convince the Vice President to commit, you'll be in Do'brai in an hour and a half. Are there any questions?"

No one moved. Vandervoos shifted the cigar. "Look, we've got three quarters of an hour. We've tried to think of everything, but you might bring up some questions we haven't considered—it could only help us."

A hand shot up from the back; it was one of the air force types. "General, the air force has always assumed the TAVs would be abandoned and the RDF would be picked up by tactical cargo craft. Are you saying that since we don't have time for any aircraft to pick us up, the TAVs are going to get back on their own?"

Vandervoos nodded. "That's right."

The air force officer rolled his eyes. "But the TAVs are basically scramjets. With the weight they're carrying they will need to be air-launched from a 747—there's no way they are going to take off on their own power. How are you planning to have them return once they get to Do'brai? Without the 747 mother ship, the TAVs can't gain enough speed on their own to ignite the scramjets."

Vandervoos looked to Lieutenant Colonel Krandel; Krandel moved forward and spoke up. "JATOs: Jet Assisted Take-Offs. While the Rapid Deployment Force is pulling off the rescue, the air crews will be refueling from the fuel bladder on the second TAV and strapping JATO units onto each craft. The JATOs we're bringing should get enough airspeed for the scramjets to start up." He paused and grinned wryly. "Or at least that's what your flight engineers at Edwards say."

Vandervoos nodded and looked around the room. "Next?"

A marine stood. "General, how was Air Force One taken over? Was there anything that might have tipped us off?"

Vandervoos shrugged. "Son, you tell me and we'll both know. It could have been anything from an on-board plant to a stowaway. Personally, I think it was an inside job, as Air Force One is protected tighter than a vestal virgin. This seems to go with our one lead: The regular stewards for these trips were in an accident, and their backups were used for the first time. But that's a moot point; the fact is that security broke down, and the President is in danger. We're double-checking the backgrounds of the stewards and any others on board just to make sure, but it won't help us now. Any more?"

Another hand went up, this time more slowly. Another flyboy from the back. "Sir, can we be *sure* the President is still at Do'brai? What if this is some kind of elaborate hoax?"

General Vandervoos's eyes widened. He studied his nails before speaking and seemed to count to himself. "Young man, I couldn't begin to tell you about all the verification procedures. We're using everything from laser phase-conjugated echo checks to seismic sensors deployed by BIG-EYE. With something as important as this, we're pulling out all the stops in the intelligence community. *Trust us!*

"Any other questions?" He waited for a moment, then grunted. "The air force will launch four preattack containers from Vandenburg as soon as you take off; they'll arrive at Do'brai twenty to thirty minutes before the TAVs get there. The canisters house the standard command sensor, biodegradation agent, runway clearer, and sleeping gas that can be carried on a Peacekeeper missile instead of the warhead. If there are no other questions, I'll leave you with Colonel Krandel. I've assigned him operational control of the mission, and he'll fill you in on the details.

"Good luck, men—and Godspeed. Our prayers are with you."

Again the room stood as Vandervoos strode out the door. Once the general left, Krandel rapped for attention and motioned the men to take seats. Facing the room of fifty marines, he swept his eyes down the rows. "If anyone in the RDF is not a volunteer for this mission, you may go to the back of the room. This will not be reflected any way in your records." After waiting a moment, and with no one moving, Krandel let his shoulders sag. "Good—I expected no less."

He straightened a stack of papers on the podium and looked around the room. "The general alluded to the fact that only two squads, twenty-four men, could go on the mission. General Vandervoos has authorized me to make the selection. I wish that all of you could go—it would certainly make me feel better if you could. However, with the limited space on the TAVs, I had to choose those with special skills. For some of you, the ability to speak Arabic was the deciding factor."

He glanced down the list of names he held and drew in a breath. "The following personnel will report through the door to your right; the rest of you are ordered to remain in this room until the backup squads for the third and fourth TAV are chosen. No contact with anyone outside this room is authorized; we can't afford to have news of this operation leak out.

"Platoon Gunnery Sergeant Balcalski." A stocky, somber-faced marine rose and strode out the door.

"Corporal Morales . . .

"Corporal Henderson . . .

"Private Havisad . . .

"Motherhen, this is Ojo-1. All the chicks are loaded and ready to roll."

"Roger that, Ojo-1. Please give the pax your stewardess briefing while we're rotating; we'll be airborne shortly."

"I copy, Motherhen." And up your ass, thought Gould as he switched off the intercom with the 747 below him. The marines didn't take more than fifteen minutes to load, and they'd been on the ground for less than twenty. Once they were airborne, he'd find out just where the hell he was going. He briefly thought about prying open the hatch that separated him from the marines in back and asking them if they knew, but he promptly dismissed the idea.

The few contacts he'd had with the "jarheads" he'd flown had not been too encouraging. For some reason they took themselves far too seriously. The officer/enlisted boundary was very distinct, and it didn't work with Gould's own style.

If Gould treated the air force enlisted folk the way the marine officers treated their men, Gould would have died *years* ago. He remembered the story about an air force wing commander at one of the fighter bases. The colonel had jumped all over some airman's ass for something completely unreasonable—the airman had his hands in his pockets, or something critical like that. After getting his butt chewed by the colonel, the airman proceeded to throw a wrench in the colonel's engine the next time the colonel tried to fly his fighter. The wing commander was lucky to have made it out of the plane alive.

You just don't mess with enlisted men—Gould had learned the lesson well. But applying that adage to jarheads was another matter. He had tried to be friendly once with one of the marine sergeants, and much to his surprise he was snubbed in a courteous but pointed way. He couldn't figure those marines out. To have another air force officer jump in his shit for fraternization was one thing, but when the *enlisted* marines did it—well, Gould just decided it was best to leave well enough alone.

So the notion of asking the marines if they knew what the hell was going on quickly passed. Gould clicked on the intercom and instructed the marines in the back to fasten all their straps, no smoking any time on board, and he'd warn them before they rocketed, thank you.

The TAV swayed slightly as the 747 lumbered down the runway. Once airborne, Gould kept an eye out for his orders to appear on the screen. The screen started bleeping and blinking, the spy icon flashing in the lower left corner of the screen. When the secure link was established, Colonel Mathin's voice came over the speaker. The orders were explained in detail, and Gould was completely immersed in the plan. He had two questions for the FTC commander once the colonel had stopped speaking.

Gould asked, "The JATO units should get us out of there without any trouble, sir, but who's piloting Ojo-2 with the fuel bladder?"

"Major Beckman was the TAV pilot on the list after you, Major Gould. She's just taking off from Edwards and will land at Do'brai about five minutes after you get there."

"Sir, you *can't* send Beckman! She's only been checked out for three months months now—"

"And if I recall, you're the one who certified her, Major.

She's the second-best stick we've got, so unless there are any other reasons she shouldn't go—besides being a woman . . ."

Several moments passed; Gould finally answered, expelling his breath. "No, sir. There's no reason I can think of."

"Good. Now what was your second question?"

It took Gould a while to clear his mind from the previous answer. "What does Ojo mean, Colonel?"

"It means "God's eye"; it's a New Mexican good-luck charm, chosen for obvious reasons. You'll need it, son. So don't step on it."

"No, sir, I won't. Uh, tell Major Beckman good luck, too, sir."

"I will. And remember, this is your final transmission. You're authorized to break radio silence with Ojo-2 only in case of an emergency."

"Roger that, sir."

Do'brai

They took the hood off his head, and he could finally breathe without gasping. The heat was almost unbearable; Montoya blinked in the light and squinted, trying to make out several shapes that hovered at the edge of the glare. A large lamp—it almost seemed to be a spotlight—pointed directly at him. Montoya felt naked, as if under a microscope.

A voice cut through the haze. "Make yourself comfortable, Mr. President. Feel free to stretch out in your chair." It was the same person who had met the steward on board Air Force One and driven him to this place. Was it General *Kamil* that the steward had called the man?

Montoya held up a hand and peered through the glare. "Who are you?"

"Who I am is not important. I trust you have been thinking about what to say when we present you before the news media?"

"You're damned right I've been thinking about what I'm going to say. Now who the hell are you, and what have you done with my plane?"

"Shortly, Mr. President, you will be moved to another location and meet several representatives of your news services. At that time you will make a short apology for the crimes your nation has committed against the people comprising the ALH.. Peace-loving people who, because of your nation's policy in arming aggressive states such as Israel and Egypt, are now suffering."

"What are you talking about? We—"

Montoya was interrupted; the speaker's voice rose a hair. "There are too many starving and homeless people your nation has neglected for you to protest. There would be no suffering, no dying, if it wasn't for your nation meddling in our affairs. You have done our people a disservice, and for the world to know that we are serious about turning these affairs around, you must make a public apology for your nation's crimes."

Montoya thought fast. The general had already tried and convicted him; no amount of logic or arguing would turn his point of view. Montoya played for time. "What is it you want me to do?"

"Make the apology." Then the voice hesitated. "I am aware that your American word of honor is not dependable; you would lie, as you have done in the past, to make things turn out the way you want. So I must be assured that you will truly apologize."

"No—you misunderstand me. I'll apologize; I'll be sincere. . . ." Montoya felt sick to his stomach. He couldn't bluff his way out.

"I do not believe you, Mr. President. But we have a solution for that, a way to *remind* you that when you apologize before the news media, it will come from the bottom of your heart." The voice spat a guttural language. Two men came from behind the light and grabbed him. They jerked his hands behind his back and lashed his arms together. They tightened the ropes until Montoya's elbows met. Montoya bit his lip to keep from crying out. They looped the rope around his elbows, then threw the line up over a crossbeam.

One man knelt and tore off Montoya's shoes and socks. Once he was barefoot, the voice behind the spotlight spoke again. "We have a short speech for you to memorize, Mr. President. We have a few hours to practice, so you will have plenty of time to get it right." He spoke again in the foreign tongue.

As he finished Montoya was jerked in the air, suspended by his elbows. The pain tore through his back; his arms and shoulders were ripped out of their sockets. He felt faint, and his breathing came in short, painful gasps.

A hand grabbed his right foot.

"An interesting technique to remind you to do what we want—and a way that doesn't leave any visible scars when you give your speech—is to slowly remove your toenails. We'll practice your speech, Mr. President, and for every mistake you make, a toenail on your foot will be ripped back and slowly torn off. And just repeating the speech isn't good enough. As you yourself said, you have to be sincere." Kamil clicked his fingers. "Repeat carefully after me."

Montoya felt a burning sensation in his feet. He cried out; the pain wouldn't go away. It was an effort just to concentrate on what was being said.

Vandenburg Air Force Base, California

Two of the air force's three shuttles were absent from the launch pad. The third, the *Antares,* waited in the sweltering heat, unfueled but otherwise ready for its launch the next week. To the southeast—over the ubiquitous golden-brown hills, and out of sight of the Western Launch Complex—a dozen missile silos were buried in the ground. These silos did not contain any of the operational Peacekeeper missiles; at least not those armed with the nuclear warheads that made the Peacekeeper the deterrent that it was. Rather, the missile silos comprised the Western Test Range. Top missile crews came from their U.S. bases to test-fire missiles—to test both the active inventory and the crews' skills.

Now only one of the silos was loaded with a "hot" missile, but it remained dormant for a different purpose.

First Lieutenant Marvin Chiu studied a text in macroeconomics. The only reason he didn't prop his feet up in the silo was that the console was too high. But the readings from the Western State master's program—something practically required of every launch officer while serving time in the hole—tended to put Lieutenant Chiu to sleep. In fact, the course was duller than an imitation Swiss knife.

Chiu's head bobbed off his chest when the intercom squawked above the console. "Bravo, tango, echo, alpha, sierra, six. Authentication: charlie, zulu, X ray, niner. This is not a test. I repeat, this is not a test. Targeting information to follow in five parts. Stand by, one."

"Shit." Chiu's body was flung forward and his feet hit the floor all in one motion. The message was repeated as Chiu sprinted across the room. Second Lieutenant Dubois, the only other person in the launch control room, and Chiu's trainee, made it to the red safe that was embedded in the wall. He arrived just as Chiu got there.

Chiu took a deep breath and said formally: "I received authentication charlie, zulu, X ray, niner and am opening the safe." He ignored Dubois, twirled the knob, and completed the first part of the opening sequence.

As he finished, Dubois announced, "I, too, received authentication charlie, zulu, X ray, niner and am completing the code." He entered his part of the combination and took a step backward.

Chiu reached inside the small safe and withdrew an envelope, which he tore open. As he scanned the contents his shoulders sagged minutely. "That's it; the authentication matches." He looked up. Dubois hadn't been in the hole for more than a few weeks, and now he got a live one on his first tour of duty. Chiu tried to put the younger officer —younger by all of two years—at ease. "Everything agrees with the code. Let's get the targeting computer ready for the feed."

"What do you think's up?"

"No telling. With any luck we're not at war. At least we're not in a hole in Minot; otherwise they'd be launching the real things, and we could kiss our asses goodbye."

"Some consolation."

"Hey, you volunteered for this, didn't you?" Chiu shot a glance at the wall clock. "Let's get a move on. The targeting feed hits us in thirty seconds."

They moved to their respective consoles, and each inserted a small key hanging from around his neck into a three-positioned hole. The keyholes were the standard twelve feet apart, preventing one person from turning the keys simultaneously on command, as required for loading the targeting information and launching the missile. As the wall clock's hand swept past the seconds the intercom came back to life. "Prepare to open the feed link on my count. . . .Three, two, one, *mark*."

At the sound Chiu and Dubois turned their keys. They had no idea of the targeting information being downloaded into the missile's one-board targeting computer. The message was scrambled, requiring on-board crypto to decode the information. The only confirmation they had that the information was being received and decoded was a small green light that burned above the keyholes.

The green light blinked off as the intercom squawked once again. "Targeting information echoed and verified; your launch window is open for the next twenty seconds. Twenty, nineteen, eighteen . . ."

As the voice counted down, Chiu shouted above the din. "Ready, ready . . . *now*." They both turned the keys. Chiu felt as though his key would break off, but a satisfying click filled the air as the keys popped into position.

Three hundred feet away, separated by layers of concrete, steel, and dirt and buoyed by springs, the seventy-foot Peacekeeper popped out of its silo in a cold launch.

Once clear of the ground, the missile's solid fuel rocket ignited and rose like a roman candle in the California sky. The silo was relatively unharmed; within minutes, a new missile could be inserted and the silo used again.

"I wonder where the hell we sent it."

"Turn on the news. If it's anything big, we'll find out soon. But it couldn't be too important; they aren't loading in a new missile yet. If this was the big one, we'd be popping those babies out of here like they were going out of style."

"Yeah," said Dubois. "Some consolation."

Do'brai

Montoya's screams pierced the room. President-for-Life Ash'ath viewed the scene without emotion from behind the spotlight's glare. Montoya hung from the ceiling, barely a foot off the ground; blood dripped onto the floor, mixing with tears from Montoya's sobbing. Ash'ath spoke to General Kamil without turning his head. "How much longer until he's through?"

Kamil bowed slightly. "We will finish the foot we're working on now and probably do one toe on the other foot."

"Even if he memorizes the speech correctly?"

"We are not worried about that, Excellency. He already knows the speech without error. He must be convinced that the apology is true and is his own."

Ash'ath raised an eyebrow. "Is that possible?"

"With enough pain, anything is possible."

Ash'ath studied the man a few moments longer before turning away and walking down the corridor. "Pity. The last time I met him I was impressed by the amount of aid he wanted to give our country. Too bad there couldn't be another way to vault the ALH into worldwide attention."

"You yourself convinced us that this would be the only way to clear up the ALH question, Excellency. Only when the world knows that the ALH can strike anyone, anytime, will this matter be put to rest. Then Do'brai can stop playing haven to ALH politics and take overt control of the united Arab front. You will emerge as the most powerful leader in this hemisphere."

"And you the second most," retorted Ash'ath dryly. Kamil bowed his head. "But I don't need to be reminded of the obvious. I just despise doing things this way for now."

"Your name will never be attached to this, Excellency."

Ash'ath snapped, *"Do'brai* must never be connected with this. Have the servants that are working on President Montoya eliminated once they are through with him. And those ALH scoundrels—"

"Hujr ibn-Adi?"

"Yes. And his cohort, and that Ghazzali fool—dispose of all of them. When the ALH delegates arrive, only you and I will know what has happened. As far as everyone else is concerned, President Montoya is simply to be loaded on board the ALH plane once it arrives. How he got here and what happened to him must never be known to the West. There must be no connection to Do'brai."

"And the remainder of the people who were on Air Force One?"

"Take them to the airport with Montoya. Once the ALH plane clears Do'brai airspace, load them on Air Force One and destroy it. Afterward we will broadcast an alert to the American authorities telling them we offered to help Air Force One, but the plane was commandeered by ALH terrorists who kidnapped Montoya and destroyed his plane."

"Will they believe us?"

Ash'ath shrugged. "How can they not? With no witnesses, they can only take us at our word. Especially when we serve Hujr's head up to them on a platter as proof."

Kamil's mouth parted, revealing a thin smile. "So Do'brai will remain in favor with the West. And once the American President is dead, you will no longer need the ALH to unite the Arab front."

"That is right, my friend. I will no longer need the ALH —for the other African states will flock to Do'brai. They are not fools; they will know Do'brai's power, even though the Americans will not. Just remember, Kamil. What is happening here is unknown to everyone. You and I, Kamil —that is all who should know. That way, we may be completely innocent when we tell the West that we had nothing to do with the ALH."

Kamil bowed at the request.

⫸ 8 ⫷

0230 ZULU:
SATURDAY, 8 SEPTEMBER

If you greatly desire something, have the guts to stake
everything on obtaining it.

Brendan Francis

If you start to take Vienna—take Vienna."

Napoleon Bonaparte

Ojo-1

The decision for Krandel to go—and to be first out—was
entirely his. He massaged his neck, trying to relieve the
tension that had mounted at the back of his head, and
thought for the twentieth time about the decision. Hell,
yes, Weston was angry that he'd relieved Weston of his
platoon. Weston was poised to lead the platoon himself—
that was part of his training. But when the decision was
made to take only two TAVs, what else could Krandel do?
The RDF *had* to be split up; someone had to stay behind.
Krandel had no other choice. Weston knew that dragging
another officer along would have been taking deadweight,
but for Weston to take the order to stay from someone
without operational experience was the final blow.

Krandel rolled his head to ease the tension and jumped

as an intercom set into the bulkhead crackled to life. "Attention in the hold. We have received final approval from the White House: The mission is a go. Stand by to rocket in three minutes."

A cheer ran through the compartment. Inwardly excited, Krandel kept the smile off his face and nodded to himself. He could hardly believe it. After all these years, he finally had a live one. And it wasn't like the White House was trigger-happy, either. After the Mexican fiasco, no politician was willing to risk American lives for *anything*. Public support for any type of military action had dwindled to nothing; this could be his only chance at combat.

The TAV began to shake. Buffeted by the winds, the 747 below them prepared for the nose-down maneuver that would release the TAV into the atmosphere. "Thirty seconds!" Krandel finished strapping himself in and sat back, rigid against the webbing.

The waiting was the worst. Once you started, things happened too fast for you to worry about them. His thoughts drifted to his first parachute jumps with the men. The first three had been night jumps—not because it was dark outside, but because his eyes were tightly shut. . . .

He opened his eyes as the TAV was released from the 747. He was almost weightless; the bottom seemed to drop from below him. . . . Then he was squashed into his seat as the TAV jerked up and to the right. The maneuver had been honed to perfection with the early space shuttle.

The TransAtmospheric Vehicle accelerated upward as the scramjets hungrily gulped air. The scramjets strained as they fought the craft's inertia, trying to build up the TAV's speed for maximum efficiency; slowly, the acceleration increased.

Krandel forced his head to one side and tried to wet his lips. The effort wasn't worth the trouble. His face drew back in a tight mask as the TVA pulled more and more g's, clawing for the upper reaches of the atmosphere until its ramjet would extinguish in the rarefied air.

This was a critical period; with a launch over California, the distance the TAV had to travel dictated a maximum velocity trajectory insertion. With the TAV's low glide ratio, unless they reached the correct insertion point, they would fall short of their destination, dropping like a rock.

Krandel was pressed harder into his seat; the air was squeezed from his lungs. He breathed in short, laborious gasps, then suddenly the pressure lifted and he floated up against the straps. His stomach flipped; he gulped, then was all right. The craft was bathed in an eerie silence; most conspicuous was the absence of the buffeting winds.

A voice broke the silence: "Twenty minutes." Krandel jerked his head to the left and stared at the battalion sergeant. Gunnery Sergeant Balcalski looked like the relic from the nineties he was. Krandel flushed involuntarily; fifteen years his senior, Balcalski made Krandel acutely aware of his fast-burning road to lieutenant colonel. Try as he might, Krandel didn't have the effect on others that the sergeant had; Balcalski seemed to ooze confidence. It was the way Balcalski carried himself.

Balcalski's battle uniform told the story. A row of hash marks barely visible on his desert-brown camouflage—thirty years' worth—ran up his left sleeve. His field experience overwhelmed Krandel's; all Krandel could boast about was putting out fires at the Pentagon. But how could Krandel compete with someone like Balcalski—especially when a staff job was the *only* way to get ahead in the scaled-down military?

Krandel raced through his own career: Distinguished grad from Annapolis volunteers for the marines and makes lieutenant colonel while the rest of his classmates are still captains. And with no field experience. But that's the beauty of getting staff jobs at the Pentagon. Management's the key—and if you can get sponsored by a fast-rising general, then *hold on tight!*

But Krandel couldn't compete with someone like Balcalski. While Krandel was at the Pentagon, sitting on his fanny, Balcalski had led the Fightin' Fourth up Atcapotzalco, right before the massacre that brought the boys home. There was just no comparison.

Balcalski released his straps. Floating upward, he

grabbed the webbing to steady himself. He held Krandel's eye. "Twenty minutes until landing, sir. Is there anything you want me to pass on to the men?"

"No, Sergeant. Just have your squad leaders check for anyone with the willies or who's spacesick. I've done my bit. Anything more I try to do will only make them nervous."

"Very well, sir." He twisted to leave. "Colonel, these are the best men we've got. We'll get you to hell and back."

"Thank you, Sergeant." Krandel hesitated for a moment; he felt he needed to say something appropriate. "When we land I want those men out of here fast. I want them so close behind me I expect to have a rifle jammed up my butt on the way out. Now get with your squad leaders—their men should be primed and ready to go."

"Yes, sir." Balcalski nodded and turned, pushing off for the rear of the craft. As he left, Krandel watched him float down the narrow line of men. Unlike Krandel's walk before the launch, Balcalski joked with the men. Holding on to the webbing, he tightened a helmet strap, slapped an ammo clip to see if it was secure; Balcalski *belonged,* while Krandel felt he was forcing it.

No matter. In sixteen minutes the TAV would swoop down, decelerating from Mach 25 to subsonic speeds, and —he hoped—surprise any air defenses that might be in place.

Krandel studied the hastily scribbled plastic checklist floating up from his belt. Each event was preceded by a time; times were given in plus-and-minus touchdown times.

He glanced at his watch; at touchdown minus fifteen minutes the second preattack canister launched from Vandenburg should pop above the airfield, releasing the biological agents. The "little buggies," as the troops called them, had a genetic defect that, once exposed to air, gave them a half-life of three minutes. By the time the TAV landed, over ninety-five percent of the little buggies should be dead. Good thing, too, as the little buggies had a voracious appetite for rubber. Things like wheels, plugs, gaskets, and seals would all be "eaten," or at least damaged beyond use, by the time they landed.

And according to plan, their own silicon-coated rubber wouldn't be affected.

According to plan.

Contact with Base Ops through AFSATCOM and BIG-EYE was disrupted as the TAV nosed back down into the atmosphere. The parabolic path took the vehicle back into the depths of the atmosphere where, because of the TAV's speed, electrons were stripped from air molecules. The resulting plasma covered the TAV, preventing any radio signals from leaving or entering the craft. It was an eerie feeling for Gould, even though he'd experienced the radio blackout on every other TAV flight he'd flown.

He was all alone now; he was totally in charge of the craft, not dependent on any calls from Base Ops or the White House to tell him what to do. The marines in the back didn't count. He was the aircraft commander, having the same authority on board his craft as any naval commander would have while at sea. It didn't matter that there was a marine lieutenant colonel who outranked him in the back of the TAV; as long as they were in the air, it was his ball game.

He didn't usually think about the responsibility, the authority, because every other flight had been for practice— just a rigidly controlled test. But now it was for real. If he screwed up, he could kill twenty-five people: Twenty-four marines' lives, and his own life, were riding on his judgment.

And what if he was waved off the field, told to scrub the mission at the last moment by that nervous Nellie in the White House? Would he do it? *Could* he scrub the mission if so ordered?

Gould felt uneasy in his seat and tried to shift his weight to make things more bearable. He didn't like the answers he kept coming up with; he didn't care for the responsibility. The macho image he flaunted, the image that Delores had so easily cut through, wouldn't hold up under the pressure.

It was common knowledge that fighter jocks, and now TAV pilots, were tolerated only because their egos had to be stroked. If they weren't incessantly told they were the greatest pilots on earth and that their shit didn't stink, would they really strap themselves into screaming hunks of metal and meet almost impossible odds head-on? Gould started to doubt it—but he also started to see that he couldn't put up with being two-faced about it. There had to be more to it than putting on a facade to boost his ego.

The TAV's computer screen started to flicker, then flash the red-blue-red-blue on-and-off sequence, indicating that contact with BIGEYE was reestablished. With their speed sufficiently slowed they popped out of radio blackout, and communications were up and working. The speed indicator finally made sense—Mach 20—and by the timetable, the landing wasn't more than eleven minutes away.

The screen confirmed that his mother ship was on its way to Reagan International, near Washington, D.C. He only hoped he would be able to meet it back there in the two hours allotted the mission; if the mission continued going the way it was, he shouldn't have any trouble meeting the deadline.

They'd be going in on a steep glide, and there'd be only one chance at it. The cockpit canopy reconfigured to IR mode. In the far distance he could make out a scattering of dwellings, lighting up in the infrared as wavering, ghostly objects. The mission was still a go; the no-return point was coming up fast. The best the White House could do now was to have him ditch in the desert if they decided to scrub the rescue.

Things were going to start happening fast, and he sure as hell didn't need some fat-assed politician breathing down his neck while he worked. He jabbed at the screen, allowing a message from BIGEYE to come through, then shut the communications gear down. He'd pass on to the marines the news he had just received, but as far as he was concerned, nothing short of a crash on landing would prevent him from carrying out the rescue.

He only wished he could talk to Delores and make sure she would do the same thing he planned to do. But then again, he realized, she had probably already made the decision herself.

Balcalski swam back to his seat and strapped in. Krandel leaned over and opened his mouth to speak when the intercom came back on.

"Five minutes to touchdown. Marines, prepare for deceleration. As soon as things slow down up here I've got some news for you from BIGEYE." Krandel barely had time to lock his body back against the webbing before the TAV gave a gut-lurching jolt. He grabbed the checklist; the third canister—the runway clearer—should have popped over the runway. If it survived the landing, the runway clearer—a miniature tanklike robot—would be waiting to shoot the hell out of everything within a thousand meters by now. Railguns, eximer lasers, fuel-air vapor explosives—all kinds of nasty devices designed to clear the landing strip of any living or moving objects for a kilometer around. A high power microwave burst would first destroy all electronics around the airport. The tank was controlled through the command sensor dropped in the first canister and would be activated only if the President had been moved—so if the President was anywhere nearby, the tank would be dormant, and they'd be landing on a live field.

The intercom crackled, abruptly pulling him from his meandering. "Three minutes till landing. The door will swing open as soon as we've slowed to fifty knots. When we've reached ten knots I want you marines to *move*. I'm turning this baby around as soon as you're off. Once refueled, we'll be ready to rotate. Those of you on the left side are to come back to this TAV; those on the right to the other TAV, dividing the President's party between the TAVs."

Krandel looked down the line of men. Sergeant Balcalski yelled over the buffeting. "He means those on the *starboard* side go to the other plane; those on the port side get back here." He shook his head and caught Krandel's eye; grinning, Balcalski gave Krandel a thumbs-up. Krandel returned it; the sergeant was on top of everything. Now if only he could do as well.

The shaking stopped, and the noise seemed to abate. "This is Major Gould again. Sixty seconds to touchdown. Word just relayed from the command post verified that the President has been triangulated to the airfield. They think he'll be moved out not on Air Force One, but by a 747. It's the only plane there, so you won't have any trouble finding it. Canister two, the biodegrader, was not—repeat, *not*—successful"—a groan went up among the men—"but the good news is that we think they don't know we're coming. They've been hit with the sleepy gas, and we haven't detected any activity around the plane. But the runway clearer has not been activated."

Silence, then: "We're coming up on five seconds . . . four . . .

"Three . . .

"Two . . .

"One . . . and *bingo*." The craft greased down on the runway. Krandel silently praised the air force pilot; he had more finesse than the navy pilots who routinely bounced down landings on carriers. The pilot continued. "We're at two hundred knots. Doors will open at fifty knots. Good luck, gentlemen."

The intercom squawked off; Krandel flipped down his IR goggles, ripped at the release locks, reached under the webbing for his rifle, and shuffled to the hatch. He stretched his legs to get out the cramps; twenty-three men stood and made their way behind him, holding the strapping for support. After what seemed to be an endless time a klaxon blared, causing Krandel to jump. Up to now he'd reacted; he hadn't had time to be nervous. Now he felt like throwing up.

A red light popped on above the hatch, and the door rotated open. In the darkness the ground rushed by, and

Krandel froze. Balcalski swatted him on the butt and barked, "Ready, sir!"

Krandel swallowed; no time to tie up now! "Ready." He grabbed the edges of the door. The IR goggles gave a ghostly tint to the runway. Hot air tumbled into the TAV, bringing with it a potpourri of smells: urine, JP-4, and a dry-hotness of the night. He knew the sleepy gas was there —at least the remnants of it—but he couldn't detect it. It was safe for them now, but had it worked?

A muffled voice came over the onrushing air, "Twenty-five knots . . . get ready, the plane will be right in front of you!" Sweat on Krandel's hands evaporated directly from the pores. "Twenty . . . fifteen . . . *go!*"

Krandel leapt from the craft, deciding at the last moment against falling to the ground in a PLF, and instead tried to keep his balance. He raced toward the lone plane, keeping low but swinging out toward the side. He caught a glimpse from the corner of his eye of the remainder of the men scurrying to his left, surrounding the craft. To his right burned the lights of the terminal. Cars were parked near the flight line; a low hum of activity filled the background as trucks creaked in the distance. The rest of the airfield was unaffected by the gas.

The TAV swung silently around to the left, keeping away from the plane. In the darkness his men stood out like burning ghosts; flipping up his IR goggles, Krandel assured himself that the men were undetectable.

No sound. There was no resistance from either outside or inside the plane.

The lone crack of a gun caused him to sprawl to the ground; a solitary figure on the top of the distant terminal was yelling. The voice was barely audible over the roar of the airport. The marines kept their cool, remembering their orders not to fire. Several other shots followed, discernible only by the pinging off the concrete runway; they hadn't been detected until moments before, or the place would have been swamped with bullets. Krandel waved a fist toward the man and pointed at Morales. Corporal Morales lifted his rifle, then shot the man down. No sound came from Morales's sonically shielded rifle.

They waited as Krandel listened for other noises; satisfied they hadn't been detected, Krandel nodded to Balcalski, who waved the men forward. Without a word they continued to the plane.

Guards were sprawled near the base of the stairway. Krandel flattened himself against a wheel. Balcalski huffed up and spoke in a whisper, catching his breath. "I don't think anyone else saw us."

Krandel nodded. Clutching his rifle, Balcalski acknowledged the hand signals from the squad leaders as they positioned their men. Krandel tried to keep the excitement from his voice as he whispered, "Ready?"

"Yes, sir."

"On the count of three, have Morales and his squad follow me up. You stay here with Henderson's squad and keep it clear for us."

"But, *sir,* we can't risk you—"

"That's an order, Sergeant; we're counting on you as a backup if I don't make it. Your *first* priority is to make sure the President gets back alive. Understand?" At Balcalski's nod Krandel jerked his head toward Morales. The corporal scurried over; when he motioned with his hands the rest of the squad followed.

Krandel drew in a breath; this was it. He whispered, half to himself, *"One, two, three."* He was up the ladder, three steps at a time, and through the hatch. Scanning the compartment, he raced down the aisle, not taking care to avoid fallen guards. As he approached the rear the fear he kept in the back of his mind reared its head: "He's not aboard!"

Crap. Disgusted, he banged against a partition on his way back up to the front as Morales's squad only confirmed what he had suspected. Thoughts of botched rescues roared through his mind: Sontay, Tehran, Mexico City. . . . Why couldn't they do anything *right?* After his adrenaline rush, the empty plane left him exhausted. He trotted down the stairs and moved below the plane.

Balcalski asked quietly, "Now what, Colonel?"

Krandel thought for a moment. This is the thing you'll never find in *Lee's Lieutenants,* he told himself. "Our first priority is still to bring the President back. We stay here until they show up with him."

Balcalski looked emotionless with his goggles on in the darkness. "Shouldn't we inform the Command Center?"

Krandel understood what he had said: Listen, dummy, don't blow the ball game by taking things into your own hands. There are too many things at stake; cover your ass first! And of course, as usual, Balcalski was right.

But Krandel hesitated. He was the commander, not Balcalski. Nor was some fat slob at the National Emergency Command Center who didn't have any operational experience.

Like Krandel . . . until now.

If only he had spent less time on staff jobs and more time in the field, where it counted. But he knew what he had to do.

He turned to Balcalski. "The Command Center can wait. Get your men who speak Arabic into those guards' uniforms. When the President arrives the ALH should be unable to tell our men from the guards in the dark. Tell them not to speak unless spoken to, and if they do speak, keep it to an absolute minimum. We can't afford to be discovered until we make our move."

Balcalski remained stony-faced. "The rest of the men, sir?"

"I want them on the plane. No, put only Morales's squad on the plane. Have Henderson's go with the TAVs as support. You go with him. I'm going to the flight deck. And send up someone who can speak Arabic. Now speed out!"

"Yes, sir." Balcalski whirled and was moving the men as Krandel raced back up the ladder. Stepping over a slumped guard, Krandel cracked open the door to the flight deck. It was empty, awaiting the arrival of the flight crew. Through the cockpit Krandel could barely make out the TAVs; the second TAV had landed while they stormed the plane and was now transferring fuel from its fuel bladder to the TAV on which they had arrived. They could wait until just before daybreak without being discovered. With any luck, the President would arrive way before then so they could get the hell out of there.

A creak at the door made him whirl. Corporal Morales motioned for him; when he approached Morales whispered, "We're ready, sir. Gunnery Balcalski wanted me to relay to you that his men are set."

"Good. Morales, tell your squad to hang in there. It won't be long."

Morales nodded; looking back over his shoulder, he motioned a marine forward. "Balcalski assigned Private Havisad to you, sir."

"Good, let him in."

"Yes, sir." Havisad moved onto the flight deck; Morales left as quickly as he had come.

Nodding at Havisad, Krandel motioned him to a position near the flight engineer's station. "Get relaxed, son. This is what they mean by the big wait." Havisad forced a grin and turned to the door; Krandel stared out the cockpit and tried not to think of what lay ahead.

His thoughts drifted to his family, and he was surprised that this was the first time he'd thought of them.

He was lucky he could see them as much as he did. It wasn't like his classmates who were *really* away: remote tours at Adak, Rodman, or pulling duty on board the ships. Or back at Pendleton, fuming, like Weston. With his staff jobs, at least Krandel was close to his family.

He felt a pang of regret; he was near them, but in his incessant climb up the ladder of responsibility he was just as remote from them as his classmates were from their families. He swore he'd make it up to them, if he could just make it through this rescue.

Once the Marines disembarked, Gould pulled the TAV sharply to the left. He was running without power and didn't want to make any more noise than necessary by using his auxiliary engines. The TAV glided to a stop, well away from the 747 on the concrete apron. He'd remain there, virtually hidden from view, until a team of four marines arrived to turn the TAV around on the runway. There was nothing to do now but wait. Wait for the second TAV, which carried the fuel that would enable them to return. He couldn't hear what was going on outside the craft, or see anything, for that matter, except a desolate view of the desert, glowing softly through the IR canopy.

If this was a place to die, at least it seemed peaceful. He did not think about the possibility that the mission might fail. His trust in the marines doing their job and pulling the rescue off was automatic. Much like their trust in him.

The second TAV arrived and startled him with its stealth. He was momentarily angry at himself for not spotting the craft, but he realized that if *he* missed it, so would anyone else at the airport. He unstrapped and hopped out of the craft. Delores met him at her TAV. They spoke in whispers.

"I've never refueled these things before."

Delores put a finger to her lips and ducked inside the TAV. She pulled out a long Teflon-covered hose. "Don't worry. I went through a crash course in this when they were fitting the TAV with the fuel bladder. All we have to do is to make sure both planes are grounded first, to prevent any sparks from igniting the fumes."

"Is this hose long enough to reach my plane?"

"They told me they installed a hundred yards of this stuff, enough to cover any situation. We're plenty close anyway."

"You're telling me. By the way, that's some pretty fancy landing you did."

"Thanks. Now are you ready to start working, or do you want to stand here and gab all night?"

"Ready when you are. Tell you what, you ground the suckers and I'll pull this hose over to my ship."

"Sure."

As she turned Gould called out, "Hey, how was the flight?" He couldn't see her grin in the darkness, but he knew it was there.

"Nice of you to ask, hotshot. It was lonely. I'll tell you about it later."

"It's a date." Gould turned his back and tugged at the

line; then, with some effort, he strained against the tension and started for his TAV, not sixty feet away.

"Help him to his feet." General Kamil stood and brushed flecks of dirt off his uniform. President Montoya tried standing without help, then fell to the floor, moaning. The two men who had tortured the President grabbed him, one under each armpit, and dragged Montoya to Kamil. Kamil studied the broken man in front of him.

Montoya's head sagged; Kamil lifted it with one hand. His cheek was badly bruised, but other than that he appeared unharmed. Montoya's eyes looked vacant; Kamil twisted an ear, and Montoya's eyes swam into focus.

"The apology . . ." gasped Montoya.

"Not now, Mr. President. Not now. You will have a few hours to rest before you make your debut, so save your strength. I will get some makeup for your face so that you will look presentable. But now you must walk."

"I can't." It came as a sob.

"You will." Kamil snapped a command, and the two men propped Montoya up against a wall. Montoya leaned heavily against the support; tiny flakes of chipped paint from the wall rubbed into his shirt. Montoya wavered, then managed to keep his feet.

"Now take a step, Mr. President."

With effort, Montoya swung one foot, then another. He grimaced, but he managed to stagger without help. Once Montoya had taken a few steps, Kamil stepped to his side and grabbed an elbow. Montoya drew his arm back, the elbow still sore from supporting his weight while hanging from the rope. Kamil swung Montoya forward.

"See, you can walk. I'll help you now, Mr. President." He snapped another command, and the two men bowed slightly before turning away. As they started to leave, Kamil fumbled with his tunic and withdrew a small-caliber gun. Holding on to Montoya, Kamil called the two. As they turned he leveled his weapon and squeezed the trigger.

He had to shoot the second man through the skull a second time before he stopped quivering.

Once finished, he turned to Montoya. "The plane is ready, Mr. President—we have to hurry. You must not keep the ALH delegates waiting."

Kamil dragged Montoya, prodding him forward. They passed through a musty corridor filled with smells of urine and dust. Sickly sweet odors wafted through the air as they passed a kitchen, and finally, near the exit, the passageway widened. A voice greeted Kamil.

"Hurry, the bus is waiting. We have the staff car for Montoya."

Kamil propped Montoya against his hip to keep the President from falling. "Have you told your ALH lieutenants about the President?"

Ghazzali sounded puzzled. "No . . . we were going to wait until we reached the plane. We agreed to display him in the air—to further incite them for the cause."

"So no one knows he is here."

"Of course not—no one else except for Hujr and Du'Ali."

Kamil raised his voice slightly. "And you have not yet disposed of those two?"

"They are my best agents—I foresee much happening with those two and the ALH," Ghazzali said apologetically.

Kamil glanced at Montoya; the President rolled listlessly against his shoulder, barely supporting himself. Kamil lowered his voice, and although the President could not understand his Do'brainese, he hissed at Ghazzali. "Orders are meant to be followed, and coming from President Ash'ath, they are certainly not to be taken as suggestions. If Hujr was to gloat about the part he had in the kidnapping, the revelation of the connection with Do'brai would be imminent."

"They will not gloat—Hujr and Du'Ali have given their word."

"Their word is as good as pig shit to me." Kamil pulled out his gun. "One mistake is too many; you yourself said the whole is greater than the parts."

Ghazzali's eyes widened. He took a stutter step backward. "You . . . you *cannot*. It was I who came up with the plan. If it were not for me, you wouldn't have the backing of the ALH—"

His words ended with a shot in the middle of his forehead. The small-caliber bullet didn't cause him to tumble backward; rather, he collapsed to the ground in a clump.

"Now there is no way to implicate Do'brai in your scheme, little man." As Kamil turned to leave, Montoya's eyes glazed over. Montoya trudged along as though he'd lost all hope.

Morales rapped lightly on the door, keeping far enough back that Krandel wouldn't accidentally harm him as he entered. "Sir, they're approaching."

Krandel tightened his grip on his rifle. "Is everyone ready?"

"Yes, sir—everyone's been briefed."

"Good. Do your job, soldier." Morales cracked a half grin and disappeared, leaving the door slightly ajar. Krandel started to curse himself for not spotting the approaching envoy, but stopped, realizing that it was part of being a commander. He couldn't do everything; and if he couldn't delegate responsibility to the men he'd trained, it was *his* fault, not theirs. He looked at Havisad; the private returned his nod.

Minutes passed. He strained to hear the motorcade. Underneath his feet he felt the bumping of fuel trucks as they topped off the aircraft's tanks; the smell of JP-4 drifted onto the flight deck. Everything was going as planned. The marines masquerading as guards were taking their jobs literally; acting stern and aloof, the guards didn't draw any attention to themselves. The guise fit the marines perfectly.

A pair of voices argued outside the flight deck. Krandel flattened against the bulkhead and peered through the crack by the door. Four flight attendants pushed past the masquerading guards and filtered to the back, straightening magazines and picking up trash on their way. As they disappeared in the back Krandel barely discerned a muffled thud as the attendants were struck; Morales's squad covered their tracks well.

Soon after, the voices of three men came from just outside the flight deck. Krandel slipped back from the door. They entered, laughing, absorbed in a joke. One, giggling as he hefted a bulky brown flight bag, stopped, startled, as Krandel stepped forward. Havisad stuck his rifle in their faces. Putting a finger to his lips, Krandel motioned for the men to move toward the front. One of them—a chubby, serious-looking older man wearing four wide gold stripes on his sleeve—nodded and jerked his head for the others to follow.

Krandel nudged them and whispered to Havisad, "Tell them if they speak, they'll die. There's no choice in the matter. I'll shoot the captain first."

Havisad quietly spat the demand in a guttural language. The captain nodded. Eliciting nods from the other two, Havisad turned to Krandel. Krandel cradled his rifle in his arm. "Have them take their positions and answer all radio calls. If they answer in an unusual way, they'll die. We have the flight attendants; they will be killed soon after. Ask him if he understands."

Havisad nodded after translating. "He says yes, Colonel."

Krandel leaned against the bulkhead, far enough away from the cockpit so as not to be seen from the outside. "Good. We wait, then. Tell the captain to get on with his work."

The crew reacted slowly, sullenly going about their preflight checks. The captain looked at Krandel before giving the go-ahead to go to auxiliary power; Krandel nodded and allowed the man to continue. As the flight deck lights came on, Krandel and Havisad stepped away from the cockpit. At the first radio contact Havisad pressed his rifle's muzzle against the back of the captain's head. Havisad translated. "They're bringing the President's convoy; the captain responded that they will be able to take off as soon as he is aboard."

The wait seemed to go on forever. With each minute the

chance increased that someone would be discovered; the thought gnawed at Krandel's stomach.

The captain turned on the plane's exterior lights. Coupled with the plane's strobe flicking on and off, they bathed the area in an eerie, pulsating glow. A convoy approached out of the darkness into the light: Three trucks, a bus, and a staff car, flags waving from the hood, moved to the front of the plane. Krandel leaned forward and whispered, "Tell him to wave."

"They can't see inside, can they?"

"It won't hurt—and we're too close now to blow it." The captain waved a hand jerkily back and forth until Krandel growled, "That's enough." A moment later the staff car pulled around to the side. "If we could only see . . ."

Noises came from outside the flight deck; several people milled outside in the cabin. A knock came at the door. Krandel whispered, "Answer it." Holding the rifle to the captain's head, Havisad breathed the translation. The captain's reply seemed to satisfy the voice outside the flight deck.

The noises grew louder outside the cabin; they were bringing him in! Krandel felt jumpy, and yet optimistic that they might pull it off. He moved toward the door.

The copilot started yelling shrilly, suddenly breaking the silence. Krandel was out the door even as Havisad put bullets first through the pilot, then the copilot.

Krandel didn't hear the flight engineer die.

As he sprang from the cockpit shooting erupted down the aisle. Krandel dove at the President, bringing him down in a tumble. Bullets flew overhead; Krandel felt a tearing pain rip through his right leg. It felt as if someone had laced a hot needle into him and wiggled it around. Another needle went through his side.

As soon as it started, the shooting stopped inside. He began to cry out but realized in horror that the President had been hit. The President lay motionless; blood oozed from a cut on his cheek. Rolling off, Krandel gritted his teeth to stop the pain and searched for bullet wounds by running his hands over the President. Only one was detectable, near his thigh.

Krandel looked wildly around; Morales's squad thundered down the aisles. Morales bent down and asked, "Is he all right?"

"I don't know." Ignoring his own pain, Krandel crawled over and slapped the President's face. After a moment, his eyes widened. "It's okay, sir. Are you all right?"

The President took a moment to orient himself; he tried to move and grimaced. "My . . . feet . . ."

"You were hit in the thigh, sir."

The President panted. "It's . . . my . . . feet, damn it." Every word took an effort.

"It's all right, sir—we'll move you out of here as soon as we can."

President Montoya's eyes narrowed through the pain; he managed to get out, "Who . . . are . . . you?"

Krandel was astonished that the President would even ask. "Lieutenant Colonel Krandel, United States Marine Corps, sir. We've come to rescue you." Krandel flushed, feeling overly dramatic. The President closed his eyes, relieved. Krandel asked, "How do you feel?"

The President tried to speak but could only shake his head. Krandel motioned to Morales.

"He's complaining about his feet. Give them a look, then get to his thigh."

"Do you know what's wrong, sir?"

"How the hell should I know? His thigh is bleeding, but he's complaining about his damn feet. Now get to it."

The corporal broke open a medical kit and unlaced the President's shoes. "Holy shit." He grabbed Krandel's elbow. "Sir . . ."

Krandel stared at the bloody remains of the President's feet. His toes were caked with still-oozing blood. Krandel turned his head away. "Give him a shot of whatever narcotic you've got and wrap those feet up. We've got to get him out of here."

"Yes, sir." Morales started wrapping the President's feet, then moved to his thigh to work on the bullet wound. After

administering a shot he moved to Krandel. Sporadic gunfire continued outside.

A high-pitched whining grew louder outside the plane;
one of the marines backed in from the top of the stairs and
announced, "The TAVs are in position, sir."

Krandel pulled his pant leg down when Morales finished
wrapping a hasty bandage. Morales broke out a hypoder-
mic and cocked an eye at Krandel; Krandel hesitated, then
said, "You're right, I might need it for later." Morales gave
him a shot of morphine. Grimacing, Krandel asked, "How
does it look outside?"

"The runway is almost clear; Henderson's squad has the
area around us under control. We found the rest of the
President's party in a bus headed for Air Force One. Everyone's all right, but we're missing two stewards who were
listed on Air Force One's manifest. The pilot said they
were the ones who pulled off the hijacking. They killed the
flight engineer while still in flight."

"Bastards." Krandel looked up at the guard still covering
the front stairs. "Is it clear?"

"We're ready to head for the TAVs as soon as you say,
sir."

Krandel surveyed the aisle. The remainder of Morales's
squad had assembled by the two exits, ready to disembark.
"What about ALH reinforcements? What's the situation
around the terminal? Can the NECC give us any info?"

The radioman spoke up. "BIGEYE reports their motion
sensors are all still operational. There's no movement
within several klicks of the airport. They say we're safe for
a quick departure."

Krandel muttered, half to himself, "Yeah, and these are
the people who said the President was already on board this
plane." The President shivered and raised on an elbow; he
studied the serious-looking marines. Their gaunt, lean
faces glistened in the cabin's light, reflecting their inten-
sity. Krandel motioned with his head. "Morales, I'll help
the President; half your squad will lead and get the President's party from the bus. Have the rest cover the rear."

"Can I help you, sir?"

Krandel waved him off. "I need you to direct your squad; I'll take care of the President."

Morales nodded, then began barking orders. Havisad took the point and silently led the way.

Emerging from the smoke-filled stuffiness of the plane, Krandel draped the President's arm over his shoulder and made his way down the steps. His leg and side ached, but the pain grew more numb from the morphine with each step; he felt a warm glow work through his body. The President stumbled once, but Krandel caught him and gave the chief executive a wordless grin. They moved away from the taxi ramp toward the two sleek TAVs, which were quietly running their engines at the end of the concrete apron. The President moved with effort, masking any pain he might have felt.

Krandel concentrated on each step. The euphoria of the rescue was coming to a close, and the wound and the physical strain of carrying another person began to wear on him. But through the pain, one thing gnawed at him: the President hadn't complained once since they had started, as incredible as it seemed. It went against his stereotyped pushover personality.

"That's it." Gould started back to Delores's TAV, Ojo-2, with the Teflon-covered hose. A spring-loaded pulley hauled the hose into the TAV as Gould approached.

A marine poked his head from around the side of the TAV. "If you're finished, sir, we'll position the TAVs so they'll point up the runway."

Delores jumped, momentarily startled. "Wait until we're back on board, then we'll have you turn them one at a time. I want one of you to stand between the planes just to make sure that the wings don't touch. We don't want another debacle like the Iran mission.

"Yes, *ma'am*," said the marine, obviously shocked at hearing Delores's voice. "We'll wait for your signal." He sprinted off to get help.

Delores started for the hatch to boost herself up when Gould reached for her arm. "We'll see you at Reagan?"

"And two to one I'll beat you there, hotshot." She hesitated, then suddenly leaned over and kissed him. She caught Gould by surprise, but he managed to draw the kiss out; her mouth tasted faintly like warm bread. He didn't want the moment to end. . . .

She drew away, out of breath, and whispered, "I'll take you up on that dinner offer—the one where the dinner comes on a boat. . . ."

"It's a date. Just be careful on your flight back." He pushed her gently back toward the hatch. She shot him a smile and disappeared inside.

Gould stood still for a moment and was startled as four marines rounded the side. He pointed to Delores's TAV. "Position this TAV first and wait for me to signal before you turn the other one."

"Yes, sir."

Gould broke out running for his plane. *Damn,* this was exciting! He couldn't remember when he'd felt so good.

Krandel positioned the President once more and finally thought they were going to make it to the TAVs. The TAVs were within fifty meters when the shooting started up again.

That's when Krandel saw the truck. A two-and-a-half-ton carryall roared down the runway, its lights out, heading for the TAVs. Henderson's squad encircled the TAVs, crouching and firing point-blank into the oncoming truck. The men didn't move from their ground.

The truck's windshield shattered, broken by expertly placed bullets, but the truck lumbered on. Bullets glanced harmlessly off the tires: The truck bore down, weaved, and slammed into the starboard TAV, igniting the craft in an eruption of flames. Thick black smoke rolled out from the inferno; a few men staggered away, holding hands over their eyes.

The President froze, halting their progress. Krandel jerked him forward and yelled over the roar. "We've got to get you out of here—the other ship can take us." He sped the pace; Morales took off for the burning TAV to help. As they circumvented the smoking craft the heat from the debacle almost overwhelmed them. Krandel kept his face away from the fire and pulled the President along, finally reaching the surviving TAV and shoving the President aboard. The rest of the President's entourage were herded on.

Krandel limped up to a marine just coming from the other TAV. "How many were on it when it blew?"

The marine dully shook his head; his face was covered with oily smudges. A gaggle of men appeared behind him and started for the surviving TAV; a good twenty marines congregated outside. Spotting Morales, Krandel managed to collar the corporal. "How many were on the TAV?"

Morales coughed and spat to the side. "Just the pilot. The rest of the men were either on the protection line or were covering the rear."

Krandel's stomach churned; the acidity in his gut tore at his insides. "Get the pilot of the surviving TAV out here."

"Yes, sir."

A moment later a nomex-suited officer jumped from the craft; the pilot looked dazed. Krandel moved up to him. "How many men can your TAV hold?" The pilot shook his head; Krandel raised his voice. "Major Gould, did you hear me? How many men can your—"

"I hear you, now just *leave me alone!*"

"Major!" Krandel whipped his hand across Gould's face twice in quick succession. "Listen to me, damn it. I know that was your buddy in that other plane, but you've got to put it behind you. You're the only way we can get back— I'd shoot you right here and now if I didn't have to depend on you. So pull yourself together. You're acting like a little girl out here."

Gould sobbed. "Oh, *please* . . ."

Krandel drew back to hit him again, but Gould cringed. "No, wait." Gould sniffed, then sobbed out, "Just let me—"

"Shut up, Major. Listen, we've got twenty-three marines and twenty-one other people in the President's party. What's the max amount of people this craft can carry?"

It took a moment, but Gould answered, "Let me think." What was it that friggin' aeroengineer had told him? Why couldn't he pay attention to the details? "If we throw out the seats and ditch some of the extra equipment—"

Krandel interrupted angrily. "We leave in three minutes, Major—we don't have time! How many can we stuff on board and still get out of here?"

The pilot wet his lips, drying his eyes on the back of his sleeve. "I'd say thirty-two, maybe as many as thirty-five people, if they're skinny, Colonel. It will take an hour to get rid of enough weight to get all your men in. And even by packing the TAV with thirty-two, none of your men can carry anything back with them: no guns, helmets—nothing."

Krandel decided instantly. "Then some of us stay. We've got to get this baby in the air before any more reinforcements arrive. Major, prepare to leave in two minutes. *Move!*" He shoved Gould toward the hatch and looked wildly around; taking a quick head count, he said, "We're two short. Get Gunnery Balcalski and have him get eleven marines to go on this TAV; married men—the youngest and skinniest we've got—go first."

Morales spoke quietly. "Balcalski and Henderson bought it with the explosion, sir—and we're going to have trouble getting the marines to go back on this TAV unless everyone goes. They won't bug out on their buddies."

Krandel's knees wobbled: Balcalski *dead?* He wavered, then thought: A competent commander doesn't spook his troops! He had to put on a good show. Drawing in a breath, he managed to get out, "Correction: You screen them, Morales. We've got to get as many out of here as possible, or the third TAV won't be able to carry all of us back."

Morales's brows jumped. "Do you really think the President would risk another TAV to rescue us, sir?"

Krandel shot a glance at the TAV; hell, no, he thought. Not if he acts the way he said he would when he was elected. "Yes, he will, Morales. Now get to it. Have those staying assemble on the other side of the runway."

Morales turned away and barked the order. Krandel gingerly pulled himself into the TAV. The morphine didn't mask his pain, nor the grief he felt for Balcalski. Moving down the cramped aisle, he came to the President and placed a hand on his shoulder. "It will only be a little longer, sir. You'll be taking off in a few moments."

The President studied Krandel, then forced a nod. He turned back to his side and closed his eyes, seemingly oblivious to what was going on. Krandel felt a surge of emotion well up inside him but quickly clamped it down.

Angrily, Krandel limped to the hatch. The last of the eleven marines who were going back entered the TAV; they tossed their rifles to those on the runway and sullenly found a seat in the crowded TAV. Some had to position themselves on the floor to find room.

Krandel stood at the hatch; this was it. He spoke up over the growing roar of the engines and said, "Men . . ." He choked, then turned to the President. Montoya had his eyes closed. Hesitating, Krandel turned and let himself slowly down to the runway.

The hatch swung shut: Through the cockpit window Major Gould gave him a thumbs-up sign. Krandel returned it, then slowly saluted. Krandel shuffled to the edge of the runway, the pain in his side and leg growing steadily.

⫼ 9 ⫼

0410 ZULU:
Saturday, 8 September

Never give up and never give in.

Hubert H. Humphrey

When a thing is done, it's done. Don't look back. Look forward to your next objective.

George C. Marshall

Facing it—always facing it—that's the way to get through! Face it!

Joseph Conrad

Do'brai

Hujr wallowed in the revelry surrounding the kidnapping. He lay on his back, smoking a hashish-laden hookah, as the woman massaged him. She moved sensuously up his body, gently rubbing scented oil into his skin, kneading his muscles with her fingers. As her hands moved in firm, slow circles Hujr felt he had finally achieved the coup of his career; the mellow lightheadedness the hashish brought on added to the pleasure.

After presenting Kamil with the American President,

Hujr was treated royally. Escorted in Kamil's private staff car, Hujr was whisked away and kept apart—which Hujr interpreted as being kept "aloof"—from the rest of his ALH comrades-in-arms. Even Ghazzali, as his mentor and the undisputed ruler of the ALH, was not permitted access to him. Food, drink, and the exciting pleasures of this drugged nymph kept Hujr entertained. Kamil had explained that an unprecedented promotion was in store for him; the glory and honor due him for pulling off the kidnapping would have no equal. Kamil had even hinted that President-for-Life Ash'ath might have a royal appointment for him. The President's personal man-at-arms, perhaps? If this was so, then Hujr would be on call for any nefarious task that Ash'ath deemed necessary.

Hujr knew that he had done well, and for him to single-handedly kidnap the leader of the most powerful nation on earth—he realized the kudos were well earned. After all this time of being an underground hero, living with harassment and even fear for his life, it was finally time to step up and collect his reward.

And it was to be in *this* life, not as a martyr, that he would enjoy the bounty. Hujr was a practical man. The prospect of martyrdom did have its appeal, but because of his unorthodox upbringing it didn't have the deep-rooted allure it would for a native Do'brainese. Hujr's bitterness toward the West certainly fueled his hatred, but it did not drive him to accept blindly the doctrines of the Jihad. If there was a way to enjoy the privileges of this world without making the ultimate sacrifice, then so much the better.

Hujr took a long pull on the water pipe and allowed the smoke to fill his lungs. The euphoria again rolled over him, and, expelling the drug, he reached down and pulled the giggling woman on top of him.

General Kamil strode down the corridor and paused before the guarded room. A man followed him, dragging a limp, dead body, and stopped behind Kamil. A single Do'brainese militiaman, smartly decked out in a sand-brown uniform with red tabs, snapped rigidly to attention. Two more militiamen were at either end of the passageway. Their weapons were drawn and pointed at the door where Kamil stood. Their orders were to shoot if any attempt was made to escape. Hujr could not slip away from the chamber unharmed.

I shouldn't be here, thought Kamil. If that dung-eating Ghazzali had taken his orders seriously, then this puppet Hujr would be as dead as his stupid assistant, Du'Ali.

Ghazzali had wanted Hujr to live, but Kamil knew the Do'brainese half-breed was too undisciplined—too cocky—to trust. The fool bounced from place to place, always enticed by the highest bidder for his allegiance. There was the chance that he might sell out, even to the unspeakable American devils, if the price was high enough.

After hustling the American President into his personal staff car, Kamil had collared an enlisted driver to transport Montoya to the airport. The man knew better than to try to identify the general's clandestine passenger—for all the driver knew, it was another one of Kamil's lovers being whisked out of the country, or a government accomplice being paid off for some unspeakable deed.

Leaving strict orders that he be notified as soon as the plane carrying the ALH delegates and the President departed, Kamil raced back to the compound where Hujr was being held. Once the plane was clear of Do'brai airspace, Hujr and his assistant would be hailed on board the plane as martyred heroes; simultaneously, back at Do'brai, Kamil would announce to the West that he had captured and killed the ALH terrorist who had kidnapped the President. With Hujr dead there would be no one to dispute the fact that Do'brai was still loyal to her western allies.

To get rid of the rest of the evidence, Kamil himself would ignite the fire that would destroy Air Force One and the passengers on board. Only he and President Ash'ath would carry the true knowledge of what had really happened.

Kamil nodded to the militiaman behind him; the dead

man's body lay at his feet. "Leave the corpse here. After Hujr dies, we'll take both bodies to the airport." As far as Kamil's troops were concerned, Hujr would simply be executed as the terrorist who had captured Air Force One. Not even his own men were privy to the truth; the kidnapping was far too important for any leaks to occur.

Kamil grunted at the militiaman still standing at attention by the door; the guard saluted and backed up. As Kamil reached for the doorknob a shout from the rear of the corridor stopped him.

"General!"

"What is it?" Kamil growled, turning.

The messenger ran up breathlessly and, without rendering a salute, gasped, "The airport, General. The airport is under attack."

"Attack? By whom?"

"I do not know, General." The messenger bent over, trying to catch his breath. "We have lost contact with the pilot and crew of the plane that was supposed to fly out. There are garbled reports of gunfire all around the airport. That is all I know."

"'Ifrit! Get back and call a general alert. Every man available is to converge on the airport. I will headquarter at the control tower." He gave the messenger a shove; the man stumbled down the hall and disappeared around the corner. Kamil pointed at the armed militiamen at either end of the corridor. "All of you, come with me." He kicked open the door and took aim with his gun. A nude woman was lying on top of Hujr. She screamed as the door crashed open; Hujr swung her around toward Kamil. General Kamil's gun cracked three times in succession; Hujr and the woman lay still, blood gushing from wounds in each of their bodies.

Kamil tried to pull off another two rounds, but his pistol clicked empty. The woman twitched slightly. Cursing, Kamil started to reload his weapon, but when Hujr didn't move, he turned from the room. "You." Kamil motioned with his eyes at the militiaman who had guarded the door. "Make sure they are dead, then join us at the airport."

"Yes, General."

Running down the hall, Kamil withdrew a cartridge from his belt and reloaded his pistol. As he turned the corner with the remainder of the militiamen, the one guarding the door entered the room, keeping his rifle pointed at the bodies.

The woman lay limp to one side; blood oozed from a small wound in her back. The man was still.

The woman groaned and moved an elbow. Her breast came into view, and the guard stopped. He caught his breath as he followed her curvaceous figure with his eyes. He moved back to the door and listened in the hallway; he didn't hear a sound. Kamil and the troops had left, leaving no one around.

Satisfied that he wouldn't be disturbed, he quietly locked the door behind him. His breath quickened; he kept an eye on the woman and quickly started removing his clothes.

The engines started like a charm. Gould performed automatically, like a machine. The TAV ran through its computerized checklist, the screen finally flashing green when all systems indicated a go.

He punched on the JATOs, giving no warning to the passengers in back. He didn't care who was back there; all he wanted to do was to get back home. And start over.

Delores . . . God, the first time he had found someone he really cared for . . .

But he couldn't think of her now. He had to concentrate on what he was doing. With the TAV filled to the max, he couldn't afford to make any mistakes.

He tried to push her from his mind. He tried to convince himself that there would be a time and place to grieve, a time and place to think about it. Why the hell did it have to happen like this? It just wasn't fair.

The runway looked clear. Through the IR canopy, the

nine thousand feet of asphalt looked like a long, shimmering ribbon. To his right the horizon was bathed in a dull glow, which grew brighter with every passing second. The sun was rising. He decided to keep the canopy on IR until he took off, just in case those Do'brainese crazies decided to throw another truck his way. Another suicide attempt and he'd be dead, along with the President and those fearless young marines who had rescued the chief executive.

To his left, Delores's TAV burned as a yellow-white glow. A funeral pyre, belching an orgy of streaming flames, demarcated Delores's grave. Even the smoke showed up on the infrared-sensitive canopy as a rising cloud of brilliant, turbulent heat.

He could almost hear Delores now: "Okay, hotshot—so you're not a fighter pilot after all, but just a rotorpuke who should be out flying helicopters. You don't even have the gonads to get the hell out of here."

No, she'd never say that—she was too good to put herself above *anybody,* himself included.

What would she do? She'd get the hell out of Dodge, that's what she'd do. She sure as hell wouldn't be feeling sorry for him if he had died instead of she; at least she wouldn't be letting it get in the way of what she had to do.

Oh, what the hell. Before running up the JATO units Gould grabbed the intercom and made the announcement for the passengers to strap in. That's the least she would have done.

The marines gathered the weapons of the eleven who were on board the TAV. They moved to a shallow depression to the south as the TAV's engine noise began to grow. With a sudden explosion, blue fire burst from the JATOs as the units ignited, and the craft rolled down the runway. The roar washed over the marines; they covered their ears to block out the white noise.

The TAV lifted and clawed into the sky. The craft seemed to crawl forward, moving upward with a sagging gait. It barely advanced but grew perceptibly smaller in the distance. As it flew from sight it made a sudden nosedive, picked up speed, then shot up into the sky as the scramjets kicked in. Within seconds the pop of the scramjets' ignition reached them.

The sky was just starting to show a tinge of red along the horizon. In the desert silence the burning TAV smoldered at the runway's middle, belching white smoke along with the black. The dry air smelled sweet, strange . . . Krandel hadn't noticed it before, but the place was almost serene. If he had been here any other time, it would have been pleasant.

Half a mile away sat the 747. It was quiet, too, and it was hard to fathom that only a short time before all the shooting and chaos was centered about that jumbo jet.

They prepared their spot in the depression and sat with their backs to one another, watching through the dawn, keeping an eye out for the troops they knew would come.

Through his growing pain from the wound, Krandel finally felt a part of the unit. The unspoken camaraderie bound them together. They sat, alert, ready to finish their job, and still they kept the hope that their brothers would be back and would not forget them.

Camp Pendleton

The waves rolled to the shore, crashing onto the beach not twenty feet from where the children played. Maureen Krandel put down her book and squinted into the setting sun. She held up a hand to shield her eyes. Justin and Julie squealed with pleasure as they ran to and fro on the sand, playing tag with the water as it came, then receded into the ocean. A red bucket and a bright yellow shovel dropped by Justin lay near the water, where the waves grew perilously near.

The two and a half hours in the sun started to show on the children: They both wore white T-shirts, and they had plenty of suntan lotion on their faces, but the beet-redness from a sunburn still showed on their skin. They got their fairness from their mother, and no matter how much protection Maureen tried to bestow upon them, they could never hide completely from the sun.

It was the same way with her husband—not with the sun, but with his devotion to his job. No matter how much she tried to protect him, his job doggedly sought him out, enveloping him and always taking him away. After he had left their home she had spent an hour on the phone with the other wives. No one knew what was going on, and no one wanted to talk about it.

In desperation, she tried to contact General Vandervoos, but his phones were tied up. Camp Pendleton was closed tight, and no information, no matter how mundane, was leaking out. The news media were as much in the dark as she—no news of any sort surfaced on the TV. She couldn't imagine what it was, but she was certain that it wasn't "just an exercise," as her husband had tried to convince her it was.

He was gone; for how long she didn't know. As to where and why, they were only incidental to the one question she feared most: Would she ever see him again? She realized that, with his job, he might be called away at any time. And although she didn't fully understand the true nature of what he was doing out there, the possibility existed that he would be away for a long time.

What's a long time? At least in war, one could be conditioned against seeing her husband for months on end. But in peacetime? A *day* could be a long time—if she wasn't ready for it.

The marine camp was mum on when he'd be back; she just prayed that he *would* come back.

Her meanderings were interrupted by Justin's shrill screams. The plastic shovel he had used while playing in the sand had floated out into the ocean. Julie was holding him back, preventing him from going after it; turning her head, the girl yelled for Maureen to help her.

The yellow shovel bobbed up and down as it slowly moved away, spinning as the turbulent waves rocked it. Maureen stood and called the children back to her. As they approached she gathered them into her arms and started crying.

Ojo-1

The President groaned when shaken awake. "Sir, we're over the worst of it. Our ETA into Reagan International is in twenty minutes."

The President shook his head. The whole trip—the capture, the rescue, those god-awful g's when the ramjet had lit, and now this weightlessness—seemed a nightmare . . . except for those marines. . . .

"We have contact with the National Emergency Command Center, if you want to speak with them."

"Yes . . . put them on." The marine swam to the cockpit and came back, unrolling a line of wire and a pair of headphones as he held the webbing. Montoya studied the marine as he came forward. One side of the man's face was blackened by soot and oil; underneath the grime, tiny blisters could be seen. They were raw and red, almost ready to pop.

Montoya asked the marine, "What happened to you, soldier?"

The man held out the headphones to Montoya. "Nothing much, sir."

"Soldier, you look hurt."

The marine seemed embarrassed. "Just some burns, sir. I was trying to help some of my buddies get away from the fire."

"Looks like you might have received some third-degree burns. I want you to get help as soon as we land. And if there is anything I can do for you, I'll do the best I can."

"Yes, sir. Uh, sir?"

"Eh?"

"Begging the President's pardon, sir—but there is one thing you can do."

"Well? What is it, soldier?"

"You could call us marines, sir. We're not dogfaces—soldiers, that is, sir. We're United States Marines." The marine reddened. "Sorry, Mr. President. I know it doesn't seem like much, but we're mighty proud of the corps."

"My mistake, marine." Crap—Montoya felt lousy. Here these young men risk their lives for him—a few even get killed—and he doesn't have the decency to call them by their right title.

"'S all right, sir. Here's the line to the NECC."

"Thank you." The President fumbled with the set and secured it to his head, wincing as he inadvertently hit his foot while moving.

Vice President Woodstone was on, apologizing. "The rescue was our *only* option . . . and we thought it wouldn't hurt you in the polls. After all, none of your party was harmed, and I don't think we upset either the ALH or the Do'brai government too much—"

The President cut in. "Do you know we had to leave eleven marines behind? And one air force pilot, as well as two marines, died."

The Vice President sounded puzzled. "Of course, but we've been in constant contact with the Do'brainese embassy, and they've assured us that once they've found them, the marines will be unharmed. And more important, they've promised not to reveal the rescue operation to the press if we keep this, uh, contretemps quiet. You see, the Do'brainese swear they had nothing to do with it. It was all an ALH plot to try to discredit them and the United States. I *tried* to hold off as long as possible, but you know how insistent Baca and that military chief of staff can get. Anyway, the Do'brai government wants us to have our marines give up. They *promise* to return them—"

The President coughed. Holding his side, he spoke dryly. "Just like they promised to treat me well, no doubt. I may be a pacifist, Percy, but I'm no fool. Have the air force launch the remaining five TAVs. Get our marines out of there."

The silence was deafening. The Vice President came back slowly. "I must have misunderstood what you said. We have a bad connection—"

"You heard me. *Get our boys home!* I want the air force to close up Do'brai tight as a drum. I don't care if we have to keep our planes in the air for twenty-four hours straight —our marines are coming home. *Nothing* is to leave Do'brai—by air or ground—unless we're in control of it. Do you understand?"

After a moment the headphone came back to life. Woodstone answered with an edge to his voice. "Yes, *sir*, Mr. President . . . I understand."

Montoya sounded weary. "Very well, keep me informed." The President relaxed, tearing off the headphones. His feet hurt like hell, and his thigh ached, but thank God, he was still alive. He studied the men around him. Across the aisle a young marine slept with his mouth open, confident that the TAV pilot would bring him safely home. Montoya swore to himself that he would do everything in his power to see that those they had left behind would make it as well.

Do'brai

Hujr tightened his body when he heard the yelling outside the door; he couldn't hear what was going on, but he could hear Kamil's voice. The young nymph moved demurely over Hujr's body, urging him to continue in the lovemaking, but Hujr remained tense, unsure of the turn of events.

The small sanctuary Kamil had offered him was a piece of heaven on earth, and he was grateful for it—but he had also been promised at least a day's rest before he would be disturbed. Kamil had told him the American President wouldn't be moved until the following day, and with the assurance that he would be left alone, Hujr felt safe in the general's hands.

But now the rumblings outside the door put Hujr on edge. The girl started to protest, but Hujr quieted her with a finger to her lips.

The door blew open, and Hujr reacted instantly, rolling to his side and pulling the girl with him. He didn't feel the first bullet; it ripped into the girl, and she screamed, her legs jerking spasmodically, almost throwing her away from him. The next two bullets found Hujr, one grazing his forehead and the other digging into his shoulder.

The shooting stopped. Hujr allowed his body to twist and fall from the elevated mat, feigning death. It was difficult to lie still with the pain, but he forced himself to be dormant. If he could keep immobile, he could swing out and jump the assassin when the person moved closer to finish him off. . . .

The expected shot never came. An empty chamber clicked off. Kamil's voice cursed at someone in the hall; then all Hujr could hear was the pounding of feet as troops raced past his door. The room was still for several heartbeats. The woman moaned lightly, her arms twitching against the mat.

Hujr was about to move when the door creaked shut. There was movement in the room. Someone had walked in and was inspecting the chamber. Hujr held as still as he could, trying not to breathe lest the person detect that he was alive. A moment passed. Hujr was prodded with a foot; a grunt from the stranger informed Hujr that the man took him for dead. Hujr heard a rustling of clothes, then the sound of something hitting the floor. A buckle clanked against metal as it was unfastened, and the girl was rolled off Hujr.

Hujr waited for several minutes until the slow, rhythmic sound quickened, then he swung out with his feet and chopped the man on the side of the head. Before the man could cry out, Hujr was on his back, digging his hands into the man's throat.

The guard sputtered, then choked as Hujr finished the job. Hujr pushed the guard away in disgust; his shoulder throbbed from the bullet wound. The girl was still unconscious, bleeding from her own injury. Hujr dressed quickly, and before he left he paused to put a bullet through the man's head. At least he would be sure the man would never catch up with him, a lesson that the guard should have learned.

He listened at the door and, satisfied that no one was on the other side, cracked it open to survey the hall. The place was deserted except for a body slumped in the middle of the corridor. From Hujr's position, the body looked faintly familiar. Hujr crept out and turned the body over. His pulse yammered at him: It was Du'Ali! Seemingly unrelated events began to click in his mind. His seclusion in total secrecy, even from Kamil's own troops, now made sense: Kamil wanted no one to know of Do'brai's involvement in the kidnapping.

Hujr backed into the room and gathered the guard's weapons: a knife, a pistol, and a high-powered rifle. Wrapping a soiled handkerchief around his upper arm, he was able to halt most of the blood still oozing from his wound. He'd have to move out, and fast—he didn't know when to expect the troops back. He was used to moving clandestinely through Do'brai; that presented no problem. But wherever he went, General Kamil would have a price on his head. He wasn't sure why, but that didn't matter.

He was used to being wanted, but for someone to double-cross him—that was unforgivable. There was only one thing he could do. He made up his mind to hunt the general down.

U.S.S.S. *Bifrost*

"So what if we've never done it before? How the hell is that going to stop us? Give them control of the runway clearer, damn it." Lieutenant Colonel Frier jutted out his jaw and stared defiantly at the army general filling his monitor. So what the hell were they going to do to him if he talked back to the chairman of the Joint Chiefs of Staff —take away his birthday? They sure as hell couldn't court-martial him up here. Not now, anyway.

Blackie Backerman's face remained impassive for a fraction of a second; the delay was due to Frier's transmission bouncing off two geosynchronous satellites, to the White House and back to BIGEYE again. When Backerman's expression did change, the general wore a scowl.

"Listen, George, we can't afford to relinquish control of the runway clearer—"

"You mean *you* can't afford to relinquish control, General. You're the only one in the NECC who knows what the hell is going on at Do'brai."

"All right," conceded Backerman. "*I* can't afford to let you control it—"

"But I wouldn't control it, I'd only relay Colonel Krandel's aiming instructions. Krandel is in direct contact with BIGEYE, and he's the one whose ass is on the line. All he's asked for is for control of the tank—that way, firepower can be controlled directly from the ground rather than relying on the whim of the NECC."

"I understand that, George—"

"Damn it, do they want these boys to live or die down there? Just tell that pantywaist staff that ever since Vandenburg launched the runway clearer, the NECC has refused to let it do what it was designed to do. Whose side are they on, anyway?"

"We thought the President was near the runway. You know we couldn't allow that runway clearer to let loose its salvo."

Frier sounded weary. "I know that. But now that Krandel's men are holed up, let *them* direct its firepower. All they have to do is relay their orders up to BIGEYE, and we'll shoot the coded directions down to the runway clearer. It's a piece of cake."

Backerman gnawed on his lip. The delay seemed a little longer than usual this time. The general replied, "Giving Krandel control of the runway clearer would ruin the Vice President's plan to get out of this situation with no injuries. I'll see what I can do—but I can't promise anything." Frier started to grin as Backerman came back: "And you're lucky you're not coming down to Earth anytime soon, George, or I'd have you strung up for insubordination." He paused, then added, "But thank God someone besides those marines has balls. I'll let you know ASAP, if not sooner, on that."

Camp Pendleton

"Men, I'm not going to give you any rah-rah bullshit this time. I'll lay it out for you straight: Eleven marines are fighting for their lives in Do'brai. Six hours ago I let you know that the President of the United States had been kidnapped. Our men have successfully rescued him; he's due to land at Reagan in fifteen minutes. But he wasn't freed without a price. Two marines—Gunnery Balcalski and Corporal Henderson—and an air force TAV pilot died in the rescue. One of the TAVs we sent in was destroyed, and now eleven of our brothers are depending on us to get them back.

"We're sending in the five remaining TAVs. Three of them will carry fuel to get you back; the other two will transport the remainder of the RDF to Do'brai." General Vandervoos paused and tried to chomp on his unlit cigar. When the stogie fell apart in his teeth, he threw it wearily to the side.

The man looked beat. Deep, dark circles enveloped his eyes, and his face was gray, but his voice still had an edge to it. "So I'm not giving you a pep talk. If you need one, you shouldn't be here. You men are all professionals—and I don't mean like some reg-happy son of a bitch who'd rather see a rule followed than the job get done. I mean professional in the sense that when you know a fellow marine is dying, you're going to go out there to rescue his ass. Even if it means you may die trying. You'll do it because you're a marine; because there are things like God and country, duty and honor and freedom, which mean more to you. . . ."

Vandervoos stopped, glassy-eyed, and almost choked on his words. He surveyed the group of forty men, but none batted an eye. Only Captain Weston, standing guard over his platoon in the rear of the lecture room, nodded his head.

General Vandervoos ran a shaky hand through his hair. "God, I'm getting old, rambling on like that. But damn it, I'd go with you if I could. I . . ." He straightened and spoke in a whisper. "Men, your brothers are out there. You're going because if you were in their place, they'd be coming after you." There was silence for several moments. He lifted his head. "Captain Weston, do you have anything to add?"

Weston spoke up from the back. "Only some tactical information, sir. BIGEYE has Colonel Krandel's men holed up in a small depression east of the runway. We'll be coming in on the TAVs from opposite directions to try to confuse any enemy fire that may be present. The plan is to disembark and cover the three TAVs coming in with the fuel bladders, refuel, and get the hell out of there."

"Good. Good. Any last questions?" The atmosphere was tense. "I know you men haven't contacted your families in over six hours now, but we still need the news blackout. Your TAVs load in ten minutes. Good luck, marines."

Vandervoos strode abruptly from the room. The men jumped, knocking over chairs in their haste to stand at attention as the general exited.

Once the general cleared the door, Weston moved to the front. "You heard him—nobody screws up and nobody dies. Let's go." He threw open the door, and the men filed silently out, keeping their thoughts to themselves. They knew the general was right. If they were the ones in Do'brai, they would be the ones being rescued. And *nobody* wanted to screw up his own rescue.

Do'brai

General Kamil reached the staff car on the run. He commandeered the vehicle, threw the driver from the seat, and tore off for the airport. The militiamen scrambled aboard a military bus and rumbled after their leader. Kamil drove steadily through the dusty streets, keeping his cool, but pressing the car even faster. The traffic was sparse at this time of the morning, but he still had to swerve to miss carts and animals as early-morning hawkers gathered to display their wares at market.

He reached the airport as the sound of an explosion filled the air. His first thought was that something had happened to the plane carrying Montoya and the ALH. But a glimmer caught the corner of his eye. Looking up, he could barely make out the sleek outline of a black jet, a jet unlike any he'd ever seen before. The jet staggered into the air, lurching like a lowlife who'd partaken of too much hashish.

Suddenly, a ball of fire erupted from the jet, and the plane took off into the sky with its tail on fire.

Kamil slammed the car door shut and ran into the control tower just as the bus carrying the militiamen pulled up. Reaching the tower offices, Kamil burst into the control room.

"Quick—someone tell me what is going on."

A man pointed a finger at a fire smoldering at the far end of the runway. "We were attacked."

"By whom?"

"I do not know. They took the bus and killed most of the ALH representatives."

Montoya struggled, causing the agents to stop their progress. "Hospitalize me, like hell! I want a chopper out here now."

"Mr. President—"

"Young man, that's a presidential order. I've got to see to the rescue." The President grabbed Gould as the pilot emerged from the TAV's cockpit. "Son, you've got to make sure those marines get out of there. You pulled me out of Do'brai—you've got to do it again."

Gould was taken aback. "Yes, sir . . ." He glanced at the doctor. The President held Gould's hand tightly, refusing to let go.

The doctor raised his brows at Gould. "If you can help us get out of your plane, I'd appreciate it." He then nodded to the agents. "Let's get him out of here."

Gould went with them as they moved out of the hatch and into a waiting ambulance. Montoya continued to protest, becoming violent. The TAV was ringed with guards, the majority of them in the dark business suits of Secret Service agents, but there was a smattering of military, state, and local police mixed in with the rest. Once inside the ambulance, the doctor pulled out a syringe.

"Mr. President, this shot will make you feel better." He injected the needle and slowly pushed the plunger.

"It better the hell not dope me up. I've got too much to do when I get back. And where's that helicopter? I thought I told you I want to return immediately to the White House."

"It's coming, Mr. President. We've just had to lay you down for a while."

"It had better get here." Within moments Montoya slowly started muttering in Spanish. He giggled to himself. When his head rolled to the side, the doctor ordered the driver: "Let's get out of here—and fast. He's in bad shape."

Gould released the President's hand as he moved from the ambulance. "Is he okay?"

"He won't be unless we get him out of here. He's got dehydration, shock, loss of blood, and what we call the kidnapper's syndrome: His blood pressure is sky-high, and he'll die if we don't settle him down. We're lucky the White House warned us about his condition. Look, we've got to go." The doctor slammed the door shut, and the ambulance screamed away.

Gould watched in silence as they left, ignoring the marines filing out of the TAV behind him. An emptiness filled him, a void left over from the rescue and Delores. Great, he thought. What the hell was he supposed to do now?

Do'brai

Krandel fingered his rifle and fought to keep his eyes open. The clouds above them turned cotton-candy pink as the sun just hit their periphery; the desert's red horizon turned brighter and finally evaporated into a glaring blaze as the sun began its journey across the sky.

To Krandel's left the TAV had stopped belching smoke, but the smell of JP-12 still reached them, mixing with the delicate morning breeze. They sat in a circle with their backs to one another, waiting and watching for the reprisal. An hour had passed since the TAV had left; except for sporadic gunfire and shouts from people unseen, no contact had been made with the Do'brainese forces.

It made the men uneasy. And Krandel shared in their worry but didn't voice his concerns out loud.

"Colonel, how much longer until they attack?"

Krandel answered automatically. "Fifteen miles."

"Oh—yes, sir," the puzzled voice came back.

His flippant retort didn't seem as funny now as it had back then—was it fifteen years before?—when Krandel, one summer while still a midshipman, was a ranger for the Boy Scouts at Philmont Scout Ranch. The sprawling scout ranch where Krandel spent one summer taking Boy Scouts up in the mountains brought back hidden memories. The scouts were usually ill-prepared for the arduous mountain hiking, and when the groans and griping started, their incessant cry soon became: "How much longer, Mr. Ranger? How many more miles until we get to camp?"

And the reply would come: "Fifteen miles."

No matter how much farther, no matter how much longer—even if the campsite was just around the bend—"fifteen miles" was the standard reply.

Fifteen more miles. Krandel wished it could be that simple now—achieving sanctuary after a fifteen-mile jaunt through the mountains. It would be a piece of cake.

But things were different now. Like it or not, he was their commander. A genuine, combat-trained, service-ready jarhead—and he was in control. But what could he do?

If the NECC would allow him to control the runway clearer from here, it would add immensely to their firepower. The tanklike device squatted not two hundred yards away—an ugly but fully operable piece of equipment controlled through the satellite link with BIGEYE. They had planned to destroy it by blowing it up once both TAVs had left.

He felt momentarily ashamed that he'd been flippant with that marine a moment earlier. The man actually looked up to him, and how often had that happened? His thoughts drifted to when he was at the Pentagon. There he was lucky to get even a nod with all the brass jumping around.

Krandel half turned to the men and said in a stage whisper, "They're waiting until it's light enough to see clearly. The airport is barely up to international standards, so it's an even bet that the rest of the country doesn't have any sophisticated gear to see clearly in the dark. Which reminds me—if you haven't taken off your IR goggles, go ahead and do so now."

"Shall we toss them, Colonel, or do you want us to keep them handy? They might get in our way later on."

"Eh?" He hadn't thought of that. He started to tell them to toss the gear, but he realized that he should be keeping the men's morale up, too. "No, we may be here for a while—it may take until nightfall for us to get out of here if the TAVs take that long—so don't throw the goggles away. Keep them in the center with the rest of the gear."

"Aye, aye, Colonel."

Krandel turned back to cover his area as the men tossed their goggles behind them, into the center of the depression. The sun was above the horizon now, and the first rays were lighting up Do'brai's terminal. A low hum of activity permeated the air, and Krandel strained to catch voices in the distance.

The drone of a truck engine caught his attention. He felt an overwhelming urge to urinate, but he fought it down. His heart started yammering, and he grew short of breath. Damn! Something was going to happen, and soon. It was the same feeling he had had just before he jumped from the TAV. The sound grew louder.

"Behind you, Colonel. They're coming from the opposite end of the runway."

"All right, this is it." Krandel twisted his hands on the rifle stock; it was already slippery from his sweat. "Wait for my order before you shoot, unless you see some son of a bitch about to kill us. We'll wait this out as long as we can to save ammunition. Cover the area in front of you, and sing out if you see anything." He wet his lips, then called again while keeping his eyes glued to the area in front of him, "Morales?"

"Yes, sir?"

"Inform BIGEYE we're about to get shit on. Find out the rescue mission's ETA, and have BIGEYE relay the bad guys' positions to them so they can take countermeasures when they land. And have them tell Washington to get off their fat asses about the runway clearer. We want control of that sucker *now*."

"Yes, sir, Colonel."

The sounds grew steadily louder; the tension mounted, but the marines held their post. Krandel had a sudden wild thought: What if they attack from all sides? Just throw men at us, wave after wave, until they use their own dead for protection against our fire? It had happened in Korea. . . . He suppressed a shudder and realized they couldn't do that. They didn't have nearly as many men as the Chinese had had in Korea. But the thought didn't comfort him.

He called to Morales again with a slight edge to his voice. "What's the holdup, Morales?"

Nothing; then: "BIGEYE can't get through to the TAVs, sir."

Krandel relaxed. "Good, that means they're just about here. They're going through the communications blackout when they reenter the atmosphere."

"Sir?"

"What, Morales?"

"Sir . . . BIGEYE reports it's too early for the communications blackout with the TAVs. They don't answer BIGEYE's query."

Shouting started on Krandel's left. A horde of men swarmed over an embankment, scrambling down the earthen side and into a ditch, where they were positioned out of sight of the marines. Suddenly, a high-pitched whistle came from above.

"Incoming!"

The marines sprawled flat, automatically collapsing in a prone position. Shrapnel sprayed the air as the mortar exploded. All hell broke loose, but the Do'braineše stayed hidden. There was no one to shoot at, and the marines didn't have any ballistic weapons with which to respond.

Krandel yelled over the firing, "Tell BIGEYE to position the runway clearer."

"The NECC hasn't released it yet, Colonel."

Another round exploded, landing to their right; the next one would be a bull's-eye.

"When will they, damn it?"

"I don't know, sir."

Another shell hit; Krandel yelled with his face in the ground, "The TAVs—when did they take off?"

"I don't know—*I don't know!*"

Hujr crept around the building, stopping to tighten the bandage around his shoulder before moving on. He made good time; the sun was starting to rise, and already he was not more than five kilometers from the airport. Slipping in and out of the alleyways was like second nature to him. He appropriated some fruits and nuts from a cart near the marketplace, not looking at it as stealing, but considering it the right of one who lived off the land.

He was dressed as a Do'brainese peasant—loose, flowing robe, tattered headgear, and, if one viewed him from a distance, a walking stick, which was actually the high-powered rifle he had taken from the militiaman. He had but one purpose in life at this time: not revenge for Du'Ali's death, but a settling of debts. Kamil had promised him fortune, fame, and notoriety. Instead he had been double-crossed and almost killed. And to repay the debt—following the dictum "an eye for an eye"—death permeated Hujr's mind.

It didn't matter how many people were around, or who would witness Kamil's death; Hujr was prepared—the same way he had been prepared to martyr himself with the President of the United States—to bring Kamil to his final justice.

The sound of gunfire and bombs exploding startled Hujr as he crept toward the airport. The airport was the only logical place for Kamil to be, and if he wasn't there now, he would have to show up sometime. The distant sounds of combat convinced Hujr even more that he was headed in the right direction.

Wrapping his robe more tightly about him, he stealthily made his way across the remaining distance.

The small depression looked even more inviting to Kamil now than it had half an hour earlier. The sun was rising, and the foreigners could be seen as motionless specks. Soon it would be time.

"Americans," spat Kamil, the name leaving a nauseous taste in his mouth. "They have no concept of what it means to fight to the death. As soon as they realize their situation is hopeless, they will quickly surrender—and then they will pay for robbing me of their President." Kamil put down the binoculars and looked quickly around the control tower. No one appeared to be listening. They all worked busily at their jobs, ignoring Kamil as he spoke to himself.

But they heard, thought Kamil. They would not dare admit that they were eavesdropping, for they must never know what had really happened out there, he thought—that we almost had the President of the United States. Let them think we were invaded. Let them think the intruders failed to take over Do'brai; it could only fuel the resentment against America.

He brought his binoculars back up and surveyed the remainder of the runway. The giant 747 that was to carry the ALH sat dormant. The smoking remains of the Americans' plane were at the end of the runway, next to where the invaders hid. But something curious—large and unwieldy, looking almost like a tank—sat off the runway, halfway between the Americans and the tower. It was left over from the Americans' raid and would have to be investigated, but only later, when Kamil had time.

The sun was fully up now. If the Americans fought back, Do'brai would have casualties, but they would be insignificant; after all, soldiers were expendable.

Bringing the binoculars down, Kamil spoke without turning. "Radio the assault force to capture the Americans. They may scare the Americans, but if any American dies, both the soldier who killed him and his commander will be gutted."

The order was acknowledged, and the troops that were moved into position only a half hour before began their assault. Mortars, coupled with the tinny sound of machine-gun fire, could barely be heard through the tower's thick windows. The firepower was only designed to pin the Americans down, but it still made an awesome display.

Reagan International

Major Robert Gould stood with his hands on his hips and glared at the colonel in front of him. Two solid hours of debriefings by a team of air force, CIA, DIA, FBI, OSI—and probably XYZ—agents had pushed Gould to his limits. Colonel Rathson was very insistent, but Gould was arguing, "Colonel, the President of the United States *told* me to make sure those TAVs are launched. I really don't think you can get it from any higher authority than that. They need my TAV back at Edwards, and they need it fast."

"Nevertheless, Major, I can't release your craft. Regulations are regulations. You've passed your sixteen hours of duty time, and you've got to have your crew rest. I appreciate the fact that you're the only TAV pilot here, but you simply cannot fly your craft back to Edwards until you've had the proper rest as prescribed in the regs. Nothing you can say will make any difference. Now, I suggest that you check into a hotel, and in twelve hours I'll release you."

"Oh, hell." Gould slammed a hand on the table.

"And Major."

"Yes, Colonel?"

Colonel Rathson looked around the briefing room and lowered his voice. "Major, in any other situation I'd have you hauled up for disrespect. Your attitude is completely unprofessional. Get the message?"

Gould counted to ten under his breath. "Yes, *sir*—I understand." The whole affair was getting ridiculous. His 747 mother craft had flown cross-country to meet him at Reagan International as soon as he had launched from Edwards not eight hours earlier. Using the air force reserve facilities at Reagan, the TAV was fitted on top of the 747 and was ready to go—except that permission for Gould to fly the craft had been denied.

Rathson had flown out from Langley AFB to coordinate the recovery of the TAV, but he had his head so far up his ass going by the book that he'd thrown Gould's plans to fly the TAV back to Edwards into an uproar.

Gould fumed and was ready to stomp out the door when a thought hit him. "Colonel?"

"Um?" Rathson lifted his eyes from a note he was reading.

"Colonel, is there anything to prevent the 747 crew from flying back to Edwards carrying the TAV?"

Rathson put down his message. "What? Did I hear you correctly, Major?"

"Yes, sir. I know that I can't fly the TAV back myself, but is there any regulation against the 747 crew flying back with the TAV?"

The colonel mulled it over. "Well, they'd have to stop at least twice to refuel with that additional weight . . . but I suppose there's nothing that says it can't be done."

Gould stepped forward eagerly. "Then let's do it, Colonel. I've got to get that TAV back to Edwards in case they need it for another mission." So he was telling a white lie, but what the hell?

Rathson pulled at his jaw. "Your 747 did bring along an extra crew, so they don't have the crew rest problem you do. I suppose that as long as it's not in the regs, it shouldn't matter." Rathson straightened and said firmly, "Go ahead, but you won't be able to file your flight plan for the TAV. I'll have to clear it with Langley."

"Thanks, sir."

Gould was out the door as Colonel Rathson finished his sentence. Bursting into the crew lounge, he caught the 747 pilot by the arm and explained the situation. The crew gathered around. They were agreeable to Gould's suggestion, as they wanted to get back home without an unnecessary overnight stop. They grabbed their gear and left for their 747, planning to leave as soon as possible. Before heading out to the plane, Gould made a quick stop at the operations desk; there was one last thing he had to check out. The colonel from Langley was nowhere in sight.

Gould collared the sergeant in charge of the ops desk. "Do you know if the TAV fuel bladder is full?"

The man checked a status board. "Yes, sir, but we have strict orders that you are not allowed to file a flight plan for the TAV."

"I'm riding back with the 747 crew."

"Oh. Well, in that case we'll have to drain the TAV and the fuel bladder before you take off. The regs forbid you to transport a fueled vehicle on board an aircraft. And since you're not going to rocket, that reg applies to your TAV."

Gould thought fast, then shook his head. "Can't. Don't you know that Air Force Reg 869 specifically states that the TAV must be mission-ready at all times?"

The sergeant frowned. He answered slowly, "I don't think I've ever heard of that one, sir."

"Check with Edwards if you've got questions, Sergeant. It's paragraph 5, subparagraph L. That reg was made specifically for the TAV, and your unit—being a reserve outfit —probably doesn't have a copy of it."

"Well, sir—"

"We've got to get going, Sergeant. Thanks." Gould spun on his heel and left the room, breaking into a run when he got outdoors. Instead of boarding the 747, Gould scrambled aboard the TAV. Once inside he informed the crew below him he'd rather sit out the flight in his own surroundings. Besides, they'd be too nervous knowing both the TAV and the fuel bladder were topped off with fuel.

He fretted through the preflight procedures, but when the 747 engines started up he finally began to relax. He didn't feel comfortable until they were airborne and on their way to California. Then he was sure that Delores would have been proud of him.

White House

Gentlemen, the President's condition is stable, but he is still asleep."

"Thank God." Vice President Woodstone let it slip out, and the others around the table looked up. Woodstone put up his hands. "I only meant I'm glad that he's stable. Aren't we all?"

"Yes, *sir*," growled Backerman, obviously displeased that Woodstone had let out his true feelings.

Woodstone arranged in front of him the small pile of papers that had accumulated during the afternoon and night. It was late at night, and everyone was starting to feel punchy. Woodstone said, smiling, "Well, gentlemen, now that the President is safely back, I'm afraid we must turn our attention to more mundane matters."

Baca coughed after no one spoke up. "You mean the marines that President Montoya ordered rescued."

Woodstone folded his hands. "Precisely. Gentlemen"—he waved a small white paper, bordered in red—"we all know that the President ordered a rescue. Since that time, we've put the remaining five TAVs on alert. Correct, General?"

Backerman glanced up at Colonel Welch. Welch cleared his throat. "Yes, sir. The TAVs are orbiting with their mother ships, waiting for your final orders. But there's still the question of releasing the runway clearer to Colonel Krandel's control."

Backerman pounded on the table. "Mr. Vice President, Colonel Welch is absolutely right. If you're not going to commit the TAVs, then you've at least got to release the runway clearer. It doesn't do any damn good for that piece of equipment to sit out there; Krandel's team is in trouble."

"Have the marines been attacked yet?"

"Yes, sir, they have."

"But has anyone been harmed?"

"No, sir, damn it—but that's not the point!"

"That *is* the point, General." Woodstone slouched back in his chair and waved the red-bordered paper again. "I have a personal communiqué from President Ash'ath—"

"President Montoya already told you what he thought about that promise not to harm our marines."

"But this is a clarification of that first message." Woodstone smiled, almost sweetly. "President Ash'ath promises that no harm will come to the marines, and in addition he promises to deliver to us the hijackers that commandeered Air Force One. I'm sure that your marines will confirm that no shells have hit them. President Ash'ath assures me that they are simply trying to keep our men in one spot."

"That's a helluva way to do that, sir." Backerman raised an eyebrow at Baca; Baca shrugged. Backerman tapped a pencil on the table. "Mr. Vice President, I don't like this at all. It doesn't seem right."

"He's got a point, Mr. Woodstone." The attention turned to Baca. "The President was very adamant about the rescue. If you weren't already in control of the situation here, I think the President's doctor would not have sedated him, and Mr. Montoya would be here right now. And ten to one he would have launched the rescue."

"But the President is *not* here, Mr. Baca." Woodstone bristled. "And I think we've argued this moot point enough." He turned to Welch. "Colonel, please transmit an official reply to President Ash'ath that we accept his gracious offer. We will instruct our marine detachment at Do'brai to unconditionally surrender—if and only if we have President Ash'ath's personal word that no harm will come to these men. Also, please order our men to surrender—with honor, if it is at all possible."

"Yes, sir." It took an effort, but Welch turned toward the door.

"Good." Woodstone smiled widely. "Gentlemen, there's always a way out of these things. To paraphrase a quote: 'Violence is the last refuge of the incompetent.' I can't remember who said it, but I think we've upheld its spirit. Just think of all the casualties we're going to avoid—American and Do'brainese alike."

Backerman stood up, his face red. "If you'll excuse me, sir."

"Certainly, but stay close by, General. I think we should man the NECC until the situation is well in hand."

"Yes, sir. Pardon me then—I have to throw up."

Do'brai

Hujr was right. General Kamil and his staff were assembled in the control tower at the airport. He couldn't see the general from his vantage point, but he knew he was in there. When the troop carriers roared past, militiamen hanging on to the sides, holding on to their rifles, they held clenched fists high in the air, saluting the tower. There was too much activity around for the general not to be present.

Hujr waited in the brush. The dirt and ants kept him company, but at least he was hidden from view. He was on a slight rise and had a perfect line of sight to the door of the control tower.

He was content to wait. He fingered the trigger on his weapon for the hundredth time, and although eager for the general to appear, he constantly reminded himself not to rush things. Afterward, he'd be able to lose himself in the city. So he waited, growing ever happier, with the thought that revenge would soon be his.

"We have some new orders, Colonel." Corporal Morales ducked as he spoke; another mortar went off, not fifty yards away.

"Well, either crap or get off the pot—out with it, Morales." Krandel was getting irate. The shelling had been going on for nearly an hour, and either the Do'brainese were the lousiest shots in the world or they were playing cat-and-mouse with them. The shelling went on, and although nothing came close enough to injure the marines, every time they tried to move they were pinned back into the depression. It was obvious they were being held there.

Crawling over to Krandel, the corporal held out the headphones. "You'd better verify the orders, Colonel. I don't like the sound of them."

"Get back to your post, marine," growled Krandel while taking control of the set. He spoke into the throat mike and after some moments tore off the headphones. He threw them aside and swore.

"What's up, Colonel?"

"Damned friggin' bureaucrats sit on their fat asses and play Monday-morning quarterback—"

"Colonel?"

Krandel composed himself. "That was General Backerman, chairman of the Joint Chiefs. The TAV rescue mission has been called off. Our orders are to surrender."

"Surrender?" The depression was alive with talk as the marines sputtered out their disbelief. "But, *sir*—"

"That's it, men. We're to surrender immediately. The Do'brainese forces have promised to transport us back to the airport unharmed and to hand over the people who hijacked Air Force One."

"Sir, do you really believe that?"

Krandel was quiet for some time. Morales spoke up. "Sir, did you see what they did to the President's feet?"

"The hijackers—"

"*Sir*, the President said he was tortured here. It wasn't the hijackers who did it; he was hurt here. You heard him!"

Krandel mulled it over; all the time explosions continued to go off around them. Morales was right. But Krandel had orders, and as a commissioned officer in the United States Marine Corps he was duty-bound to carry out those orders. He had sworn an oath to do it.

But on the other hand, what happened to his men was the on-site commander's responsibility. Why hadn't he paid attention to those philosophy courses at Annapolis—the ones where they discussed when an officer had to follow a higher law? They showed at Nuremberg that an officer cannot be within the law by simply "following the orders of his superiors" when those orders were illegal. He had to make the decision. Could he take a chance and trust the judgment of someone thousands of miles away?

He knew the textbook answer: It was an unqualified yes. But if those who gave him the orders to surrender were wrong, his men would die.

But if Backerman was right, and Krandel disobeyed those orders, he'd be court-martialed.

General Vandervoos had told him a command would be the best thing ever to happen to him. Krandel wasn't so sure of that now. It was his ass on the line, and he had his men to think about.

"Morales, get me a white flag. Use a T-shirt, underwear, anything."

"Sir, we're not going to surrender, are we?"

"Shut up. You heard me. Now listen up, men." He drew

them near and, over the explosions, explained to them what they were going to do.

And as they got ready he thought that Balcalski would have been proud of him.

"Are you sure it's a white flag?"

"Yes, General. Look for yourself."

Kamil scanned the area, then put down his binoculars and smiled. "Inform President Ash'ath that his message has gotten through. Unless it's a trick, the Americans have surrendered. I will accept their surrender myself." He handed the viewing instrument to his aide and smoothed his shirt. "Inform the assault commander that I will be at his position in five minutes. I will accept the surrender." He held up a finger. "But have him station sharpshooters around the depression where the Americans are hiding. If anything appears suspicious, all the Americans are to die. Understand?"

"Perfectly, General." His staff snapped to attention and held the position until Kamil was out the door of the control tower. His aide followed as he left, scurrying to keep up.

Kamil stepped from the air-conditioned coolness to the morning heat. Although the sun had only been up for an hour, the temperature had begun to soar. He moved to his staff car and decided at the last moment to let his aide drive. It had been a long day—almost too long—without a rest. He'd be able to pull his thoughts together and prepare the precise words for the Americans during the drive.

Hujr brought the rifle up and squinted into the sight. Kamil stepped from the control tower and moved toward the car. This was almost too easy. Hujr carefully squeezed the trigger, mentally preparing to pump several bullets into the general once the first had found its mark. The bullet would hit as Kamil opened the car door. . . .

"'Ifrit!'" Kamil whirled away from the door just as Hujr was about to squeeze off the round. Hujr abruptly jerked his finger free of the trigger. He held his breath; he thought the sound could be heard from kilometers away, but the soldiers coming from the control tower paid him no attention.

Kamil entered the passenger side of the car, moving in a motion that looked as if it was calculated to prevent Hujr from shooting him. Hujr dropped the rifle and swore to himself.

The staff car took off and took a turn down the frontage road, heading for the plane at the end of the runway. Hujr eyed the plane; it wasn't over three kilometers away, and if he went through the desert, the distance would be much shorter. He reasoned things out: Kamil must be going to where the shooting was occurring. It would take Hujr time to get there, but if Kamil was going to be at the end of the runway, he would be exposed.

And if he killed Kamil there, there was a chance that he would not be caught. The blame might be laid on those whom Kamil was going to meet.

The rationalization sounded so good that Hujr had to restrain himself and wait until the last soldier roared off from the tower. He crept around the side, keeping out of view of the control tower. As he scooted clandestinely from bush to bush he was consoled that no one would be looking for him.

U.S.S.S. *Bifrost*

Major Wordel spoke up, breaking the silence in the space station. "Colonel Frier, I've got a request to relay a message from *Ojo-1* to Edwards."

"Tell him to clear the channel, damn it. His mission is over. We need this link for monitoring the situation at Do'brai."

"I think you'd better listen, Colonel." Wordel persisted. "He's taken off from Reagan, piggybacking back to Edwards, and he wants us to notify Edwards that his TAV will be available for the Do'brai rescue in thirty minutes."

"Thirty minutes?!" Frier exploded; he propelled himself across the communications chamber to Wordel's screen. "What the hell is he going to do, rocket back to Edwards?"

"I think that's his plan, Colonel. He wants us to download his semiballistic burn vectors from the CRAY."

Frier slapped at the screen; Gould's face appeared, enveloped in the red-bordered security link. "Okay, Gould, what's the story? Why the hell do you want to rocket back to Edwards? You had better have a good reason."

Gould answered instantly, as if reciting from a transcript. "Simple, Colonel. I was ordered by the President of the United States to make sure the marines were rescued. The quickest way for me to do that is to get my TAV back to Edwards so they can use it for the rescue. I've already got a fuel bladder ready for them, so all they have to do is get a new crew for her."

"You'd be flying without authorization—"

"It was a direct order, Colonel."

Frier turned red. "Gould, don't try me. I know you think you're doing the right thing, but it won't help. Now don't piss anyone off by rocketing back. Just sit back and enjoy the ride."

Gould chewed on it, then said slowly, "What do you mean, it wouldn't help if I rocketed back?"

"The rescue mission has been called off. The RDF was ordered by General Backerman to wind down the operation. All TAVs are back at Edwards, and the alert has been downgraded to a level three. The marines at Do'brai have surrendered—or rather, they're in the process of surrendering—and will be transported back to the U.S. with the President's hijackers."

There was a long silence. When Gould came back over the comm link there was an edge to his voice. "Colonel, did I misunderstand you? The marines are *surrendering?*"

Frier could only force a nod. He hoped Blackie knew what the hell he was doing at the NECC. There were times when you just had to do something that you didn't want to do. But he had it easy; all he had to do was to relay the bad news. Colonel Krandel back at Do'brai had the hard part.

Frier said, "Gould, you got the President back alive. That's more than anyone could ask."

Gould came back, his voice hard. "I want the burn vectors for Do'brai, Colonel."

"What? You're crazy, Gould."

"Do'brai. I want them downloaded."

"You're nuts; you're out of your mind. Do you know what's going to happen? You're going to get to Do'brai and the marines won't be there; they'll be on their way back home. You'll not only be arrested for invading a foreign country, but you'll give Do'brai one of our TAVs—and to top it off, you'll be court-martialed if you ever get back to the U.S. How does *that* grab you?"

"Download the burn vectors, Colonel—I'm not going to ask you again."

"And what the hell are you going to do if I don't give them to you?"

"Do it by the seat of my pants. My on-board computer can get me within twenty miles of the Do'brai airport; I can get the rest of the way on my own, VFR. But with your help I'll have a damned better chance of making it. Now, are you going to do it or not, Colonel Frier?"

Frier started to get advice from Blackie, then decided against it. Instead he said, "Gould, listen to me—"

"Colonel, do you really believe Do'brai intends to release our marines?"

Frier's reply sounded feeble. "I don't know, Gould, but Blackie said they promised—"

"Colonel, there's a right thing to do and there's a moral thing to do. The moral thing is to rescue those men, and you know as well as I that if we do, we'll get fried by our own people when this thing is over. So you can be on the right side and cover your ass, or you can help me out. Those men are depending on me, Colonel.

"Now give me those burn vectors, or I'm going without them. I intend to be in Do'brai in forty-five minutes with or without your help. God willing, in three hours I'll have those marines back home."

Frier closed his eyes. Getting away, taking command of

the *Bifrost,* seemed the perfect way for him to abdicate the authority that came with command. He had screwed things up once and ended up killing a student pilot; he had made a bad decision on pulling out of a stall, and someone died for it. It was a command, although small, that went astray.

That's what was nice about BIGEYE; you only did what you were told, and although you had responsibility, you had no authority. And no chance to be blamed if you screwed things up. He was useful here, but he didn't make decisions.

He could run, but—although he'd run three hundred miles straight up—he just couldn't hide.

Frier's fingers danced on the touch-sensitive screen below Gould's picture. Icons and rows of figures sprang up at his touch until the screen blinked green.

"Prepare to accept the vectors, Major Gould. Please echo-check them ASAP . . . and good luck."

"Roger that, BIGEYE."

Frier kept quiet through the echo check. Wordel, silent throughout the exchange, floated up next to him and handed him a slip of paper. Frier scanned it, then said to Gould, "Major, I have an urgent note here from Base Ops at Reagan."

"Better hurry, I'm rocketing in twenty seconds."

"It says they couldn't find a DOD Reg 869. You're to return to Reagan soonest unless you clarify which regulation you quoted about flying with a completely fueled TAV —signed Colonel Rathson."

A laugh came over the screen. "Too late, Colonel. Tell Rathson better luck next time. There ain't no such animal."

The link clicked off. Frier stared, then switched to survey his satellite monitors. Wordel spoke up. "Shall we inform the NECC, Colonel?"

Frier chewed on his lip before answering. "Yeah, might as well give them a heads-up on this. It's too late for them to screw anything up for Gould now." As Wordel moved to make the report Frier caught himself thinking that maybe he had finally found a way to make it up to his student's family.

Do'brai

Hujr slipped behind the bush undetected. He was not more than a hundred meters away from the depression where the Americans were, but he was hidden from both them and the militia. He was halfway between the Americans and the 747 on the runway.

Hujr settled into the sand, pushing away the grains by wiggling until he was comfortable. He brought the rifle around and looked through the sights. The Americans huddled together, conferring about something. One of them had fashioned a white flag made from a T-shirt and tied it onto a radio antenna.

He relaxed. That ensured Kamil would make an appearance—he wouldn't miss a surrender for anything in the world. And when he showed, he wouldn't escape.

"I thought the Americans surrendered."

"We did too, General. Would you care to look through the binoculars?"

Kamil grunted; his aide brought the viewing instrument up, and Kamil surveyed the area with a slow sweep. "I can't see anything."

"They're hidden in a depression, General. The control tower can see them, and they report the Americans have brought down their white flag."

"Then what is the holdup?"

"The Americans are grouped together, probably praying to their God. I doubt they trust us."

Kamil allowed himself a smile. "Ah, but their leaders do. And that's the difference between us and them. They cannot act autonomously; they have to rely on directions from halfway across the world. They would not die for a cause—it would cause too much bad publicity." Kamil handed the binoculars back to his aide. "Inform me as soon as their flag goes back up. If it is not flying in ten minutes,

212

then lob some mortar rounds in their direction to speed them up."

The ten men clustered low around Krandel. Although no one was in sight, he spoke in a whisper. "This is it. Everybody ready?"

The marines remained silent, expressing their affirmation with grim nods. Krandel drew in a breath. He almost felt like taking a vote to see if the men really wanted to go along with this harebrained stunt of his.

But he couldn't. He didn't know why, but he just *knew* that they'd die if they surrendered. No matter what the NECC promised. So this was their only option. After they acted, maybe the NECC would get off their butts and call the rescue back on. And if they didn't, the marines still had a better chance doing it their way.

Krandel nodded to Morales. "All right, let's get this show on the road."

Morales sprang to his feet with the white flag and started waving it slowly back and forth over his head. Krandel spoke quietly in the microphone to BIGEYE, explaining their plan.

"General, the flag!"

Kamil bolted upright and snatched the binoculars from his aide. "Have the militia disperse along the runway. I will accept the surrender myself."

"Yes, sir." The aide barked the orders, then drew a revolver to join his general.

Kamil unbuckled his gun belt and, throwing it to the ground, shook his head at his aide. "I'll be going alone."

"But, General—"

"It's a matter of honor for the Americans. They will be so thoroughly demoralized, this will be the final blow to them: the unarmed commander coming to accept their defeat."

The aide protested. "General Kamil, I implore you. It could be a trap."

Kamil raised a brow. "The militia will shoot to kill—"

"Let me accompany you as a backup. They will at least expect an aide to do your bidding."

Kamil decided after some thought. "Very well, but keep your weapon hidden. And use it only if we are threatened."

"Yes, General." Scrambling down the sandy embankment, they passed several of the militia, dug in the sand. Soon they passed the last guard and reached the runway. The Americans lay before them.

Movement. Hujr fingered the trigger and spotted Kamil through the sight. The general bounced in and out of view, walking next to his aide. Hujr could kill the aide and hope that Kamil would be so disoriented that he wouldn't dive for cover, but the man was too good for that. Hujr would just have to wait for the first opportunity.

He allowed the two to continue toward the depression.

Krandel stood with his hands above his head as the officer approched. Morales had put another shot of morphine into Krandel's leg, so he was feeling slightly cocky, but at least the pain had gone away. From the ribbons, medals, and paraphernalia the officer wore, Krandel reckoned the man had not missed Sunday school for twenty straight years. A taller yet obviously subordinate man, probably the officer's aide, followed to the officer's left. When they reached Krandel the superior spoke in a guttural language.

Krandel saluted. "Lieutenant Colonel William J. Krandel, United States Marine Corps, 227-68-7269. Do you speak English?"

The officer returned the salute, obviously pleased that the Americans were groveling. "General Kamil, commander of the Do'brainese militia forces. We will speak English if we must. There is no one among you who speaks the Do'brainese tongue?" The man surveyed the marines; Havisad kept silent. Krandel wanted the translator as his trump card in case something went wrong. The general spat rapid-fire sounds, but the language fell upon deaf ears.

Krandel's men merely shrugged at the questioning. The

general turned to Krandel. "You are the commanding officer of this commando detachment, Colonel?" The word colonel came out as *kor-nal*.

Krandel drew himself up. "Yes, sir, I am. I present my unit to you in an official act of surrender under the codes of the Geneva Convention. We are all class-one military members, and we insist upon the recognized sanctions of the International Red Cross, of which both the United States and Do'brai are signatory members."

"You are in no position to barter, Colonel. You have launched an unprovoked attack upon Do'brai—"

"We did *not* attack. It was a rescue attempt to free our President from a kidnapping."

The aide's eyes grew large. Krandel noticed the expression and, watching the superior officer, knew that President Montoya's presence here was not known to all.

"I do not know what you are talking about, and that is not the point of my presence here. I am ready to accept your surrender; have your men throw down their arms." Kamil made a slight motion with his hands. Krandel spotted movement from the corner of his eye; he saw Do'brainese militiamen moving toward the marines. For the first time, Kamil moved away from his aide.

"Very well, sir." Krandel turned to his men. "Gentlemen, as Knute Rockne said, 'Let's win this one for the gipper.' *Hike!*"

Krandel tackled General Kamil. Instantly, the popping sounds of rifle shots peppered the area. Morales brought down the general's aide, and once on the ground he knocked the man unconscious with a blow to the head.

Krandel straddled Kamil's back, holding an arm to the general's windpipe. "You have five seconds to stop the gunfire. If you don't, you're going to die with us." Krandel yelled for Havisad to wave the white flag. Within seconds the gunfire ceased, and Krandel jerked Kamil to his knees. "All right, let them know we've got you."

Krandel let up his grip on Kamil slightly. The general started to shout, but Krandel stopped him. Still on his knees, Krandel directed his question to Havisad. "What did he say?"

"Something about not listening to him and following his orders, Colonel. His voice wasn't too clear."

"Then tell the general in Do'brainese, Private: no funny stuff, or he dies."

The general's shoulders sagged as Havisad repeated the orders; the general realized that indeed the Americans had the upper hand. "Do . . . not . . . press . . . so . . . hard." Krandel let up the pressure slightly; Kamil rotated his neck. "I will do as you say."

Krandel and Kamil rose to their feet. Havisad translated as the general shouted instructions in Do'brainese. Havisad remained on the ground, out of sight of any snipers, and held a rifle at Kamil's midriff.

When the general was finished, several of the militiamen stood and threw their rifles to the ground. They started backing away with their hands up, and when they were some distance from the depression they turned and ran.

Krandel watched the retreat, thinking that it had almost been too easy. With his arm on Kamil's throat, he turned his attention to the next detail: how to get them the hell out of Do'brai. "Havisad, radio BIGEYE and tell them we're busting out of here. If a TAV is not on its way to get us out of here, we're going to commandeer a crew for that 747 where we rescued the President. And tell them we need control of that damn runway clearer to cover us when we leave."

Hujr shot off three bullets in a row, then drove his head into the sand. He could hear the sounds of shots. He stiffened in anticipation of one of the bullets hitting him, but nothing happened. Still the shots continued. The militia couldn't be that poor as marksmen; they should have hit him when he tried to kill Kamil.

Hujr jerked his head up, then back down, trying to catch a glimpse of what was going on. The shooting was directed at the depression, and nothing was coming his way. Shouting—a hoarse, familiar voice—rang over the din: "Cease immediately! As chief of staff of the militia forces, I order you to lay down your weapons!"

Hujr moved his head from the ground. General Kamil, held from the back by an American, repeated the orders. No wonder Hujr wasn't peppered with bullets—he had shot at Kamil the same instant that the militia were firing at the Americans. But would Kamil survive the American capture? Probably. Americans were notorious for turning the other cheek once the situation was in their favor. So if Kamil survived, Hujr was still in danger. If not now, then years from now.

He had to kill Kamil. Depending on where the Americans took the general, Hujr's best chance was still here, hidden as a sniper.

U.S.S.S. *Bifrost*

"Why the hell do I have to be the clearinghouse for all this crap?"

Wordel allowed a thin smile. "Colonel, it's not like they'll kill the messenger for bearing bad news."

"I know that, damn it; it's just that I'm always on the receiving end." Frier slapped at the communications screen. He shoved the remains of a sandwich down his throat before Colonel Welch came into view. With the marine rescue vacillating between stop-and-go status, Wordel brought in the food and relieved Frier only when the colonel had to use the rest room.

Colonel Welch looked ragged. He, too, only played the part of a messenger, but his superiors—Vice President Woodstone and General Backerman—did not temper their emotions toward him. Welch rubbed his eyes, trying to get the story correct. "Now let me get this straight: Major Gould has launched his TAV for Do'brai and will arrive within the half hour, and Colonel Krandel has chosen *not* to surrender and wants a Do'brainese flight crew to fly him out of Do'brai. Is that right?"

"He doesn't trust the Do'brainese, Colonel. Krandel will try to commandeer the 747 that the President was rescued from. He urgently requests that total control of the runway clearer be given to his men, or else—"

Welch exploded. "Or else *what?* Krandel isn't in a position to barter with the White House, Colonel."

Frier bit his lip. "I know that, Colonel, and you know that, too. Let's face it: we have one crazy marine down there, determined that he and his men are going to make it out of Do'brai alive. No matter what they have to do."

"I see." Welch ran a hand through his hair. "Stand by, one. Let me see what I can do." He was back shortly. "You've explained to Krandel that he's violating a direct order?" Frier only stared. "Crap—and it's too late to stop that renegade Gould; he's already on his way." Welch's shoulders sagged. "Give me another minute to plead their case."

The wait was longer this time; when Welch finally appeared he looked more haggard than ever. "Woodstone has released the runway clearer to Krandel, but only because there's a chance that something could happen to Gould on the way down. Once Gould is on the ground, they're to get the hell out of there." He cocked an eye at Frier. "Woodstone is pretty pissed about this whole affair. He really wanted to come out of this smelling like a rose, so don't do anything to screw things up any more than they are."

"I copy that—"

Frier was interrupted. "And Frier, no more off-the-wall requests. I've been bounced off so many bigwigs, I don't know which way is up."

Frier grinned. "Don't worry, we've got you covered. I guess that those marines must not be too crazy if they're still alive."

"You hit that nail on the head."

Frier slapped off the screen and turned to Wordel. "Get Krandel on the comm link and tell him to have fun with his runway clearer. We'll bounce his aiming coordinates directly back to Do'brai. And tell them the TAV will land in twenty minutes."

▥ 11 ▥

0630 ZULU:
SUNDAY, 9 SEPTEMBER

This is not the end. It is not even the beginning of the end. It is rather the end of the beginning.

Winston Churchill

Do'brai

Gould's adrenaline level was sky-high when he jumped from the TAV. The 747 lay to his right. As he came down over the remains of Delores's burning TAV he suppressed the emotion he'd felt earlier about her. The important thing now was to get his TAV turned around and transfer the fuel from the bladder in the hold to his wing tanks.

Four marines poured out of the 747 and sprinted to the TAV's stubby wings. Gould directed traffic. "Turn her counter-clockwise; swing her around so she's facing the other way." As the marines started moving the tiny suborbital craft Gould jumped back inside and started the electric pumps to transfer the fuel. Satisfied that the fuel was flowing unhindered, he pushed the JATO units to the hatch. He'd get the marines to attach the units to the craft.

Suddenly gunfire erupted outside, beating a tattoo against the runway. Gould pushed away from the JATOs and stuck his head outside the craft; the marines kept turning the TAV, ignoring the bullets. Gould yelled, "You men get down!" Do'brainese militiamen took potshots at the marines. Gould set himself, expecting the TAV to be punctured by a projectile at any moment.

The marines ignored his cry, determined to get the plane ready for takeoff. Gould was about to bellow another order when a strange sound came from beyond the runway. A squat, tanklike object rolled onto the asphalt and swung its turret around with blinding speed. A whooshing sound came from the object. Explosions erupted down the runway.

Gould's jaw dropped. "Holy shit . . . what the hell is *that?*" His question remained unanswered as the miniature tank swiveled, picking off snipers, vehicles, and anything Do'brainese that moved. He stood mesmerized by the apparition until a lone figure zigzagged from the 747 to the TAV.

A marine ran up breathlessly. "Sir, I'm Corporal Morales. Colonel Krandel requests your presence on board the 747 when you're free."

Requests his presence? Where did Krandel think he was —in the O-club bar? "Right." Gould dropped from the TAV and ran bent over. He followed the corporal the fifty yards to the jumbo jet. Once on board, he was led to the cockpit. When Krandel turned to him, Gould was astonished at the man's appearance. He looked as if he'd aged ten years—and it was less than eight hours since Gould had last seen him.

Gunfire continued outside the plane, and the whooshing sound dominated all the explosions. Gould could make out the tanklike vehicle through the cockpit as it continued to neutralize the Do'brainese forces.

Krandel drew his lips tight. "Major Gould. I'm surprised it's you, but welcome back. How soon can you get us out of here?"

Gould turned his attention from the view outside the cockpit. "As soon as I'm fueled. It shouldn't take more than fifteen minutes to transfer what I have in the bladder.

All that's left is strapping on the JATOs. If we do that now, we could rocket in twenty minutes."

"I don't know if we can hold them off that long."

Gould pointed to the tanklike vehicle. "You guys aren't doing so bad from here. Is that thing on our side?"

Krandel looked surprised. "The runway clearer? Sure. You flyboys launched it from Vandenburg with the bio-package and sleepy-gas capsule. Washington just turned control over to us. We've got it on auto to shoot anything except for what's in our area. I wish we could have had it earlier. It would have made life much easier for us, but that's another story."

"What's it shooting?"

"Everything from railguns to lasers—but look, good as that thing is out there, I'm not sure we can hold out another twenty minutes. The sooner we can get out of here, the better chance we have for surviving."

"It still looks like your runway clearer is doing its job."

Krandel came back impatiently. "Look, Major, it can't keep everything out of our hair. Sooner or later the Do'brainese will figure a way to lob something past it. Is there any way we can get out of here pronto?"

Gould chewed his lip. "Well, we might be able to save a few minutes if we started loading everyone now, rather than waiting for the bladder to empty."

"What would that gain us?"

"About five minutes, but it's against regs to have anyone in the TAV while it's refueling." Gould cracked a grin.

Krandel nodded, not smiling. "I don't think that another broken reg will hurt us. All right, then, let's get everyone on board. Once you're refueled, we'll rocket out of here."

"Right." Glancing around the cockpit, he sighed. "And to think I gave up flying one of these babies for TAVs. I would probably be doing the LAX–Honolulu route now."

"And not having half the fun."

Gould grinned wryly. "You said it, Colonel." Only then did he notice the two nude prisoners tied together with their backs to each other. They sat on the deck, out of sight of the front of the cockpit. A marine private silently held a rifle on them. "Who're the prisoners?"

"I think the short one is the one who masterminded this whole debacle. Right now he's our insurance for staying alive."

Gould grunted and started to leave but stopped when a thought came to him. "Can you control that runway clearer from the air?"

"Sure. We were planning on having it cover us on the way out. Why?"

"I'd want that thing to cover our front as well. I don't want to meet any surprises on the runway when we're taking off."

"Good idea; we'll work on it. Now get those JATO units on."

"Right." Gould exited the craft. He made the short run without trouble as the gunfire abated. Gathering the marines who'd turned the TAV around, he instructed them on how to strap on the JATO units.

When the dormant tank started firing, Hujr had swung his rifle around. At fifty meters, he could clearly see the hatch and would have an excellent shot at Kamil.

The tank was spraying its destruction, keeping the militia well away from the Americans. This would be Hujr's last chance, and if he could do it without drawing the tank's attention to him, he just might be able to make it out alive.

Hujr didn't wonder what made the tank go, why it awoke when it did, or even what type of weapons it possessed. He was used to accepting things as they were, and since the tank obviously was directed against the Do'brainese, he respected the fact that he would not be shown any favoritism. So he waited—he was used to it now—and with every second he waited, his determination grew.

"Major Gould said he's ready for us, sir."

"Right. Let's get ready to make the transfer." Krandel pushed up from the seat and rubbed his eyes. With any luck they'd be out of this nightmare in ten minutes and he would not have to worry about the pain anymore.

As the flight deck emptied of marines Krandel crouched and spoke to General Kamil, who was gagged as well as nude. Krandel said, "We'll notify your troops as soon as we're out of here. Let this be a warning to you: Don't mess with us. Next time you won't get off so easily."

Havisad stuck his head in the cockpit. "We're ready, Colonel."

Krandel stood and bade Kamil farewell. "Remember what I said, General." Heading out the door, he met Morales, dressed in Kamil's uniform. "We'll do this just like we did with the general. We've got to make the Do'brainese think he's still with us so they won't try attacking the TAV. Ready?" The men nodded. "Let's go."

Drawing in a breath, Krandel ignored the pain that started growing in his leg and shoved Morales out the hatch; they moved in the same spiraling motions as they made their way slowly to the TAV. Their weaving dance seemed to move imperceptibly faster as the men became more anxious to reach the TAV's sanctity. Krandel felt elated. It was almost unbelievable, but they were finally getting the hell out of there.

Hujr brought his weapon around and followed the Americans. As before, Kamil was in the center of the group, randomly moving to the outside and back to the center again. Hujr didn't have much time; the Americans were almost to the mysterious aircraft. He remembered to breathe normally and slowly squeezed the trigger. He got off three, then four shots.

He hit Kamil! The Americans were scrambling about; the general jerked in spasms on the ground.

Hujr kept pulling off the shots, delirious that he was finally through. Each crack of the rifle was like a blessing.

The Americans were shooting back! Dust clouds rose from the sand in front of him, pinging bullets flew over his head. Raising his head, he started cursing. Kamil was climbing on board the plane on his own! Hujr was infuriated; Kamil's wound was not fatal. In a rage he reloaded his rifle and methodically started to pump bullets into the black aircraft's fuselage.

"What the hell?! Hit it!" Krandel shoved the group of men to the ground and rolled away. Morales screamed in pain; Krandel started barking orders as bullets zinged around them. "Nail that sniper!"

The men split up, crawling in different directions toward the sniper.

Krandel swiveled on the ground and started spraying bullets in the sniper's direction. The shooting stopped momentarily. Krandel shouted, "Morales, are you all right?"

"They . . . got my shoulder, sir."

"Make a run for the TAV, and we'll cover you."

The response came back slowly. "Aye, aye, sir." The corporal pushed up unsteadily and made a broken path to the TAV.

Krandel yelled, "Whoever's on the TAV, get BIGEYE and have them expand the area of coverage of the runway clearer. Tell them a sniper managed to squeeze through a seam of the coverage."

The sniper started shooting again, but Morales was inside, out of danger.

The marines started converging on the sniper. Havisad reached the 747 and was making his way to the plane's rear. Krandel started to call him back but decided against it. The private should be able to keep the sniper busy until the runway clearer was redirected.

Gould dropped the fuel line in the rear of the TAV. When the shooting started he attempted to increase the flow rate, trying to speed the refueling process. Pinging noises and the dull, deep sound of the reverberation of metal upon metal rang through the ship. Suddenly, all he could smell was the heavy, musklike odor of TAV fuel. He was not alarmed at first, for the viscous JP-12 had a very high flash point. But an image of Delores's burning TAV raced through his mind. What if one of the bullets started a spark? Gould panicked.

"Holy shit—everyone out!" Gould scrambled to the back. "We're hit! Get the hell out of here!"

Gould crawled over the bladder; he slipped, then picked himself up. He felt suddenly drained. The volley of bullets started up again. He turned wildly around. Krandel was still outside, as were most of the marines. One marine had crawled inside; dressed in the general's medal-laden uniform, he clutched his shoulder. Gould yelled, almost hysterically, "We've got to get out!"

"Sorry, sir—"

"Great." Gould grabbed the marine under his arms and lowered him to the ground. Moving outside the TAV was like going from the frying pan to the fire.

Yelling erupted from the runway: "We got him! We hit the sniper!"

A lone marine sprinted from the rear of the 747 to the desert. The marine reached down and yanked a robe-covered man to his feet. After a brief struggle, the two staggered back toward the TAV.

Krandel pushed himself up and started forward, favoring one of his legs. "Gould, are you ready?"

Gould waved him and the others away. "Back to the 747! That sniper hit the bladder, and fuel is spilling out like crazy. If a spark hits it, it will blow!"

A few of the marines kept their ground in disbelief; Krandel's voice didn't even crack as he directed, "You heard him, get the hell out of here!"

Pulling the marine onto his back, Gould started for the 747. Krandel limped over, and they moved off. The runway clearer ensured that there was no opposition from the Do'brainese.

When they reached the jumbo jet Krandel helped ease the wounded marine to the deck. "Somebody take care of Morales." He turned to Havisad. The marine had climbed on board moments before with the sniper. He stood with a foot on the sniper's back, holding a rifle to the Do'brainese's head.

"I thought you'd want him alive, Colonel."

"Like hell I do. Put him up with the general."

"My pleasure, sir."

Krandel spoke to Gould. "Let's move to the back, where we can talk."

As the men made their way down the aisle marines moved out of the two officers' way. When they reached the back the sound of Do'brainese curses erupted from the cockpit. Krandel turned and yelled, "Shut those prisoners up!"

The sounds continued. Krandel said irritably to Gould, "Just a minute," and he stomped to the cockpit. "What the hell is going on in here?"

The sniper yammered in broken English: "General Kamil—he is behind the kidnapping! General—"

"'*Ifrit!*" A sharp rebuke poured from the general in Do'brainese. Kamil had somehow managed to work his gag loose.

"I was only trying to kill the general; I have no quarrel with you. You must believe me! Kill him right away—he is responsible for kidnapping your President!"

"You lying pigdog; shit comes from your mouth." The general squirmed and shouted at Krandel over Hujr's rantings. "Do not listen to him. This is the kidnapper. He is the man who brought your President here—".

"Shut up, both of you!" The noise stopped abruptly. Krandel turned to Havisad. "All right, what's going on?"

Havisad shrugged. "I'm not sure, Colonel, but the sniper and the general aren't on too friendly terms. They accuse each other of kidnapping the President."

Krandel thought for a moment. "Well, keep them apart for now. Gag them again, and if they start acting up, quiet them with your rifle butt."

"Aye, aye, Colonel."

Krandel left and met Gould in the back. Krandel muttered, "Even the squirrelly Do'brainese hate each other."

Gould slumped against a bulkhead. "What now, Colonel?"

Krandel eased into a seat. His leg started to throb. He thought about getting another shot, but he didn't want the morphine haze that enveloped him to get any worse. "I don't know. I guess the only thing to do is tell BIGEYE and try to get another TAV sent here."

Gould shook his head. "I don't think they'll do that, Colonel. We've already lost two TAVs, and besides, it will take at least an hour to get another one here. Longer if they don't have one with a fuel bladder ready."

"We'll see." Krandel turned to a marine guarding the hatch. "Private, have Havisad raise BIGEYE and request another TAV pronto."

BIGEYE only confirmed Gould's assessment: "Washington refuses to budge on this one, Colonel. Vice President Woodstone had the deal all worked out with Do'brai, and you're only making things worse. I've been told to relay a direct order to you: Surrender immediately and don't cause the situation to get any worse."

Krandel muttered, "What does he mean, get any worse? What the hell does he think we're doing, having a birthday party out here?"

Gould raised an eyebrow. "What do you think, Colonel? They say we've got a guarantee from Do'brai's president himself."

"I think that's bullshit. We surrender and we'll never get out of here alive." Krandel looked around and ran a hand through his hair. They were so close—it just wasn't fair. To have Gould come all the way back—and for what? A pilot without a plane is like a bus driver without a bus. There had to be something else they could do.

Krandel closed his eyes. Ten hours ago he was getting ready to spend an afternoon at the beach. With all that had happened since then, he couldn't just roll over and allow the Do'brainese to get the best of him. He had been incessantly drilled to consider all options, to uncover all possible avenues. It was like taking a test; he had to do things right the first time under pressure.

He reviewed what he had: a plane without a pilot . . .

Without a pilot! He opened his eyes and spoke excitedly to Gould. "Okay, you're a pilot. How about flying us out of here in this?"

Gould nearly choked. "In *this?* You want me to try to fly this trash hauler?"

"Look, you said you could be flying this plane on the Los Angeles–Honolulu route—"

Gould straightened. "I said I *wished* I was. Colonel, there's a big difference between knowing how to do something and *wishing* you could do it. They spend months learning how to fly this thing. If this were a helicopter, or a TAV, I could do it. But fly this? No way."

"A plane's a plane!"

"But they're all different," Gould said with an edge to his voice. "I could kill us. Besides, it's too dangerous. And what if this baby has bullet holes in it? We'd never be able to make altitude." He shook his head. "I just don't know how to do it."

Krandel was silent for a minute. "Gould, did you see the President's feet?"

Gould hesitated. "No, I didn't. He was pretty well banged up, though, from what the doctor said when we got to Reagan."

"*I* saw them. He was tortured, Major. His toenails were torn out, and he was pretty badly beaten. And if they would do that to our President, can you imagine what the hell the bastards would do to us?" Krandel searched Gould's eyes. "Are you married, Gould?"

"Eh?"

"Are you married—do you have any kids?"

Gould was silent for several heartbeats. Krandel felt he must have struck a nerve. Finally Gould whispered, "No."

"I am—and I intend to see my family again. I left my wife and children without a word of explanation. I don't want them to remember their daddy as someone who was too busy to care, too busy to say goodbye. I want to see them. And the only way I'm going to do it is if you get us the hell out of here."

"I told you, it's not that simple. I don't know how to fly this thing—"

Krandel interrupted angrily. "If there was a truck out there and I didn't know how to drive it, you'd better the hell believe I would give it a try. I don't want to die because you're too scared to fly something you've never flown before. I'd rather die trying than give up. Now get your ass up there and *fly* this bastard, Major. That's an order."

The two stared at each other, hard, for what seemed to be an hour. Gould finally spoke, closing his eyes. "Can you get me a link with BIGEYE through the plane's radio?"

"We have one up now."

Silence, then: "I'll need that, and someone's help on this end—one of your men who has some technical training to help me fly this thing."

"That will be Havisad."

Gould opened his eyes. "Then if we can get BIGEYE to relay me instructions, I'll give it a try."

Krandel struggled to his feet. He put a hand on Gould's shoulder. All he could manage was, "Thanks."

Gould threw off Krandel's hand and headed for the cockpit. He said almost bitterly, "Don't thank me—thank her."

Puzzled, Krandel started to speak, but he had more important things to do. He collared a marine. "Tell Havisad to get with Major Gould and do whatever the hell he wants him to do. The rest of you secure the doors and the prisoners; we'll allow them to disembark right before we take off."

He caught himself; the general was their only way out of this quagmire. And the general would provide an alibi for their disobeying NECC directives and failing to surrender. With the enmity that the sniper and the general had for each other, it might explain some of why all this had transpired. And what if one of the two had really kidnapped the President? He could not afford to let either of them go.

He said forcefully, "No, belay that order. Secure the

prisoners in a seat. Make sure there's no way they can escape. We're taking them with us."

"Aye, aye, Colonel."

It had been a while since the men had tackled a job with such enthusiasm. Now if only Gould could come through for them.

The 747 showed up as a burning, bright-red dot on the runway clearer's IR sensor. A single line extended from the dot: the runway. New instructions from BIGEYE made it clear that the dot was sacrosanct, so the runway clearer swung its turret to other matters.

The runway clearer was fitted with OTH backscatter radar, finely tuned, so that it could detect motion even from its squat height. An array surrounding the runway clearer's turret was packed with action, sound, and seismic sensors. Each sensor was queried, updated, and adjusted every one hundred millionth of a second.

It detected movement: two hundred twenty-seven point zero three meters, point eighty-nine radians from north. A swoosh and the runway clearer let loose another round from its railgun.

The movement ceased.

The runway clearer kept up its sentinel, unmindful of the time. Soon the red dot grew bigger. It moved down the runway, going even faster. The runway clearer was deaf to the plane's roar.

The runway clearer detected a volley of fire directed at the dot. True to its orders, the runway clearer snuffed out the bullets in flight, vaporizing the metal slugs with its free electron laser. One projectile after another was destroyed along its way. When the bullets were stopped the runway clearer turned to the bullets' source. The shooting stopped also.

As the red dot lurched from the runway the runway clearer reviewed its instructions: the self-destruct code was given in myriad different ways so that misinterpretation was impossible. A signal was sent; electrons trickled down to the runway clearer's nuclear-driven core. The pile was shut down, disassembled, so that the atomic plant could never be used. Then two thousand pounds of explosives reacted with laser chemicals, blowing a crater fifty feet across. Do'brai's runway was destroyed by the runway clearer's death.

Bethesda Naval Hospital, Washington, D.C.

"Young man, I don't care who the hell you are. If you don't get my Secret Service escort in here, I'll kick your butt all the way to Hawaii. Now *move!*"

The nurse scurried out of the room, slamming the door behind him. The room, although tastefully decorated, still had that drab, military-hospital look about it. The windows were secured, and the outside doors were probably locked as tight as the inside.

Montoya's legs were wrapped from the thigh down. He tried to move his feet, but he couldn't feel anything. Seconds passed, and a man entered the room.

"Mr. President—"

"Get me the White House on the phone."

"It will take a few minutes to get the secure link through, Mr. President."

"I don't care if you get them over a pay phone. I said now, dammit."

"Yes, sir." The agent backed out of the room. The door didn't completely close, so Montoya could overhear frantic whispering. Almost immediately a phone with a long extension cord was rolled into the room. "It's an open line, Mr. President; we've got the connection. Please remember not to discuss any classified information—"

Montoya grabbed the instrument. "Hello, Colonel Mathin? Put Woodstone on the line. He's not there? Then put on General Backerman." After a few seconds he continued. "Tell me what the hell has happened, Blackie."

After Backerman's assessment, Montoya nodded. "I see. Well, then, launch whatever fighters you've got in the area.

Try to clear them through each country's airspace, of course, but I don't care where they have to go—as long as they can escort that 747 back. Yes, go ahead and send up any AWACS, tankers, and whatever the hell you need. The safety of that jet is your first priority. I'm in charge now, so if Woodie shows up and gives you any crap, tell him to talk with me.

"Is Baca there? Well, see if you can round him up, too. And keep me on top of things. Bye."

Montoya slammed the phone back on the receiver. A Secret Service man rolled in another phone. "The secure link is here, Mr. President."

Montoya shot a glance at the apparatus, then relaxed back in his bed. "Thank you, Paul. See if you can scare up the Vice President and have him meet me here as soon as possible."

"Yes, sir, Mr. President. Anything else?"

"No, that's all. Wait—bring me a Tecate with salt and a lime. Make that two of them."

"Yes, sir; I'll see what I can do."

As the agent left, Montoya raced through the events as General Backerman had related them. If the marines did indeed have that Do'brainese general on board, and if the general was who Montoya thought he was, then Montoya was *really* perplexed. He didn't know who he was going to kill first: Woodie or the general.

38,000 Feet over Do'brai's Northern Border

Gould eased up on the throttles, allowing them to cut back once they reached cruising altitude. The sky above was a deep, dark blue. He felt he could keep going up, all the way to space. It wasn't as breathtaking as being in the TAV, but it felt one hell of a lot better.

He'd overcompensated at first, rising from the runway with a jerk; but once he was over his nervousness the flight had gone smoothly. A piece of cake, he thought. He might even enjoy flying a trash-hauler like this. But hell, he was a test pilot, so this *should* be a piece of cake. It's one thing to be cocky if you never have to test yourself; it's another thing entirely when other people depend on you during that test.

He sat mesmerized for uncounted minutes, his eyes fixed to infinity, until Havisad grabbed his elbow and pointed. "Look, Major."

Gould squinted. Below him and to his right came three four-ship formations of XL-16 fighters from his six. One approached until it was less than twenty yards away and rocked his wings; the pilot saluted through his cockpit. Holding his hand up longer than usual, Gould returned the salute as the fighter moved out to pace him. The other eleven planes surrounded the 747, keeping the jumbo jet tucked safely away.

Exhausted, Gould relaxed back in his seat, comfortable at last. Now he could grieve for Delores.

SUSPENSE, INTRIGUE & INTERNATIONAL DANGER

These novels of espionage and excitement-filled
tension will guarantee you the best in
high-voltage reading pleasure.

__FLIGHT OF THE INTRUDER by Stephen Coonts 64012/$4.95

__THE LANDING by Haynes Johnson & Howard Simons 63037/$4.50

__DEEP SIX by Clive Cussler 64804/$4.95

__ICEBERG by Clive Cussler 67041/$4.95

__MEDITERRANEAN CAPER by Clive Cussler 67042/$4.95

__THE PLUTONIUM CONSPIRACY By Jeffrey Robinson 64252/$3.95

__DIRECTIVE SIXTEEN by Charles Robertson 61153/$4.50

__THE ZURICH NUMBERS by Bill Granger 55399/$3.95

__CARNIVAL OF SPIES by Robert Moss 62372/$4.95

__NIGHT OF THE FOX by Jack Higgins 64012/$4.95

__THE HUMAN FACTOR by Graham Greene 64850/$4.50

__WARLORD! by Janet Morris 61923/$3.95

__JIG by Campbell Armstrong 66524/$4.95

**POCKET
B O O K S**

**Simon & Schuster, Mail Order Dept. SUS
200 Old Tappan Rd., Old Tappan, N.J. 07675**

Please send me the books I have checked above. I am enclosing $_____ (please add 75¢ to cover postage
and handling for each order. N.Y.S. and N.Y.C. residents please add appropriate sales tax). Send check or
money order—no cash or C.O.D.'s please. Allow up to six weeks for delivery. For purchases over $10.00 you
may use VISA: card number, expiration date and customer signature must be included.

Name _____

Address _____

City _____ State/Zip _____

VISA Card No. _____ Exp. Date _____

Signature _____ 318B-05